Acknowledge

Many thanks to the people of Idle and Thackley for their help, knowingly or otherwise, in the creation of this novel. Without their input, interest, and encouragement it would not have been completed.

Special thanks to Adie Womersley for providing the image for the book cover and to John Higgins and Adam Flaxington for finding the time to take part in the photoshoot. Thanks also to Martin Steele who allowed me to use his allotment as the site for the disposal of a (fictional) body, and to John and Nicky and customers for their hospitality at the Ainsbury.

This is a work of fiction. Although many of the places referenced in the book are real, some characteristics have been changed to fit the story. The characters and events in this book are products of the author's imagination or are used fictitiously. Any resemblance to actual persons, living or dead, is entirely coincidental.

To The Idle Book Club.

Best wishes

CHAPTER 1

Stephen Marks was seated at the kitchen table having a coffee when his daughter, Penny, knocked and walked in.

"Hi, dad. Just passing and I thought I'd call in. How are you?"
"Fine, love. The kettle's just boiled if you want a coffee."
"Thanks. I'll just have a pee first, if that's OK?"
"Go ahead."
"You busy?"
"Remember I told you a while ago I fancied trying to write a book?"
"Yes, I remember. Don't tell me you've done it!"
"No. But I've made a start."
"Can I read it?"
"If you want. It's only a draft, though."
"What's it about?"
"It's a crime novel. I thought, maybe, I could pick your brains now and then, seeing as you're a PCSO."
"I doubt you'll get much of interest from me, but I'll let you know if I come across anything unusual. Anyway, I'm glad you've found something to occupy your mind until you find a job. Anything turned up, yet?"
"No, love."
"What are you looking for?"
"Anything except stacking shelves in a supermarket. I'm not doing that again. If I'm honest, I'm glad they sacked me."
"I'm sure something suitable will turn up. Anyway, can I have a quick read while I'm here?"
"I'll go get it."

He walked to the dresser and opened a drawer, extracting a wad of A4 paper and handed it to Penny.

"Here. It's only a draft of the first chapter, though, so don't be too critical."

She began to read as she drank her coffee.

<u>Killing for Pleasure</u>

It had all gone to plan so far. As he expected, she'd been in the pub as she usually was on a Saturday night, with her two girlfriends. They'd had a few drinks and a natter until closing time when they went outside to wait for their taxis. It was drizzling but not too cold and they sheltered in the doorway, forcing customers to squeeze between them to get out. He was watching from his car parked at the roadside twenty yards from the pub, hoping tonight would be the night. He watched as a taxi drew up outside the pub, two of the girls got in and it drove away. So far, so good. The attractive girl with long dark hair was left at the entrance, alone. He'd go for it. He took a deep breath, started the engine and drove up to the pub entrance, stopping and opening the passenger side window. He leaned over, smiling, and asked.

'Need a lift?'

She was taken aback but smiled and answered.

'No, I'm OK, thanks. I'm just waiting for a taxi.'
'Where are you going?'
'Calverley.'
'I'm going to Rodley. Hop in. Get out of the rain.'

She deliberated for a second, looking at the face of the attractive young man smiling at her. Why not, she thought and got into the passenger seat. He smiled and introduced himself.

'My name's Rob. I've seen you in the pub before.'
'I'm Melanie. Me and my mates often meet up there on a Saturday night.'
'Well, I'm pleased to meet you, Melanie. I have to say, I find you really attractive.'
'You don't waste much time, do you?'
'Sorry. I didn't mean to offend you.'
'I'm not offended. I just wasn't expecting it.'
'It must happen to you all the time.'
'Well, yes, occasionally. But they lose interest as soon as they learn I'm engaged.'
'Oh. I didn't know.'
'He goes out with his mates on a Saturday night, so I go out with the girls.'
'Do you ever get picked up?'

'Men try occasionally. But they soon find I'm not interested. You can let me off at the end of the road down there.'

She indicated the spot she meant. He drove right past it.

'Stop, please. You've missed it.'

He smiled at her.

'I'll take you down to mine for a nightcap. You'll love it.'
"No! Let me out here. Now!'

He continued to drive. She tried the door. It was locked. She turned to face him to express her anger, but he reacted quickly, punching her in the mouth, grabbing her by the hair and banging her head hard against the dashboard until she almost lost consciousness. He pulled the car off the road at Thornhill Drive and drove to a quiet dark spot surrounded by trees. He ran round to the passenger side and dragged his victim out, kicking her hard in the stomach. As she lay motionless on the grass, he tore off her clothes and sexually assaulted her, ignoring her pleas until he was finished. Melanie lay sobbing while he zipped himself up, grinning.

'You liked it, didn't you?'

She looked at him in horror before everything went black as he kicked her several times in the head and about the body until he was satisfied she was dead. Breathing heavily, he dragged her body further into the wood before returning to the car to get a shovel out of the boot. He dug a shallow grave, pushed the body into it and covered it with soil and branches.
Satisfied with his night's work, he got in the car and drove home to Greengates, where he lived, not to Rodley, as he'd falsely told his victim.
He would sleep on his night's adventure before planning his next killing. He was calm and pleased with himself.

****

Penny put the manuscript down and said 'Wow'.

"What do you think?"

"I wasn't expecting this."

"Yes, but did you enjoy it?"

"Yes. It's a good start. It makes me want to read what happens next. Where do you get your ideas from?"

"Straight out of my warped imagination."

"So, who's the next victim?"

"I haven't decided yet. I need to do some research. I need to get to know this area better. This is probably where everything will happen."

"Well, good luck with it. Sorry, I'll have to get back to work."

"Thanks for calling, Penny. I'll see you later."

Alone, Stephen read through his story once more, making some minor amendments before copying it to a USB stick. The task completed, he removed the flash drive and took it upstairs. He pulled out the left-hand drawer at the bottom of the wardrobe and attached the drive underneath with Sellotape before replacing the drawer. He walked back downstairs and deleted the file from his laptop. The hard copy went in a drawer in the kitchen. He sat at the kitchen table and planned the next chapter.

He was delighted that Penny failed to associate his story with an instance of a missing person – a young lady on a night out with friends some months ago – with what she'd just read. He could now turn his thoughts to his next venture and plan how he would carry it out.

****

It had been quiet in Bradford CID for a while, so DCI Gardner had taken the opportunity to grant some overdue holiday requests from his staff. Lynn and Andy were on holiday leave – abroad together, their relationship not yet confirmed but close to becoming public knowledge, while Teresa was at home re-decorating her house, although still on call in case of emergency. Gary, Paula and Jo-Jo were attending a training course in Manchester. Scoffer, though, was a workaholic who seemed to thrive on the pressure and had to be persuaded to take the occasional day off. So far, Brian Peters wasn't missed. As far as the team knew, he had handed in his resignation, and was not to be contacted under any circumstances. Only DCI Gardner and Teresa knew the truth, which was his resignation had been rejected and he was on extended sick leave. Gardner had made that decision without informing even Brian; the resignation letter was still in his desk. Gardner wanted him back and was prepared to wait for a while in case Brian had a change of heart.

****

Stephen Marks finally stopped typing, stretched his back and exhaled. It was almost 3am and he'd been typing for over an hour, desperately trying to ensure he'd remembered and recorded every detail of what had happened. He was tired yet exhilarated as he sat back and poured himself another glass of whisky. He read quickly through it, making minor changes on the way until he was satisfied that he'd given an accurate account of what had happened and how he had felt about the incident. Finally, he saved the file, shut down his laptop and went to bed, hoping he would be able to sleep without the incident weighing heavily on his mind.

But he slept badly; the incident kept playing over and over in his head. Each detail was clear. Each sound, each movement was crystal clear and fresh in his mind when he woke just before midday. He switched on his laptop and opened the Telegraph & Argus website. There it was. The lead article. He read, slowly, checking every reported detail against the details stored in his brain and on his hastily written manuscript.

'BURNT BODY FOUND BEHIND SUPERMARKET

The badly burnt body of a man as yet unidentified was found early this morning at the rear of a supermarket in Greengates, among smouldering rubbish, after firefighters were called to the scene by a passing motorist.

The victim is thought to be a homeless man who was often seen in the area and was known to sleep among the cardboard boxes stored at the back of the supermarket awaiting collection. It is not yet known how the fire started. A police enquiry has commenced and there will be limited access to the car park until the police and forensics team have concluded their investigation.'

He felt a frisson of excitement as he read the article once more. There was no mention of arson. Nobody was seen in the area at the time of the fire. He copied and pasted the T & A's article to his laptop in a newly-created file which he saved as 'Supermarket killing'.

It had gone exactly as planned. He'd set off just after 1am for the short walk to the supermarket, taking a roundabout route avoiding Greengates junction, where there were traffic cameras, and instead approaching the site via Stockhill Road, then Carr Bottom Road and Ashgrove, before finally crossing the car park, hood up and head down as he edged his way towards the skip and cages full of cardboard. He knew exactly where the security cameras were, and that there was a blind spot behind the skip which he could use to his advantage. He could already see the sleeping figure, piles of cardboard pulled closely round his body to keep out the cold. He approached slowly, pulling the lighter fluid from his pocket and sprinkling it over the cardboard. He opened the bottle of turpentine and spread it liberally over a pile of paper he'd dragged from a skip. Then, he struck a match and lit the edge of the paper before walking quickly away from the scene.

The fire took hold immediately. He didn't look back until he thought he was safe. He smiled, seeing the flames, and then was gone. Five minutes later, from the safety of his house he could see the glow in the sky and hear the sirens as police and a fire engine were summoned to the scene. Mission accomplished. He could now take his time to plan the next event.

****

He ate a light breakfast as he planned his day. His first task, naturally, would be to visit the scene. He hurriedly wrote a shopping list and set off towards the supermarket, a broad smile on his face. As soon as he reached New Line, he could see the cordoned-off area, the TV vans, and the crowd of onlookers. He recognised a BBC news presenter flanked by a crowd of people hoping to get their face on TV, but walked straight past and entered the store, listening attentively as shoppers discussed the incident. He smiled when he heard an old couple debating whether it was an act of terrorism, whereupon they were interrupted by a tall man who was adamant it was the work of hooligan teenagers from the Ravenscliffe estate.

****

Acting DI Gary Ryan, back from his course that morning, had been alerted about the incident but was waiting for a call from Forensics to confirm whether a crime had actually been committed. There was always the possibility that death was accidental, caused perhaps by a dropped match or by the victim having lit a fire to keep warm. However, the phone call came within minutes.

"Gary, it's Allen. It's a suspicious death. We've ascertained that the victim wasn't a smoker for a start. He had no matches on his person, and we also found the remains of a container of lighter fluid and a bottle of turps at the scene. There was no indication that he used the fluids to get high – no trace was found in his lungs, so it appears that the fluids were used to ensure the fire spread rapidly. So, unless the victim was suicidal, we can class this as murder. I'm sending you a copy of the full report."
"Thanks, Allen. We're on it. By the way, has the victim been identified yet?"
"No. He's regularly seen in the area, standing outside supermarkets and shops asking for money, but security guards keep moving him on. Somebody told us his name was Arthur, but that's all we know."
"OK. Thanks."

He checked his whiteboard for active investigations before calling DC Schofield over.

"We've got a murder inquiry, Scoffer. Fancy joining me on it."
"Absolutely, boss. Ready when you are."

He brought Scoffer up to date with the case during the drive to Greengates where two uniformed officers were still on site ensuring it remained undisturbed until they were instructed otherwise, and after a quick look around, Gary dismissed them. They spoke to the store's staff but were unable to gain much knowledge about the victim apart from the fact that he was considered a nuisance. Scoffer was incensed at their attitude.

"Has it never occurred to you that the way he lived might have been forced upon him by circumstance? Do you really believe he chose to live this way, begging and sleeping on the streets? You should count yourselves lucky. This could happen to anybody."

After checking the images from the security cameras, the two officers split up. Gary headed for the nearby St John's Community Church, while Scoffer visited the local shops. They met up afterwards in a nearby café to compare notes.

"Nobody I've spoken to had a bad word to say about him, boss. He never hassled people. He always expressed his gratitude if anyone gave him a sandwich or a cuppa, or some small change. He just accepted his lot and tried to get through each day. Apart from that, nobody seems to know anything about him apart from his Christian name."

"OK. I had more luck at the church. He went there regularly when the weather was bad and regularly got hot food and drink. From what I've been told, he was a veteran of the Falklands war, so he was probably in his sixties, but nobody seems to even know his surname. I think we'll need to put out an appeal in the T & A."

"Well, whoever he was, he didn't deserve to be murdered. He might have been down on his luck, but he did no harm to anybody."

"Well, it was certainly no accident. Whoever killed him had clearly done his homework. He knew *exactly* where the security cameras were located and worked out there was a blind spot. Anyway, there's no more to be done here. Let's see if the T & A can come up with anything. At least we've got a recent photo of the victim having a Christmas dinner at the church hall last year."

It was later confirmed that he'd left the army after the Falklands War but suffered from PTSD and was unable to adjust to life as a civvie. Eventually, he left his wife in Manchester after saying he was going out for a walk. It seems he just carried on walking.

****

He was staring at his manuscript, wondering how to continue when the doorbell ring. He closed the open file before he opened the door. It was his daughter, Penny.

9

"Hi, Dad. I was in the area and thought I'd call."

"Come in, love."

"How are you?"

"Fine. You?"

"OK. We're busy trying to keep people away from where the body was found. People keep turning up to take selfies."

"Have they found out what happened yet?"

"I don't know. It's with CID, and they don't let information slip out unless we are actively involved in the investigation."

"There must be rumours."

"Well, yes. All I've heard is what's probably a conspiracy theory."

"What are they saying?"

"That Asda had him killed because he was putting customers off."

"That's absurd."

"I know, but you know what Facebook's like."

"Yes. A load of nonsense. So, how are you and your boyfriend getting on?"

"We're fine, Dad."

"No wedding in the offing, yet?"

"No. We're taking our time. Making sure we're both secure in our jobs with some money in the bank."

"And what about your mother?"

"She's OK."

"Is she still seeing that bloke?"

"I think so. She doesn't talk about him much. Anyway, I can't stop. I just wondered if I could have a pee and then get back to work."

"'Course you can."

"Thanks. You still working on your novel?"

"No progress. Still thinking about it."

"Don't worry. As soon as you get going, you'll whizz through it."

"Let's hope so."

"Anyway, a quick pee, and then I'm off."

"It must be a hard life being a PCSO."

As soon as Penny had left, he included a note in his manuscript to the effect that the supermarket had the homeless man killed because he was putting customers off. That done, he checked the weather forecast on his laptop, put on his coat and walked up the road towards Idle for a pint. He felt he deserved it and was in good spirits as he walked up Albion Road, whistling softly. He took little notice of the two young lads who rode their bikes past him on the road but was startled when a third lad whizzed past him on the pavement, passing within inches of him. He was visibly shocked and couldn't help himself shouting out.

"You stupid little sod! Get off the bloody pavement, idiot!"

The young lad, no older than maybe twelve, stopped suddenly next to his mates who'd waited for him. They blocked the pavement in front of him in a gesture of defiance, but it didn't have the effect they'd hoped. It simply made him even more angry. He glared at the kids, walking towards them with his fists clenched. They waited until he was only a few yards away before mounting their bikes and pedalling away furiously, all the time shouting obscenities. He whipped out his phone and took photographs hoping he'd get some recognisable images, but even if not, his action had the effect of frightening them away. He checked the images. They were good enough. He smiled, thinking how he could avenge their action, and how he could include it in his book. Just for a moment, he felt like Dirty Harry.

He stopped at the nearest pub, sat down with a pint and wrote furiously in his notebook all that had happened, as dramatically as possible. That done, he projected what action he might take as a result of the confrontation.

****

Initially, Brian had made good use of his unaccustomed freedom. He was fitter and healthier than he'd been for years. He regularly went running along the canal towpath for five miles or more and stuck to a healthy diet whenever possible. He was not yet tee-total but stuck to rigorous weekly allowance limits as much as he could, until his resolve broke and he would go on a bender for a day or two. The only lasting ailment was his rasping voice. He could live with that. However, he was becoming bored, and his drinking was becoming more regular and greater in volume. He read the T & A online every day, noting the latest reported crimes, and the apparent lack of progress in solving them.

****

It had been a week; a full week since Stephen Marks had last written a sentence and he felt useless. He seemed to have totally lost his direction. Not a single idea had entered his head. He got up and walked around the small room, stopping to look out of the window in the vain hope that he'd see something, anything, to trigger a response in his brain and get him back on track. He put on his coat and shoes and went out for a walk, even though heavy rain was forecast. He walked through the estate and down to the canal towpath in search of inspiration as the first raindrops began to fall. He pulled up the hood of his coat and stood under the shelter of a tree. The towpath was empty except for a couple of drenched dog-walkers. He walked on in the direction of Rodley as his thoughts turned once again to his ex-wife. She was pregnant with Penny when they married and found things difficult. There never seemed to be enough money in the house regardless of how many hours he worked and when he lost his job things got worse to the extent that their marriage suffered. There were endless rows and he drank heavily, until one day, on the way to the supermarket, he'd bumped into a friend who persuaded him to go for a pint. A couple of hours later, having spent his money, he went to the supermarket, picked up the provisions he'd gone for, and left the store without paying. A security officer grabbed him in the car park and called the police. The resulting fine and police record made it even more difficult for him to find work, and from that point on it was all downhill. The marriage collapsed.

Eventually, with help, he brought his drinking under control and found a job working on a factory production line where he worked for almost fifteen years before the business closed. Now all he had was a rented house, occasional short-term work, few people he regarded as friends, and the overwhelming desire to be a successful writer.

****

He stood at the window, drinking a mug of coffee, staring at the rain falling steadily. He was bored. It was almost 11 am but he still felt tired. He's been writing until the early hours, until he'd finished the scene he'd worked so hard at. He was satisfied with what he'd produced but now wanted to put it into practice. But he knew the rain would make it more awkward. For a start, he'd leave clear footprints at the scene, even though it was highly unlikely they'd be able to follow them all the way back to his house. He decided to use the time to perform another dummy run. He finished his coffee, put the mug in the sink and pulled on his hooded jacket, first checking his notes to ensure what he was wearing was different from what he wore on his last sortie. Finally, he pulled on three pairs of thick socks and took his pair of size 10 boots from the cupboard in the cellar. Wearing them was extremely uncomfortable but there was good reason. He picked up his backpack, made his way down to the marina, crossed the canal via the swing bridge, and walked slowly towards Rodley.

On the way, he encountered the occasional jogger and dog-walker, but the drizzle allowed him to keep his head down and avoid eye contact. He was just another person taking a little exercise and, as such, attracted minimum attention. As he rounded a bend, he could clearly see the canal boat ahead at its regular mooring. This was to be his target. Approaching the boat, he could see wisps of smoke escaping the slim metal chimney, and, though the curtains were closed, could see a light inside and hear the sound of a radio softly playing classical music. He checked the time and made a mental note. So far, so good. Looking around, he could see nobody. He made the decision. He would do it today. He'd performed enough dummy runs. He was prepared, so why miss the opportunity? He pulled on his gloves, stepped on to the boat and knocked gently on the door, steeling himself for what was to come.

The elderly woman who opened the door was totally unprepared as he pushed her backwards, stabbing her in the stomach before her husband had time to react. He quickly overpowered the old man and slashed his throat as he tried to rise from his seat. His heart was pounding and his pulse racing. He stood between the old couple as the life drained from them both before taking off his backpack and changing his jacket. He closed the cabin door behind him as he left, after checking the towpath was clear. He continued until the next swing bridge where he crossed the canal and made his way along the path to the main road which led back to Greengates, grimacing all the way home in his ill-fitting boots. It had all happened exactly as he'd written it.

****

The call came in during the afternoon. An old lady, who lived nearby and who was friendly with the couple, called on them for a chat and, discovering the scene of carnage, phoned 999. Gary and Scoffer set off immediately and parked by the nearby road bridge, walking back to the towpath which had been cordoned off. SOCO officers were already on site. They approached Allen Greaves, the head of Forensics.

"Afternoon, Allen. What have we got?"
"Two bodies, Gary. Pensioners, living on the boat. The lady was stabbed once in the stomach and bled out. Her husband had his throat slashed with the same blade. He would have died in minutes."
"Any witnesses?"
"None that we know of."
"Who found the bodies?"
"A woman who lives in one of the nearby cottages was friendly with them and often called for a chat. She called on them at about 3pm. Nobody answered the door, but it was unlocked, so she entered and found them. She called it in immediately."
"Where is she now?"
"Home. The end cottage. A WPC is with her."
"OK. Any evidence?"
"No prints. He wore gloves. We have bootprints. Size ten. So, he's a big man."
"Or a little man with big feet."
"Of course. We'll be finished soon, if you want to talk to the lady who found them."
"We'll do that now."

As they walked along the towpath, Scoffer voiced what Gary was already thinking.

"Don't you think it's a bit odd, boss? No signs of a struggle. Nothing appears to have been stolen. Is it possible they knew their attacker?"
"It's possible but think about it. They're old. If someone burst in, unexpectedly, they may not be mobile enough to leap out of their seats and confront him, or her, or them, even. As far as theft is

14

concerned, perhaps their attacker had other motives. We'll need to interview as many of the locals as we can. Starting now, with the lady who found the bodies."

****

Lynn and Andy were back at work after their holiday and quickly made public the fact that they were engaged. As per protocol, DCI Gardner, after congratulating them, informed them it would be advisable to avoid working together on the same case whenever possible, to avoid any potential conflict of interest. Andy teamed up with Paula on a new case. They were seated in the car across the road from the Chinese takeaway after they'd had a tip-off advising them that drugs were occasionally being sent out along with food orders. They'd been given a delivery address and the time it was normally delivered every Friday night. They even had a photo of the delivery driver, the make of his van, and its registration. They watched until Andy nudged Paula.

"There it is. Bang on time."

A white Ford van had pulled up outside the takeaway. The passenger got out and entered the shop as Paula compared the photo with the one she'd been given. It was a match.

"That's him Andy. We'll follow him to the house. Give Forensics the nod, please."
"Will do."

They followed the van to its destination and waited until delivery had been made, and recorded on Paula's phone, before calling the backup team to join them before they left the car and detained the delivery driver. He was handcuffed and locked in the car by the time the backup arrived to join them in arresting the occupants of the house. There were two couples, with a large quantity of heroin between them. They were already too stoned to resist arrest and were loaded into the police van and taken to HQ along with the delivery driver before Paula and Andy watched the SOCO team collect all the available evidence for further examination back at the lab. It was a successful operation, but not yet over. They drove back to the takeaway, ordered them to close for the rest of the evening and took the staff in for questioning while the premises were examined.

****

Stephen Marks was walking up Town Lane to call at The Scruffy for a pint. The road was steep and he was out of condition and found it hard work maintaining his stride. Traffic was light, but there was a kid coming towards him on the pavement on his bike. He recognised the kid immediately. It was the one who'd almost run into him previously on the pavement. Well, this time he was ready and stood his ground as the distance between them closed rapidly. At the last second, the kid braked hard and skidded into the road where he was almost hit by a car. He grinned and walked on, leaving the kid angry and swearing he'd get revenge.

****

Marks woke suddenly, sweating. He looked at the clock. 10.15. He'd overslept yet still felt tired. He dragged himself into the shower only emerging once the tiredness had left his limbs. He towelled himself dry while trying to recollect his dream. It was similar to the one he'd had regularly where a man was burned alive, but this time it was a different man, in a different location. He was still thinking about it while he ate his breakfast of cereal and coffee until it became clear. He recognised the location from the supermarket logo. He dressed and set off on a walk to Idle.

As he entered the carpark, he realised the layout was as he'd dreamed. The incident, though, was not at the supermarket, but at the side of the store adjacent to it where the waste cardboard was stored in skips and cages ready for collection. He walked around, noting the position of cameras and the general layout, before deciding to return during the early hours of the morning. He set off home by a tortuous route along the side streets, often retracing his steps until he had several escape options should he be disturbed.

Back at his laptop, he typed the backbone of his new storyline. Once the action was complete, he would return to his script and fill in the details. He was excited to the extent that he wasn't worried that anything untoward would happen to disturb his act. He had no fear. Everything would go exactly as planned. He felt invincible.

He was unable to relax and paced back and forward in his home until darkness fell. He'd been unable to eat a meal such was his excitement as he watched the hands of the clock move inexorably towards midnight, and once that time was reached, he went up to his bedroom to change into his 'working clothes', which were all black. He checked his backpack for the umpteenth time before slipping on his coat and grabbing his beanie hat. He picked up his car keys and left the house.

He parked on Hampton Place and made his way along the footpaths between the blocks of houses before emerging on Idlecroft Road. As he'd hoped, there was no traffic, apart from the occasional taxi and he was able to step back into the cover of the bushes when one passed. He walked towards the car park entrance and kept to the left where it was in shadow. The car park was in darkness except where the odd light glowed for security. Walking close to the wall, he approached the loading area, where the cages were kept, lined up against the wall. In the dim light, he could see the mound of cardboard piled in the corner, sheltered from the cold wind. He moved forward slowly, until he was able to make out the figure of the rough sleeper. He took off his backpack and removed the bottle of inflammable liquid, unscrewing the cap as he edged towards the sleeping figure. Silently, he crouched beside his victim, pouring the liquid on to the cardboard and dousing the legs of the man still fast asleep. He took out his lighter, lit a rolled-up newspaper and threw it on to the cardboard pile. The fire took hold rapidly as he ran back to the main road and hurried back to his car, unseen. He could hear sirens as he drove away, smiling.

Back home, he quickly changed his clothes and switched on his laptop to pick up the latest local news. As he'd hoped, it was there, described exactly as he'd experienced it. His excitement reached its peak when the announcement came through that a body had been found when the fire had been extinguished. He opened a can of lager, following the story as it was reported, until, finally, he switched off and went to bed.

****

The report was on Gary's desk when he arrived at work. He'd already been alerted by text in the early hours of the morning but realised there was little to be gained by coming in early as he would have to wait for the Forensics report before deciding on a plan of action. As it happened, the report arrived shortly after he'd logged on to his PC. Reading quickly through it, it was evident the crime was similar in so many respects to the earlier supermarket attack that they were linked. He called his team to the Conference Room.

"It's the work of a serial killer, or at least people who are collaborating. Rough sleepers are the targets. The venues are similar in that they are stores where recyclable materials, for instance, cardboard boxes, are kept for collection round the side or at the back of the store. Quiet areas, out of public view. Poorly lit and unmanned during the night, there are security patrols at intervals only, and their purpose is to deter attempts at burglary."

He pointed to the photos taken at the crime scenes before continuing.

"There's no doubt in my mind that this is just the beginning. The killer is targeting rough sleepers. Why? Any ideas?"
"They're easy targets."
"That's true. They are predictable. They tend to sleep in the same spot regularly, until they get moved on. Other reasons?"
"They're not really capable of defending themselves. They're unfit, undernourished...."
"Yes. These are valid points. But is it possible the perpetrator has a more visceral hatred of rough sleepers? He may see them as worthless nobodies, for instance. In his mind, he's cleaning up the streets."
"Do we have anybody who fits that profile, Teresa?"
"I'll start looking as soon as we're done here."
"OK. In the meantime, I want the rest of you looking into the history of the victims. I want to know what they have in common, apart from their lifestyle. There might be a clue in their background."
"They might use the same meal provider."

"Exactly. I want a full profile for each victim. And quick. I want to know how he picks his victims, before he tries to kill again."

****

It was early in the evening. Stephen intended to have a pint or two in Idle, just to relax, and was making his way up Albion Road when a kid on a pushbike passed him on the pavement, knocking his elbow. He shouted at the lad who stopped about ten yards ahead and turned his head, his face breaking into a broad grin when he recognised the man he'd brushed against. As soon as Stephen started running towards him, he pedalled furiously across the road in front of an oncoming car which braked violently as the cyclist crossed its path before racing away downhill back towards Greengates.

Stephen was furious and started planning his revenge as soon as he'd got a pint in his hand and time to think. Very soon, a plan began to formulate in his head.

By mid-morning on the following day, Stephen had already taken delivery of two separate wagonloads of timber and insulating material, which were now covered by tarpaulin in his back yard. He immediately began dragging the items he needed initially into the house and manoeuvring them down the narrow steps into the cellar. He spent the rest of the day sawing timber to size and attaching the lengths to the exterior walls, covering the small window and air grates. That task completed, he stuffed thick lengths of insulation between the timbers before covering them in sheets of plywood with even more noise-cancelling foam panels fastened securely on top. He checked his watch. 18.30. He was hungry but there was something else he had to do before he was satisfied with his work. He went up to the kitchen, unplugged the radio and took it back down to the cellar along with an extension cable. He plugged it in, switched it on, turned the volume to 'full' and went back upstairs, through the kitchen and out of the front door. He listened and smiled. He couldn't hear any sound coming from inside. Walking to the back of the house, he repeated the exercise. Again, no sound could be heard from the cellar. He was fully satisfied with his work and sat in the kitchen with a can of beer. From there, he could only just discern a faint noise from the cellar. He could fix that with extra acoustic tiles. Now, he had to plan his next move. He smiled as the tagline from the film 'Alien' came to mind. 'In space, no-one can hear you scream.'

Stephen was up early the next morning driving up and down the streets of the Thorpe Edge estate, watching the kids as they went to school. There was no sign of his target, which didn't surprise him. He needed a photo so he could show it around. Maybe someone would recognise him and disclose his whereabouts. He checked his watch; the school day had now commenced so he decided to park the car and check the nearby parks and play areas on foot. Maybe he'd get lucky.

And he certainly did! Within ten minutes, he'd spotted the kid on his bike, practising his 'wheelies' and other tricks in the skateboard park. The kid was totally immersed in his macho posturing, he never realised he had a spectator. Stephen looked around. The area was empty bar a couple of dog walkers some distance away. He'd take the chance. Using the cover of the bushes surrounding the area, he approached stealthily until he was practically within touching distance of the kid, and, as he raced past, engrossed in his bike manoeuvres, Stephen leapt from the bushes and dragged him from his bike, pinning him to the ground.

"Don't try to get free, arsehole. There's a knife in your ribs."

Just to emphasise the point, he pushed the sharp blade into the kid's side. He winced in fear.

"You're coming with me. You can leave the bike here. You won't need it again."
"Where are you taking me?"
"Somewhere safe. Somewhere we can have a nice little chat. So, just do as I say, or I'll kill you. Understand?"

The kid nodded.

"Say it. Do you understand?"
"Yes."
"Yes, what?"
"Yes, sir."
"Come on, then. Nice and quiet. Here, put this on."

He handed him a blindfold, dragged him to his feet and took him to the car, the knife still pressed against his side. Heavy rain was falling now, which pleased him as it meant there were fewer people on the streets. He parked around the back of the house and dragged the kid inside without being seen.

"Welcome to your new home. From now on, you do *exactly as I say*. Understood?!"
"Yes."
"Call me 'sir'."
"Yes, sir."
"Good. Now let me show you around. Just through this door."

He drew back the bolts and put the key in the newly-fitted lock. Turning to face the kid, he grabbed him by the hair, pulled off his blindfold and dragged him into the cellar, throwing him to the concrete floor.

"Have a look around. There's a sink to wash yourself. There's a bucket in the corner. It's a chemical toilet. There's a bottle of water. Two litres. That's your ration for the day. Every now and then I'll bring you some scraps of food, as long as you behave. There's no point in shouting; the room is totally sound-proofed. So, just behave and serve your sentence. Annoy me in any way and I'll make you stay here longer. Do you understand?"
"Why are you doing this to me?"
"Because you disrespected me, and you have to learn your lesson."
"I won't do it again. I promise you."
"Good. When I believe you've served your sentence, I'll let you go. So, just behave or I'll kill you. And I'll take that shoulder bag you've been clinging on to. What's in it anyway?"
"Nothing."
"I'll just have a look."

He opened the zipped bag and stared at the small, sealed packages inside.

"What are these?"
"I don't know. I just deliver them."
"Who to?"

"The addresses on the sheet in the side pocket."
"I'll have a look upstairs. I'll leave you to get some sleep."

The kid promptly burst into tears as Stephen left the room, bolting the door behind him and switching off the light. He stood there for a few minutes until the sobbing subsided and then walked calmly up the stairs, put his coat on and went out for a pint. The rain had stopped, so he decided to walk up to Thackley. Unfortunately for him he chose the wrong time - the end of the school day. By the time he was close to Emmanuel School the pavement was packed with groups of kids ambling along together, staring at their phones rather than watching where they were going. Stephen refused to give ground and ploughed through them, barging them out of the way. He was angry at their lack of manners and insouciance. Perhaps, he thought, they would be among his future victims.

****

Lynn took the call from Teresa.

"Sorry about this, Lynn, but I've had a very angry phone call from an aggressive woman who seems to think nothing's being done about her missing son. This is the third time she's called me this morning! I tried to tell her it was in the hands of the local police, but she won't have any of it."
"So, what's been happening?"
"Basically, her son's been missing for three days. She reported it two days ago, but so far, the local squad have just made general enquiries, whereas she thinks the entire force should be out combing the area in their hundreds."
"Give me her address. We'll go and talk to her."
"Thanks. Just get her off my back."

Lynn took Ruth with her to interview the woman, only to find there was nobody at home. They left a note to say they'd called and returned to base.

CHAPTER 2

That night, Stephen was roused from his sleep by a dull thudding noise. He knew immediately where it came from and dragged himself down the stairs to the kitchen where he collected a large knife before unlocking the door to the cellar. He switched on his torch to find the kid blinking, shielding his eyes from the sudden flash of light, cowering in a corner. He shone the torchlight around the room. The kid had attempted to tear away the thick covering of acoustic material without success.

"I thought I told you not to touch anything."
"I was looking for the light switch. I don't like the dark."
"Well, lad, you'd better get used to it. The light switch is outside, and I decide when it goes on and off."
"You can't keep me here like this!"
"No? We'll see about that. Now get to sleep. Or, at least, keep the noise down. You're wasting your time. Nobody can hear you outside. Anyway, nobody cares about you. You're just a loser."
"Please may I have some more water?"
"Oh, so you *can* be polite? Why aren't you like that all the time?"
"I am, normally."
"No, you're *not*! You're a little shit. And, no, you can't have any water. You've already had your ration. Now, shut your mouth and go to sleep. You never know; I might let you go tomorrow."
"I'd like that."
"Well, I'll have to decide if you're ready first. So, don't wake me again. OK?"
"OK."
"You may call me 'sir'."
"OK, sir."

Stephen turned and locked the door behind him, leaving the boy once again in total darkness. Hearing the boy sobbing, he smiled and went back to bed.

****

Mrs Stokes, the mother of the missing boy, Karl Stokes, called CID the following morning not even apologising for her absence, stating only that she'd had to go out. Lynn and Ruth went immediately to her home.

"Have you found him yet?"
"Mrs Stokes, we don't even know what he looks like. That was one reason we visited your home yesterday."
"Well, I had to go out."
"So, there was something more important than helping us find your son? Would you mind telling us where you went? And please also explain why you didn't leave us your mobile number?"
"Well, I was upset, wasn't I. I went looking for him."
"Where did you go?"
"To talk to some friends. To ask if they'd seen him."
"OK. If you want us to try to find him, we'll need your full cooperation. Understood?"
"What are you implying?"
"Just answer our questions, eh? The sooner we're done, the sooner you can get on with your daily routine."
"I don't know what your problem is. I've a good mind to report you."
"Enough of this nonsense. You either help us do our job, or I'll arrest you."
"On what charge?"
"Being in possession of illegal drugs."
"I don't know what you're on about."
Yes, you do. You've been done twice to our knowledge. We've looked at your record."
"Well, anyway, what's that got to do with it?"
"It'll make up for having wasted our time. Now, can we get on with business? When did you last see Karl?"
"Monday afternoon. He said he was going to his mate's house."
"What's his mate's name and address?"
"Keiran something or other. I don't know his address. I think he lives on the estate."
"Have you got a photo of Karl?"
"'Course I have."
"Send it to my phone."
"There."
"Thanks. Now, is there anyone else in your family he's in contact with?"
"He sees his dad occasionally."
"Have you got his address?"
"No. But he lives somewhere on the estate."
"Have you got a phone number for him?"

"No. I don't have anything to do with him."
"Give me his name, please."
"Dave Carlton."
"Thank you, Mrs Stokes. You've been a great help."

They had spent more than thirty minutes at Mrs Stokes' house during which time they learnt very little about Karl, apart from which school he attended. They drove straight there after making an appointment to speak to the headteacher. What they heard from him came as little surprise.

"Karl's attendance record over the last twelve months has been dreadful. He seems to think he can turn up and hang about until lunchtime, and then disappear for the rest of the day. And the following morning he comes up with some lame excuse, like, 'mum was ill' or 'dentist appointment'. He's close to expulsion, and he knows it. He just doesn't seem to care. He's a serial absentee."
"Have you spoken to his parents?"
"Parents? No, not to his father, anyway. We've spoken to his mother. She defends him with some excuse or other. Frankly, we're wasting our time."
"Has he any friends we can speak to?"
"He only seems close to one lad at this school. Keiran Donnelly."
"Could we speak to him, please?"
"Certainly. I'll go and fetch him."

Keiran was unable, or unwilling, to provide anything of any use. According to him, the last time he'd seen Karl was on Monday morning at school. He was adamant he and Karl were only acquaintances, and he knew nothing of Karl's activities outside school. They returned to HQ none the wiser, except they were certain Karl's mother and Keiran both knew more than they were admitting.

****

When Stephen went down to the cellar with some scraps of food for Karl, he found the boy on the floor, apparently asleep. He slapped his face until, finally, the boy showed signs of life and whispered.

"Please help me. I don't feel well. I think I need a doctor."
"What's up with you?"

"Asthma. I can't breathe down here. No fresh air. Help me. Please. I need my inhaler."

"Where is it?"

"At home."

"Don't you carry it with you?"

"Not all the time, no. I didn't expect to be kidnapped!'

"Tough. Take a deep breath, before I lock you in again."

The boy was in distress. Stephen had never considered the lack of fresh air in his efforts to soundproof the cellar. It was too late to change now. He would have to check on him more often, just in case the boy was faking it.

Later that night, he checked the cellar again. As before, the boy was laid on the floor, apparently asleep. Stephen nudged him with his boot.

"Wake up, you lazy bugger. Here's your supper."

There was no response, so he kicked the boy again, this time receiving a wheezing plea.

"Help me."

"What's up with you now?"

"Can't breathe."

He shone his torch directly on the boy's face. It was deathly white. The boy was clearly in distress. He made the snap decision to get the boy out of the house so at least he didn't die in the cellar. He ran up the stairs and grabbed his car keys, reversing the vehicle up to the back door, hoping he didn't disturb the neighbours. Carefully, he carried the boy up from the cellar and placed him in the boot. He checked he was still breathing. He was, just. Stephen drove him across town to the Bradford Royal Infirmary, driving slowly around the car park until he found a suitable poorly lit spot where he stopped and ran round to the boot. Opening it, he looked at the boy who now showed no sign of life. He laid him out in bushes by the car park before driving quickly away. He was someone else's responsibility now.

Fifteen minutes later, a middle-aged man with his wife as passenger was making his way slowly around the grounds of the

BRI, following the signs for 'Accident and Emergency' while looking for somewhere to park. His headlights shone on the bushes where what seemed to be a body had been hastily concealed. He parked the car and went back for a closer look, before hurrying back to the car where his wife was waiting patiently.

"You'll have to wait for a while, love. There's a body in the bushes. I think he's dead."

He ran into A & E where he told the lady on Reception what he'd found and waited until someone went back with him to check.

"You're right, sir. When you've taken your wife inside, you'll be asked to wait until the police arrive."
"But my wife needs attention."
"We'll see to your wife, sir. You'll just have to wait in Reception."

****

Gary was on call and was having a quiet night until the phone rang.

"Sorry to disturb you, sir, but we've had a call from BRI. Apparently, a dead body was found in their grounds tonight. SOCO are on their way."
"Thanks. Let them know I'll be there shortly."

The area had already been cordoned off and a tent set up covering the crime scene. Allen Greaves and his team had responded quickly and efficiently, as usual.

"Good evening, Gary. The victim is a young boy. We've already taken the body for examination, but one of the doctors at the scene here had a quick look and gave a likely cause of death as asphyxiation."
"He's been strangled?"
"Apparently not. All he could determine without a full examination and post-mortem examination was he'd died through lack of oxygen. From what we could determine, there were no signs of strangulation, but we'll know more when we've got him on the slab."

"OK, thanks. Any ID on him?"
"Nothing we could find."
"OK, I'll leave you to it."
"Thanks. You'll have the initial report in the morning."

Gary went into A & E and was able to speak to the man who'd found the body, and get his statement, before asking for copies of CCTV recordings to be sent to HQ. He logged a brief report of the incident before leaving the scene and went home.

Allen Greaves's initial report was waiting for him in his email inbox when he logged in the following morning.

"My initial cause of death seems correct. An inspection of his lungs indicated he suffered from asthma, so a lack of oxygen would bring on a serious attack. Interestingly, his lungs looked like those of someone who'd been buried under a rockfall, for instance. Like a miner who been trapped underground while the availability of oxygen became scarce. That sort of thing. Certainly, a person with severe asthma wouldn't last long under those conditions without oxygen.
Judging by his underwear, he hadn't had a change of clothing recently. Interestingly, he wasn't dressed for caving, but we did find some fibres on his clothing. It's similar to the stuff used for loft insulation, but this is more often found in insulation from noise rather than loss of heat."

He called Allen.

"Allen, assuming he was deprived of oxygen, how long would it be before he died?"
"It depends on the quality and amount of oxygen available. Could be several hours, or a few minutes. We would need to establish the scene of crime. The other factor would be how bad his asthma was. We would need his medical records to determine that, which means, of course, that we need to identify him first."

He ended the call and rang Teresa.

"Teresa, can you get me a list of reported missing persons, male, under the age of sixteen, please. Local area."

No more than a minute after he replaced the receiver, an incoming call from Teresa interrupted him.

"Sorry, Gary, the BRI just informed me their CCTV was out of order last night. They've got nothing for us."

While he waited for further information from Teresa, he looked at the list of new cases which had come to light within the past twenty-four hours. Following his predecessor's example, he wrote them on the whiteboard before adding the names of the officers he'd assign to each case.

1. Young male. Asphyxiation. Lynn/ Ruth
2. Drug dealing. Yeadon/Guiseley. Paula/ Andy
3. Takeaway deliveries – drugs. Paula/Andy
4. Homeless murders. Jo-Jo/ Scoffer
5. Barge murder – Jo-Jo/ Scoffer

He called the team to the Conference Room for a briefing.

****

CHAPTER 3

Brian had just dragged himself out of bed and was drinking a mug of strong black coffee to clear his head of the fog which enveloped his brain after a heavy night's drinking in the Black Rat. He'd unexpectedly bumped into some acquaintances he hadn't seen for years, with the predictable outcome and was suffering the consequences. He switched on his laptop to read the news while he decided what to do with his day. He read a brief T & A report concerning the body of a young boy found in the grounds of the BRI, paying only scant attention to it before moving on to other news. He checked his watch. His regular morning call was overdue, probably, he thought, due to the body he'd just read about. But then his phone rang. He checked the number displayed before answering.

"Morning, Teresa."
"Good morning, Brian. How are you today?"
"Fine. I'm just about to go out for a run."
"Good. Anything else on your plate today?"
"As a matter of fact, I've been considering writing a novel."
"Ooh, what about?"
"Crime."
"Why am I not surprised?"
"Well, what else do I know much about?"
"If you need any advice or information, I'm sure Scoffer would help you. He's really coming on."
"Glad to hear it, Teresa. Now, if you'll excuse me, I need to prepare for my run."
"OK. Enjoy it. I'll talk to you tomorrow. 'Bye'"

He ended the call and sat back. He had no intention of going for a run. Perhaps, later, he'd have a walk – to the pub. He'd simply said he was going for a run to please Teresa. She'd be dismayed and disappointed to know the amount of alcohol he consumed these days, and it was apparent to Brian that he was now regularly exceeding his weekly allowance. He put it down to boredom and maybe spending too much time alone. He was still grieving for his family. Perhaps, when he felt ready, he'd tackle his problem, and, just maybe, conquer it. And, if he could manage that, maybe, just maybe, he'd seriously consider writing a novel.

****

When Gary returned to his desk after his meeting, a large file awaited him, along with a note from Teresa.

"This is all we have regarding missing persons matching the criteria you specified."

He opened the file, which confirmed what he'd expected. They'd discussed it in the meeting he'd just left. The body belonged to Karl Stokes, whose mother had been interviewed by Lynn the previous day. He looked at the attached photograph. It was undoubtedly that of the boy whose body he'd seen in the grounds of the BRI. Now someone had to break the news to his mother, and as the most senior officer currently in the team, the duty fell on him. He asked Paula if she'd accompany him. She had no choice but to agree.

Mrs Stokes was angry rather than upset, even more so when Gary asked if she'd accompany them to the mortuary to officially identify the body.

"You should be asking his father to do that. It's his fault."
"What makes you say that, Mrs Stokes?"
"He was probably doing a delivery for his dad. Ask his dad. He spent more time with Karl than I did."
"What sort of delivery are you talking about, Mrs Stokes?"
"I'll give you three guesses?"
"Drugs?"
"You got it in one."
"Give me his dad's name and address, please."
"Dave Carlton. He lives somewhere on Ravenscliffe, but I don't know the address."
"OK. Get your coat. We need you to come with us to identify the body."
"Do I have to?"
"Please yourself. If you refuse, I'll call Social Services and arrange for your benefits to be recalculated."
"I'll get my coat."

While she went for her coat, Paula called Teresa requesting the address for Dave Carlton, and informed her they'd pay him a visit and bring him in for questioning.

Mrs Stokes identified her son, showing no emotion whatsoever, except disappointment that he had no possessions with him. Gary picked up on it immediately.

"If you can tell us what you expected to find on him, perhaps we can consider robbery as a motive. Did he have anything of any value?"

"Oh, no. I was just wondering."

"No phone? Watch? Money? Drugs?"

"No, nothing in particular. I was just wondering."

"You know what, Mrs Stokes, I don't believe you. I think your son was a drugs mule."

"Think what you like. It was nothing to do with me. Ask his dad."

"We will."

After dropping Mrs Stokes off, they drove to Carlton's home. He was upset to hear his son was dead. Gary thought he knew why.

"I get the impression you're not particularly upset at his death. It's more a matter of what he was carrying at the time."

"I don't know what you mean."

"I think you do. You want to know what happened with his deliveries, and the money he collected for you."

"That's rubbish. You can't prove that."

"Hand me your phone."

"No, That's private."

"OK. I'm arresting you and taking you in. We'll have your phone analysed while you stew in a cell."

"I want a lawyer."

"We'll get one for you. Stand up and put your hands behind your back."

"What if I refuse?"

"We'll call for the big boys with the truncheons and tasers to subdue you. Tasers can be quite painful, you know."

"You can't do that."

"Try me."

Carlton thought it over for a few seconds before conceding.

"OK. Look, I only use weed now and again. Karl delivers it to me. It's his mother who's the dealer. I'm just an occasional customer."
"That's not what his mother told us. Give me your phone."
"No."
"OK. You're coming with us. You might want to bring a change of underwear. Unless you're tougher than you look."
"You don't frighten me."
"Just tell us the truth. Give me your phone. Now, please."

Grudgingly, he handed it over before he was cuffed and bundled into the car.

****

The T & A had already got hold of the story, or at least part of it. They'd been told about the body found in the grounds of the BRI by a cleaner who worked there and had rung Teresa several times for more information. They were promised a statement before the end of the day. Nevertheless, they printed what they knew.

That evening, Stephen saw the story in the T & A. He was happy that they had very few facts, not even the victim's name, but he suddenly remembered the boy's shoulder bag he still had. He took it out of the cupboard and emptied the contents on the kitchen table. There were fifteen small bags. He took one and held it to the light. He was sure he knew what it contained – cocaine – and lined up the bags on the table before getting a small set of scales from the pantry. He weighed each bag; they all weighed the same. He looked at the sheet of paper which showed a list of addresses, and the amount ordered, followed by the price to be collected on delivery. He began to imagine the scenario he'd interrupted. The boy had collected the drugs from a dealer and was waiting in the park probably for someone to help him deliver them to the addresses on the sheet of paper. When they hadn't been delivered, the intended recipients would most likely ring the dealer. As a result, both the dealer and the customers would be very unhappy. He wondered if there might be another way of selling the cocaine. And there was the dilemma of what to do with the cellar. If he were to use it as a prison again, he would have to install a source of oxygen without compromising the soundproofing. He'd have to give it some serious thought. However, first he needed to write up recent events while they were still fresh in his memory.

****

The following morning, both Mrs Stokes and Dave Carlton had been interviewed and allowed to go home. Carlton's phone had been analysed, and the contacts identified had been questioned, having been warned they could face charges later. However, they had established the fact that both Stokes and Carlton were dealers; Carlton bought heroin and cocaine in bulk and re-packaged it into small bags, some of which went to Stokes for sale to her local customers, and the rest was distributed by Karl Stokes and his pal, Keiran, to Carlton's customers.

After lunch, Gary and Paula went back to the school and, with the head's permission, had a short conversation with Keiran. He initially denied having any part in distributing drugs, but eventually, under intense interviewing, he broke down in tears and confessed to his role.

"All I did was meet Karl and help him deliver the packages. For a long time, I didn't know what the stuff was. Honest. I just did it 'cos it was easy money. I used to meet Karl in the park, but I was late that day and he wasn't there. He texted me to say he was going without me unless I got there soon, but he'd already left when I arrived, and I couldn't get any answer when I texted him. So, I just went home, and I never saw or heard from him again."
"And you've no idea where he might have gone?"
"No. I didn't get to see his delivery list. He could have been anywhere."
"But you knew the addresses of his regular customers?"
"Well, some of them."
"Any of them a bit dodgy?"
"They were all weird."
"Thanks for your help. In the meantime, keep your nose clean. We'll let you, and your parents, know what repercussions there will be for your part in distributing drugs."

The next job for Paula was to re-examine Carlton's phone messages to determine who actually supplied him with the drugs. All the contacts had already been interviewed briefly, but all admitted being users rather than suppliers. Neither Carlton nor Stokes would talk, each accusing the other of being the bulk buyer.

****

Stephen had been up deep into the night writing the latest chapter of his novel. He was pleased with his work and read the section once more whilst eating breakfast, occasionally changing a word or correcting poor grammar until he was satisfied. Eventually he put his laptop aside and considered what might be his next chapter. He wondered if it might be possible to separate one of the schoolkids from the torrent which poured out across the pavements at the end of the school day. He quickly decided to have another look at the situation that afternoon. In the meantime, he searched the internet looking for a device which would ensure a constant supply of fresh air to his cellar quietly and without compromising the soundproofing. He spent hours reading all he could before deciding the expenditure and installation wasn't worth it. In future, if he took any prisoners, they would have to cope with conditions as they were. His cellar was a prison, not The Ritz.

Mid-afternoon, he shut down his laptop and set off towards Thackley, just in time for the end of the school day. As he neared the school, he turned off to the right squeezing past the cars parked on the pavement and passing Elm Tree Court and then following Ellar Carr Road, the rough track which eventually emerged on Park Road. He'd walked along the track a few times, noting that youths would occasionally gather there for a quiet smoke. He was lucky. A short distance from where the track took a sharp turn to the left, two schoolgirls were standing at an entrance to the playing field, smoking and chatting. He averted his gaze as he passed and continued until they were out of sight. He put a hand in the deep right-hand pocket of his coat and pulled out a long sharp knife. He felt powerful with it in his hand. He would do it. He turned and walked back towards the bend. The girls were still there. He quickened his pace and held his breath until he was only a few yards away, his hand gripping the handle of the knife in his pocket. He was on the point of pulling out the knife when he noticed the two ladies walking towards him, each with a Border Collie on a leash. He stopped abruptly, then continued on his way, walking past the young girls, and the two dog-walkers, keeping his head down until he was back on the main road and heading home. His heart was pounding. As he passed the entrance to the Hitching Post, he imagined he could hear the sirens, then see two police cars racing up to Thackley, followed a minute later by an ambulance.

When he arrived home, he locked the door behind him and punched the wall in anger and frustration. He would have to try again tomorrow. He took off his coat and pulled his laptop from the drawer and wrote a full chapter about his frustrated outing. Then, he wrote a new chapter about how he returned the following day and succeeded in his murderous intent and had left the scene minutes before the two ladies and their dogs came along to find the scene of utter carnage. He tried to put in words their emotions before concluding the chapter and saving it.

Next, he opened a porn site and relieved himself furiously.

The following afternoon, once again he made his way up Leeds Road towards his intended 'kill site'. He dressed differently and wore a baseball cap and glasses, but his intent was the same. Again, he walked along Ellar Carr Road and was soon able to see the two girls chatting and smoking by the entrance to the playing fields. As he approached, he glanced behind himself. There was no-one in sight. He would do it. He walked past the girls so he could see if anyone was coming from the opposite direction. It was clear. He turned and walked back quickly, again looking to see if the dog-walkers were in sight. There was no sign of anyone. He stopped next to the girls and spoke.

"Excuse me, ladies."

They turned to face him as he plunged the knife deep into the nearest girl's stomach. She gasped and fell to the ground. Her friend gasped, but before she could react, she too felt the knife slice through her clothes and pierce deep into her flesh. Her eyes were wide in shock, staring silently at her attacker as he thrust the blade into her once more. As she slumped to the ground he turned and walked quickly in the direction of Park Road, then turned right and followed the road to its junction with Park Avenue, where he turned left, walking briskly. He stopped for a few seconds to check his appearance. Apart from the odd spot of blood, he was presentable and continued to the end of the road, turning left to Thackley Corner, crossing at the pedestrian lights and walking quickly up the hill to Idle from where he made his way home to Greengates. This time, as he walked down Albion Road, he could definitely hear the sirens and as he reached the bottom, he saw the police cars and an ambulance racing up Leeds Road towards the crime scene. He allowed himself a smile. Job done!

Safely home, he stripped off, threw his stained clothes into the washing machine and took a shower in the expectation it would purge him of his sins.

****

Brian was standing at the bar in the Ainsbury when Steve, one of the regular customers, burst through the door.

"What's going on up by Park Road?"

Brian looked at him, bewildered.

"No idea. Why?"
"The police are everywhere. Ellar Carr Road's blocked at both ends. Something serious must have happened."
"I wouldn't know, Steve. It's not my business any longer."
"It's just so unusual. Nothing much ever happens around here."
"I'm sure it'll be in tomorrow's T & A. Probably a flasher showing off to the schoolgirls."
"More likely the schoolgirls flashing at the lads."

****

Marks woke early the next morning and powered up his laptop. As soon as it was active, he opened the T & A's website. There it was, already. The report of two schoolgirls stabbed in Thackley. He devoured every word before thinking how he should spend his day. He decided on a walk on the canal after he'd eaten breakfast; he was surprised how hungry he was. Hungry for the kill. Once out in the cool, damp air, he was a little surprised at the number of people who exercised on the towpath. But he didn't let it deter him. He was determined he would carry out another murder.

He walked slowly from Apperley Bridge towards Rodley, constantly looking around to see if anyone was behind him. Eventually, he saw a jogger approaching him in the distance. He was alone. Marks looked around. There was no-one else in sight. He checked continuously until the jogger was close, then pulled out a knife, stabbed him twice in the stomach and once in the chest, and then, before he sank to the ground, he pushed him into the canal. He looked around before walking briskly away. He kept looking back until the body had sunk. The area was deserted. Nobody had seen what he'd done. He took off his bloody windcheater and put in in a bag before pulling on another clean zip-up jacket. He looked around once more and walked calmly away as blood rose to the surface of the canal and dissipated.

****

News reached the team as they arrived for work. The first two on site, Lynn and Andy, were immediately dispatched to the scene to join Forensics who were already there, but soon returned as there were no witnesses to interview.

****

Scoffer had asked for a meeting of the team. He had something on his mind, and he felt sure others in the team felt the same, but nobody dare bring it up. They assembled in the Conference Room. Gary opened the discussion.

"OK, Scoffer, what's on your mind?"
"Well, nobody seems to know what their priority is. We keep getting moved from one case to the next."
"I'm trying to ensure everybody is up to date with the status of every case, so we can cover for absences more easily."
"Well, I'm sorry to say I don't think it's working."
"Ever heard of multi-tasking?"

"Of course. But I don't always think it's right in our line of work. I think we should be allocated a specific case and see it through. It's always worked when Brian was here."

"How does everyone else feel about this?"

"I'm with Scoffer."

"That surprises me, Lynn. What about the rest of you?"

"I think we're all of the same mind, boss. It's nothing personal. It's just when Brian was in charge, we always knew where we stood, what our priorities were and how we were expected to handle each case. We knew if we did well, he would congratulate us, and if we made a mistake, he'd take us aside and talk it through. There was no animosity, no criticism. We always felt that even if we made a mistake, we learnt from it, and it made us better officers. Sorry, boss, but we're all a bit disheartened. Your style of leadership is different to what we've got used to."

"I see. Well, thanks for being honest. I'll think it over and get back to you. OK. Back to work."

Every member of the team was apprehensive about the possible outcomes, but at least they'd brought it into the open. Something had to change.

Gary explained to DCI Gardner in his office how the team felt about the way he led the team.

"I'm sorry, sir, but I don't think I'm cut out to be the leader of this team. They have too much respect for DI Peters for me to fill his shoes. I'd like to be relieved of the duties, sir."

"You want to revert to being a DS?"

"Yes, sir."

"Don't you think the team will regard you as a failure?"

"Well, they'd be justified. I've failed to fill DI Peters' boots."

"So, who do you suggest should replace you?"

"I would say Lynn, sir. But I don't think she'd accept it. She has too much respect for DI Peters. Everyone feels the same. They're adamant you should ask him to return."

"I'm not sure he'd accept."

"I think I might know how to persuade him."

"How?"

"Ask Teresa to talk to him. He respects her more than anyone else here."

"They certainly worked well together."

"It's worth a try, sir. Please give it some consideration."

"I will."

"It will certainly galvanise the team, sir. You'll soon see results."

The DCI gave the situation a great deal of thought before picking up the phone and asking Teresa to come to his office. She had guessed what he wished to discuss and was prepared. She took a deep breath, knocked on the door and entered.

"You wish to see me, sir?"

"Sit down, Teresa. I'd like to discuss something with you in complete confidence."

"That's guaranteed, sir."

"Thank you. Now, Gary feels that the team members are not responding to his style of management. He's asked to step down, back to his previous role, and I've agreed. So, that leaves us with the matter of picking someone else to take the leadership position. Any ideas?"

"Only one, sir. In my opinion, there's only one person in the entire team who could hold it all together *and* get results. And I think you know who that person is, sir."

"Brian Peters."

"Exactly, sir."

"Would he be interested?"

"I'm sure he would, sir. But, more than that, he needs to work. He needs something to occupy his time. You'd be doing him a great favour by asking him back."

"That's difficult, Teresa. He offered his resignation, and as far as he knows, it was accepted, reluctantly, I admit. But it was his decision."

"What if I could persuade him to ask for his job back?"

"In that case, I would be happy to take him back, provided he is mentally and physically fit for the role."

"Then, let me talk to him. Would it be on the same terms?"

"Yes. But he would have a probationary period to prove he's fit for the job. Let's not forget, the rest of the staff believe he gave notice to quit, and as far as Brian is aware, his notice was accepted. He doesn't know the letter of resignation is still in my desk drawer.

"I'm sure he'd be fine with that, sir."

"Then persuade him to come in to speak to me about it."

"I'll go straight after work, sir. Thank you, sir. You won't regret it."
"I sincerely hope not, Teresa."

She called Brian and arranged to see him, at his flat, at six pm. She refused to tell him what it was about but asked him to refrain from alcohol until they had spoken face to face. Reluctantly, he agreed.

Teresa arrived on time, and Brian made her a cup of tea before they sat at the kitchen table.

"So, Teresa, what's the secrecy in aid of?"
"I know your drinking is getting out of hand, Brian, and I understand why. And I think I've found a way to help you."
"Go on. I'm listening."
"I think your problem is due to the fact that you've too much time on your hands, and nobody to share it with."
"So, what are you suggesting? I get a part-time job stacking shelves at Aldi?"
"No. I'm suggesting you take a job that everyone knows you're good at. A job which challenges your intellect and stamina."
"I think I can see where you're going here. You think I should apply to re-join the Force?"
"Yes."
"What makes you think I'd want to? And, more to the point, what makes you think they'd have me back?"
"Whether you want to go back is not the issue. You *need* to work. You need a challenging job to occupy your time, to keep you out of the pubs, to give structure to your life. You can't go on as you are, Brian. It's making you ill."
"OK. I agree with that to some extent. I do need to find a job of some sort, but I very much doubt whether CID would have me back."
"If you could commit yourself to doing the job to the best of your ability, they'd take you back."
"And you know this how?"
"I've discussed it already with the DCI. He wants you to go in and discuss it with him. But there will be conditions. For a start, you would have to convince him you could control your alcohol intake. And you'd have to complete a probationary period, until you prove

you're committed to the job and producing results. Don't worry, all the team will be right behind you."

"What about Gary?"

"He's in favour. He's already stepped down. He's been struggling to emulate your success. You're a hard act to follow."

"Let me think it over."

"You've got tonight. You're meeting DCI Gardner tomorrow morning, as soon as he can make some time. Be sober and convince him to give you your job back. We need you, Brian. We've a backlog of cases to be solved. Scoffer needs you. He keeps saying we need you back in charge. He's got a great future, but he's getting disillusioned."

"Tell Gardner I'll be there."

"Thank you. And no alcohol! Be sober. This is where you get your life back. Give it your best shot."

"I will, Teresa. Thank you. You're right. It's time I did something useful with my life."

"It's what Sarah would have wanted, Brian. Your parents, too."

"I know. I've just been consumed by anger. And self-pity."

"It's time that stopped. Use your time and skills to make sure it doesn't happen to anyone else. A word of advice, though."

"What's that?"

"Gardner may appear reluctant to take you back, but actually he'll be delighted. But make sure you convince him this is the right move for everybody. He's getting it in the neck from his superiors. It's a win-win situation, Brian. Please help us out here."

"You've convinced me. I'll be there."

"Thank you. I know you won't let us down. This is a new beginning for you, Brian. Grasp it with both hands."

He sat in the kitchen after Teresa had left, thinking about how he should approach his meeting with Gardner when his phone indicated an incoming message. Scoffer. He opened it and read.

"Hi, boss. Good luck for tomorrow. We need you back here asap."

He poured himself a drink – tea, then logged on his laptop and read the local news, concentrating on the reports of recent crimes. He went to bed early and slept well after receiving an email from Teresa.

"Your meeting with DCI set for 10.30am. Good luck."

****

He woke early next morning, and drank a coffee while he checked his PC, before going for a three-mile run. On his return, he showered and ate a light breakfast, mentally preparing himself for his meeting. He was nervous. There was a great deal riding on the outcome, but he was confident. He realised how much a successful outcome meant to those previously under his command. He was confident he could galvanise them, if only he had the will to do the job. But, deep down, he was optimistic. During the night, he dreamed his murdered wife Sarah had spoken to him, urging him not to give up, but to return to the job which gave him the opportunity to take criminals off the streets. She pleaded with him to do the job she believed would give him the strength to live. He dressed and went down to the car park where a taxi was waiting for him.

On arrival, he presented himself at Reception and Teresa came down to escort him to the DCI's office, where she wished him good luck and kissed his cheek. He knocked and heard the DCI's voice call 'Come in.' He entered to find DCI Gardner standing in front of his desk with his hand out in welcome. They shook hands.

"It's good to see you again, Brian. How are you?"
"Very well, sir. Thank you for seeing me."
"My pleasure, Brian. Please take a seat."
"Thank you."
"Now, I'm sure you've read the papers and are aware we have some difficult open cases."
"Yes, sir. I'd like to help you by offering my experience and acumen. The team know how I work and, in the past, have responded well to my methods. I'm sure I can help to get the results you require."
"I believe you can, Brian. Your record is testimony to that. The only thing in question is whether you have the motivation and will to do the job."
"I believe I have, sir. I believe I've reached the stage where I need the job to help maintain my sanity and health. I'll do everything in my power to return to where I was before my family were taken

from me. I admit I was in no way able to function without them. Now I realise I need the job to prevent me from a total breakdown. I've come to accept what's happened and I know that my wife and kids were proud of me and the job I did. I want to ensure they maintain that pride. I don't want to let them down. I know they're watching me, and I want them to know that, as much as I miss them, I can function knowing they're out there somewhere cheering me on. And I promise, sir, that alcohol will no longer be a crutch I have to lean to. From now on, my focus will be on catching criminals, and ensuring my team have a leader they can look up to and be proud of."

There was silence for a few moments before DCI Gardner spoke.

"Brian, I believe you. I'm willing to give you a chance to prove yourself, but it will be on the basis of a three-month probationary period at which point we'll review the situation and decide how we move forward from there."

"That's fine, sir. Thank you for giving me a chance."

"When can you start?"

"How about a week on Monday?"

"Not sooner?"

"I've booked a week at a spa for detox and help to maintain an alcohol-free future. They're highly recommended, sir. They'll help me hit the ground running."

"That's fine, Brian. Your desk will be waiting for you. Do you mind if I inform the team?"

"Not at all, sir. I hope you get a positive reaction."

"I'm certain I will, Brian. They've missed your leadership. They'll all be glad you're back. Now, is there anything else?"

"No, sir. Thank you for giving me this chance."

"I don't need thanks, Brian. I need you to show me I've made the right decision. Don't let me down."

"I won't, sir. That's a promise."

They shook hands at the office door before a smiling DI Peters made his way down the steps to the exit where Teresa was waiting. She could tell by his demeanour the meeting went well.

"So, when do you start?"

"A week on Monday."

"Why so long?

"I've booked a week of detox and rehab. This is the start of the new me."

She threw her arms around his neck and kissed him.

"I'm so proud of you, Brian. You can do this."

"I know."

"Can I tell everybody?"

"No. Let the DCI do that."

"Not even Scoffer? He keeps asking if you're coming back."

"No, Teresa. Gardner will announce it in due course. Just keep it to yourself for now."

"Awwwww!"

"Promise."

"OK. We'll see you a week on Monday. Mind if I send you some reading material to fill your time on holiday?"

"Case notes?"

"Yes."

"Please. That would be useful. Thank you. Keep it quiet."

"Will do."

"'Bye for now."

****

That evening, Brian phoned his parents. It had been a while since they'd had a chat, but it went well. It was obvious that the reason his parents used to visit so often was to see their grandkids regularly as they grew up. They shared the same sense of loss that Brian felt, making conversation difficult when Sarah and the kids where no longer there.

****

Brian drove to his destination on the outskirts of Llanberis, close to Mount Snowdon. It was an impressive hotel and spa which immediately gave him the feeling his stay would be worth every penny. And so it transpired. He attended every session and took part enthusiastically in each challenge and activity unlike some of the others who evidently were not there of their own volition. He recognised many of the participants, even though some used assumed names. There was a Labour MP, several musicians and various TV personalities. All the same, he left at the end of the week feeling like a new man, physically and mentally. He now felt totally prepared to take up his old role and he couldn't wait. He needed the challenge and was fully confident he would succeed.

****

CHAPTER 4

On the Monday morning, he was up early, feeling refreshed and ready for the challenge he now faced. He checked his look in the mirror; his suit had been dry-cleaned and he wore a new shirt and tie, as well as having had his shoes soled and heeled. He picked up the car keys, locked the door behind him and walked down the steps to begin his new career. Outside, he looked proudly at his newly valeted car before getting in and driving to work.

Pulling into the car park at HQ, he noticed his parking space had been reinstated, and pulled into it with a smile. The duty officer on Reception greeted him cheerily, adding that it was good to see him back. So far, so good! Mounting the steps, he took a deep breath before entering the office. He was early but the entire team was already there and greeted him warmly, the men shaking his hand, the ladies giving him a hug. Slightly embarrassed, he responded by thanking them and asking them to join him for a meeting in the Conference Room in ten minutes, so that they could bring him up to date regarding their workload. But first, he went upstairs to see Teresa. She showed her delight immediately and unashamedly, throwing her arms round his neck and kissing his cheek.

"Thanks for coming back, Brian. God! We've missed you!"
"It's good to be back, Teresa. Would you please inform the DCI I'm here and just getting up to date with the team. I think that's my priority."
"Of course. He's delighted you decided to come back. Perhaps a little sanity will return to the team now."
"I'll give it all I've got, Teresa. That's a promise."
"That's all we ask."

He entered the Conference Room to find his team busy ensuring the whiteboards were up to date and everything was tidy. He wasted no time.

"OK, let's have an update. Gary, you first, please."
"OK, boss. Our main focus has been on a series of murders, two of which we think are linked. In each case, the victim was a homeless man, a rough sleeper, who was doused with an accelerant and set alight as he slept. In both cases, the crime took place in the early

hours of the morning in the storage or delivery area of a retail building. Up to now, we have no leads. CCTV footage is indistinct. We believe the perpetrator did his research and worked out where the blind spots were, and what time security patrols passed. We have no leads at all."

"OK, what's next?"

"The dead body of a young boy was found in the grounds of the BRI. We believe he was dumped there. Death was due to asphyxiation; he was starved of oxygen, and already suffered from asthma. We're working on the theory that his death was accidental; in that he may have been held in captivity and his captor took him to the hospital in the hope that he could be saved. When he got there, he realised the boy had died, so dumped him. Again, there is no CCTV. We've identified the boy, who it seems was used as a drugs mule."

"OK, next."

"Two more murders. This time the victims were pensioners who lived in a houseboat moored on the canal near Rodley. They were stabbed to death in their home. The perpetrator left the scene without anyone having seen or heard anything."

"Next."

"Two schoolgirls were stabbed to death in Thackley as they were having a smoke on a quiet track behind the school after classes were over. Nobody saw or heard anything. All we have is the statement from a couple of dog walkers who saw a man in that area the previous day. Apparently, they walk their dogs there every day, but had never seen the man before, or since the incident."

"Have we got an artist's impression?"

"Yes. But we're not too confident as both women's recollections differed."

"Next."

"A jogger was stabbed on the canal towpath. His body was found in the canal. No witnesses."

"Next."

Lynn spoke up.

"These are my cases, boss. First, we have had reports of fireworks being set off close to wooded areas. We believe they are a signal that drugs have been delivered and are ready for collection, but by the time it's been called in and we've got officers there, the place is deserted. No leads."

"Anything else?"

"We have had reports that another local Chinese takeaway is being used to take orders and deliver drugs. That one's just come in."

"OK. Who's in the best position to look into the takeaway?"

"I fancy that, boss."

"OK, Scoffer. I'll call you when we've finished here, and we'll discuss it."

"OK."

"Anybody else underemployed at the moment?"

Nobody spoke up.

"Is everybody happy with the case they've been allocated?"

Again, no response.

"OK, then. Have another look at your cases. See if you've missed anything. If you have, deal with it. If not, bring it back to me and we'll take another look at it. Any questions?"

Silence.

"OK, off you go. Gary, could you just hang back for a minute."

Once the room had cleared, Brian spoke to the clearly embarrassed Gary.

"Gary, I want to thank you for the hard work you've put in in my absence. I'm very grateful."

"I'd like to say it was a pleasure, boss. But it wasn't. I'm glad you're back. I'd got to the end of my tether. I've found it very challenging, to say the least."

"As long as you did your best, Gary, nobody can have any complaints. Things should be a little easier for you now, but if ever you need to talk about anything, in confidence, I'll be here for you."

"Thank you, boss."

"OK, Gary. Back to work. I'll look at all the cases and see if we need to tweak our response to them."

He immediately called Scoffer for a quick word.

"Thanks for putting yourself forward for the takeaway case, Scoffer."

"A pleasure, boss. It will be good to be able to make a few decisions for myself."

"What are you saying?"

"Just that Gary has a different way of managing us, boss. He micro-manages. He makes all the decisions for us and expects us to do everything his way."

"Well, he does have more experience than you."

"I know, but we learn from mistakes. And, working with you, you let me decide to a great extent how to approach an investigation, and only stop me if you think I'm doing something wrong."

"We're all different, Scoffer. Gary just employs a different style. People respond differently to the way their boss works. Maybe it's just that his style regarding you needs tweaking a bit. Maybe he just needs a bit more leadership experience. We're all different."

"I get you, boss, but I am delighted to have you back."

"Then, concentrate on this case and decide how you'll approach it, who you want to partner you on it, and come back to me with your proposal. OK."

"Thanks, boss. I'll get right on it."

****

Scoffer was reading all the information they had regarding the takeaway drugs business when Ruth came over to his desk.

"Hi Scoffer, can I have a word?"

"Of course, Ruth. Pull up a chair."

"It's just I was thinking about the case you're looking at."

"And?"

"Well, I'd like to partner you on it."

"Any particular reason why?"

"Not particularly. I just thought a male / female combination would work."

"You're probably right."

"Besides that, I've been told you learnt very quickly working with DI Peters, so I thought I could pick up some tips from you."

Scoffer smiled.

"You're right. I learnt a lot from the boss. I'd be happy to pass on any knowledge I can. What are you working on now?"
"Just fetching and carrying for Gary. I don't think he trusts me yet. Could you ask him if you can take me as your partner for this case?"
"It's Brian's decision now."
"I know, but out of courtesy…."
"Leave it to me."

He picked up the phone and called Gary.

"Hi, Gary. Would you mind if I asked Ruth to partner me for the takeaway case. It's a job for a couple, I think."
"Yeah, that's fine. I can't find anything to suit her particular talents. You're welcome to her."
"Thankyou."

He ended the call.

"Sounds to me he doesn't like you much."
"I've done nothing wrong as far as I know. I've done everything he's asked to the best of my ability."
"Well, with me it's a case of listen and learn, and don't be afraid to make suggestions about how you think we could do better. Welcome aboard. I hope you're OK working mostly evenings on this."
"No problem."
"Right, I'll clear it with Brian, then we'll sit down together and work out how we're going to handle the case."

By mid-afternoon they had worked out a plan which they discussed briefly with Brian, before finishing work early in order to take a break before commencing surveillance on the takeaway later that evening.

****

Teresa was intrigued by an email sent to her from a PCSO. It read:

"My boss suggested I should forward this report to you, just for information, as there seems to be some unusual criminal activity just now. If it's not relevant, please accept my apologies for wasting your time. See attached. PCSO Stevenson."

She opened the attached document before deciding it was worth bringing to Brian's attention.

"On Friday, 7th April, PSCO Hatton and I responded to a phone call from the manager of a local retirement housing scheme, regarding the behaviour of a new tenant. She informed us that a few of the single female tenants had told her he was 'creepy', and they felt uncomfortable in the communal areas if he walked in when they were alone. On more than one occasion, he has 'touched' some of the older ladies who live alone and made sexual innuendoes. The manager has spoken to him about his behaviour, but he just brushed it off as 'a bit of fun'. She has given him a warning as to his future behaviour. We spoke to him and gave him a similar warning. He doesn't appear to have a criminal record, but I believe he should be marked up as 'one to watch'. He is now known locally as 'Uncle Creepy' after a character in a humorous novel called "the Forkham Predicament.""

Brian filed the information, rang the manager who'd raised the incident, and spoke to her for a short while, asking her to bring any further incidents to his attention and send him the man's photograph. He wrote the man's name on one of his whiteboards.

The email containing Uncle Creepy's image arrived shortly afterwards. He printed it, shut down his PC, put on his jacket and left the building, parking in Sainsbury's car park in Greengates so he could visit the pubs close to the junction. He had no intention of having a drink; this was business.

He visited four establishments in quick succession. The man in the photograph was recognised in each and was already barred from two for making unwanted approaches to female customers. The consensus of opinion was that he was a 'dirty old man'. Brian drove home satisfied with his enquiry, and pleased with himself that he'd been in four pubs without having an alcoholic drink.

****

The following day he called at the Immanuel College where he was allowed to show the photograph to many of the pupils. However, nobody was able to identify him, nor state they had seen him on the day the two pupils were murdered. Once at work, he updated the whiteboard with the recently acquired information. At that point, Scoffer and Ruth arrived after a late night shadowing the deliveries from the Chinese takeaway. They'd had some success.

"So, how did it go?"
"Very well. We've identified three addresses where we believe drugs rather than food was delivered."
"So, what's the next step?"
"I'm not sure, boss. If we raid the addresses after delivery, can we be sure we can prove they were delivered by the takeaway's driver? Or should we intercept the driver in the hope that he's carrying drugs? We need a plan which is absolutely guaranteed to provide cast-iron evidence against the takeaway business."
"How do you propose to do that?"
"Get the driver on our side?"
"And plan B?"
"Get one of our men on the inside?"
"OK. Sort out what you decide and come back to me."
"Thanks, boss."

Once they were away from Brian's desk, Ruth commented.

"That wasn't a lot of help, was it?"
"What do you mean?"
"Well, I thought he would have told us exactly what to do, to make sure we didn't slip up."
"He makes sure we get it right by asking questions. Making us think about how to handle tasks rather than blindly following instructions. He doesn't want 'yes' men. He needs people who will think about what they're doing so they can react if circumstances change. If you want to get on in this business, you need to give some thought to what you're doing, not just do what you're told."
"OK. I get it."
"Right, let's think about how we should approach this case. But you need to bear in mind that if ever the boss tells you what to do,

then that's *exactly* what you have to do, and there'll be a very good reason for it."

"OK. What if we look into the driver's background?"

"To see if we have any leverage?"

"Yeah. See if we can get his ID from Teresa's facial recognition? Or ask her to hack their payroll software?"

"You learn fast. Let's see what we can find."

Teresa was soon able to identify the driver and provided his criminal history. He had twice been convicted of distributing drugs, including cocaine and heroin, and had served time in prison. Scoffer decided to confront him in the process of delivering the drugs and asked Brian if he could organise for two uniformed officers to take him in while he and Ruth interviewed the customers. It was agreed. Just before Scoffer and Ruth walked away, smiling, to prepare for the evening, Brian called them back.

"Haven't you forgotten something?"

"What's that, boss?"

"What about the takeaway?"

"We've sorted that, boss. The Drugs Squad will hit it as soon as we've established the driver is delivering drugs. They can go in with all the necessary equipment to establish exactly what they're selling and the quantities. Plus, somewhere on the premises there'll be an address book, etc. From that we can see who's supplying the goods. I thought it best to bring in the experts, boss. Hope that's OK."

"Perfect, Scoffer. Well done, the two of you. Go get 'em."

****

They sat in the car until the delivery driver set off on his rounds, waiting until they were absolutely certain it was a drugs delivery rather than food, based on the size of the package, and stopped the driver as he was about to ring a doorbell, dragging him away around the corner.

"Excuse us, sir. We'd like a look at the delicacies you're selling."

"I'm just delivering, mate. You have to order at the takeaway."

"Well, why don't you just show us what you're delivering?"

He brandished his ID in front of the driver's face, and Ruth, with a wide smile, did the same.

"Let's have a look inside that package."

He was right. He'd seen the type of package on numerous occasions, and summoned backup to escort the driver to HQ. With the package in his hand, he rang the bell and waited until the door opened to show an unshaven, unkempt young man.

"Your delivery, sir."
"About time. You're not the usual man."
"He's not well. Will you check the delivery. Is it what you ordered?"

He opened the bag and looked at the small clear plastic bags inside.

"Yeah. All here. Thanks."

He was about to shut the door when Scoffer spoke.

"What about paying for them?"
"I've paid. I ordered them online."
"From the takeaway?"
"Yeah. What's wrong with that?"
"Just that I didn't know about the online business, so, thanks for that. Now, if you'd like to come with us."
"What you on about?"
"We're taking you down to the station for interview. You might be there for a while, but if you get hungry, we can get you a takeaway. Get your coat."

He showed his ID. The customer groaned and complied.

As they drove back to HQ, they received a message to inform them the Drugs Squad had arrived at the takeaway and closed it for business while they searched the premises.

"A good night's work that, Ruth. Fancy a takeaway?"
"Only if it's been checked out."
"I know just the place. Big portions. I don't know about you but I'm starving. I could eat a cow between two bread vans."

"You know, I really enjoy working with you, Scoffer. You make me laugh. It was never any fun working with Gary."

"I think Gary's struggling with the weight of his responsibilities. I've been lucky; working with Brian has been great. He's always treated me well. Still, we've done a good job tonight. Maybe he'll let us team up again in future."

"That would be good."

"Yeah. I think so too. Tell you what, Ruth. How about we take the takeaway back to mine? We can sit and chat, and I've got a nice bottle of wine waiting to be sampled."

"Good idea. I'd like that."

Scoffer's face broke into a broad grin.

****

"Come on, Scoffer. Wake up! Look at the time!"

"We've time to do it again."

"We haven't! I need to get home and get changed."

Your clothes are fine."

"No. I wore them yesterday. Someone will notice and they'll guess I've been out all night. And looking at the grin on your face, they'll guess exactly where I've been and what I've been doing."

"Does it matter?"

"Of course, it matters. They might not let us work together."

"OK. Let's get showered and we'll call at yours so you can get changed."

"You do understand, don't you?"

"I suppose so."

"Well, look at it this way; you wouldn't want a relationship to stand in the way of your career, would you?"

"I don't know. It depends on how I felt."

"Well, let's take things slowly. Last night was great, but we need some time to really get to know each other before we make it public."

"Understood."

"Come on, get moving."

"Time for a quickie?"

"No. We need to get to work. Now *move!*"

They drove in silence to Ruth's house, both thinking carefully about the nascent relationship and where it might lead. They were both aware of the effect it might have on their careers and knew at some point they would have to make a decision concerning their possible future together. However, right now, their work was more important, and they were forced to put their feelings aside and concentrate on their next assignment, hoping they would be able to work it together.

Arriving at work, they presented themselves at Brian's desk to report their previous night's success.

"Well done, you two. I thought you'd be good together. How do you feel about teaming up for the next assignment?"
"Fine by me, boss."
"Me too."
"Good. I want you to look into this other business which keeps cropping up. Reports of fireworks being set off to indicate, we believe, that a delivery of drugs has been made and is ready for distribution. It's so far thwarted our attempts to catch them in the act. Will the two of you look into it?"
"Of course, boss."
"OK, get the info from Teresa. And good luck."

Teresa handed over the file to the officers, and in return was informed about the drugs takeaway business's online ordering presence. She gleefully informed them.

"Their online business will soon contain a bug which alerts me whenever anyone orders drugs online."

****

Stephen Marks was out early in the morning for the short walk to Stanley Street. It was still dark but he worked quickly, wrapping around the entrance gates the crime scene tape he'd bought at a party shop the previous day. The job completed, he stepped back and took out his camera, lining up several shots from different angles. He checked the images, took a few more, and pulled off the tape, stuffing it into his inside pocket, before leaving the scene. He was pleased with his work. Nobody had disturbed him; nobody had seen him. He smiled, walking quickly home to load the images onto his laptop so he could photoshop them before writing the storyline.

****

When Brian arrived at work the following morning, a shock awaited him. No sooner had he sat at his desk than he was summoned to DCI Gardner's office.

"You wanted to see me, sir."
"Yes, Brian. Something's come up, and I have to say it was not totally unexpected. Gary has handed in his notice."
"Whatever for?"
"He's decided it's not for him. His promotion to acting DI and subsequent switch back to DS, which has happened twice now, has left him seriously questioning whether he wants to continue in CID. And, unfortunately, he's decided enough is enough."
"Have you tried to talk him out of it?"
"Of course, but he's adamant."
"Let me talk to him."
"No, Brian. He's taken leave. Let him go. It's what he wants. Personally, I'd like him to stay, but, quite predictably, he's looking at what the job's done to you and decided it's not the path he wants to follow."
"That's absurd, sir."
"I agree, but I think he's now become more aware of the problems the job may cause and doesn't want to have to go through what you've suffered."
"OK. If that's how he sees it. I'm sure we'll get by without him. We certainly won't be short of potential recruits if need be."
"I know that, Brian. The way you've been grooming your team for promotion has not gone unnoticed. We have some outstanding officers in our ranks."
"I agree, sir. And they get on well together."
"Right. So, now we're tasked with picking up the pieces from the investigations Gary was overseeing. The murders and a suspicious death of a young boy. Will you bring yourself up to speed on where we're at and get them moving forward?"
"Of course, sir. I'll get right on it."

At his desk, he read quickly through the notes of their open cases, making further notes as he read. He put aside the drug-related crimes and looked carefully at the murders, writing details on a whiteboard and drawing lines linking certain details. He was convinced that the murders of two homeless men were committed by the same person but was unable to establish a motive except that they were easy targets for someone who for some unknown reason decided to kill people. If he was right, there would be further victims, more challenging. And if that was the case, they had a serial killer, who would evolve and whose victims would be more difficult to stereotype. He stood, staring at the whiteboard as the horror of the situation sunk in.

He turned his attention to the other murders, The two pensioners on the canal barge. Easy targets. A jogger on a deserted stretch of canal towpath. Easy target. Two girls on a deserted country path, likewise. He was becoming increasingly certain they were all linked. The suffocated boy? He was unsure about that one but kept an open mind while he looked at all the other information regarding his death.

His thoughts were Interrupted by a call from Teresa.

"Sorry to disturb you, Brian. I've just had a call from the BRI. A woman turned up at A & E this morning missing a finger. She told the staff that her boyfriend had sliced it off and wants him arrested. Can we help?"
"Send me the details and we'll get someone to attend."
"Thanks."

He checked the workload and called Paula.

"Paula, can you and Jo-Jo pop up to BRI Accident and Emergency? A woman, Eileen Davies, has turned up minus a finger. She says her boyfriend cut it off."

They quickly arrived at A & E and asked to speak to the patient.

"She's out cold. We put her in a side room. It seems she's sleeping off a hangover."
"Can you get someone to wake her up. We need to talk to her."

"Good luck. You're likely to get some swearing. The doctor had to give her a sedative before he could treat her. I'll get him for you."

The doctor confirmed the woman came in a taxi, with her hand wrapped in a towel and severe bruising to her face. The third finger of her left hand had been severed just above the knuckle. She told him she'd been beaten up by her boyfriend at her home. He left her and she managed to phone a taxi to bring her here. They'd been drinking heavily.

"Can you wake her up?"
"I can try but be prepared for some foul language."
"We're used to it."

It was a further hour before they were able to speak to her and for her to answer coherently.

"OK, Mrs Davies. Would you like to tell us what happened?"
"My boyfriend did it. He beat me up and cut my finger off."
"Why did he do that?"
"He's got a temper when he's been drinking."
"OK. Talk us through what happened."
"We'd been up talking all night...."
"Drinking all night?"
"Well, yes."
"OK, go on."
"Then he started getting abusive. Slapping me, and that."
"Why didn't you call the police?"
"I couldn't get to the phone. He was beating me up."
"Did you shout for help?"
"I tried, but he knocked me unconscious."
"Has he ever attacked you before?"
"Lots of times. He's got a right temper when he's been drinking."
"So, why haven't you reported it before?"
"'Cos I love him."
"It doesn't sound like he feels the same way about you."
"He's only like that when he's been drinking."
"Where is he now?"
"Don't know. I suppose he's gone home."
"Give us the address. Please. We'd like to talk to him. By the way, what did he do with your finger?"

"Don't know. He must have taken it."

"Do you wish to charge him with assault?"

"I don't know. He's nice. Until he gets drunk."

"Give us his address anyway. We'll talk to him."

Back in the car, Jo-Jo asked,

"What did you make of that?"

"I don't know what to think. But I want to hear his version of events. Let's go and wake him up."

They drove to Ravenscliffe and parked outside a neglected semi. Paula knocked on the door and rang the bell several times until they eventually heard movement inside. When the door opened, a sleepy face appeared.

"What do you want?"

"Are you Malcolm Carter?"

"What's it to do with you?"

They showed their ID. He groaned.

"I wondered when you'd come. Is it about that whore, Eileen?"

"Yes. You've been expecting us, then?"

"She's always been saying if I stopped seeing her and giving her money, she'd report me for something or other."

"Were you with her last night?"

"No. I was working. Night shifts in Shipley. Why? What's she done now?"

"She's at BRI. She says you cut off her finger."

"Not her ring finger by any chance?"

"How did you know?"

"She couldn't get her wedding ring off. She wanted to sell it."

"She's married?"

"Divorced. He let her keep the ring, as long as she promised never to bother him again."

"Why did she bother him?"

"For money. She was always in debt. As soon as she got her Benefits, she was down to the Off-licence, or on the phone to her dealer. And when she'd spent it all, she was selling herself to anybody who needed a quick shag."

"OK, if you give us the name of your employer, we'll check your alibi and if it's confirmed, you're off the hook. Do you know where we can get hold of her ex?"

"If he's not in the Hog's Head, he'll be in the bookies by Greengates Junction."

"Thanks for your time."

They drove to Mr Carter's place of work, where his attendance the previous night was confirmed. They decided to call the BRI to query the condition of Mrs Davies, only to be told she'd discharged herself. They got her home address and pulled up outside. As they'd expected, all the curtains were closed.

"Probably sleeping off the hangover."

"Or earning her living."

They got no response from ringing the doorbell and hammering on the door. Debating their next move, Jo-Jo thought out loud.

"I wonder what happened to her finger?"

"Does it matter?"

"Well, I would have expected her to take it to the hospital with her, in case they could re-attach it."

"Good point. I'll ring them."

She made the call and received confirmation that Mrs Davies did not bring the severed finger with her.

"I wonder what she did with it."

"No harm in looking."

They went round to the back yard and pulled back the lid of the bin.

"God, that stinks!"

"Masks and gloves, then."

They lifted out a carrier bag and untied it, releasing flies and an awful stink. There, on the top, loosely wrapped in kitchen paper and covered in blood, was the detached finger.

"Let's take it to Forensics. I want to know how it was removed. It looks like a butcher's job."

They dropped it off at the Lab and returned to HQ.

The following morning, the result came through from the Lab, by email.
"The finger was detached by two sharp blows, probably by hammer and chisel to the proximal phalanx. Marks on the skin indicate a ring would have been worn. Looking at the proximal interphalangeal joint, which was swollen (probably arthritis), the only way the ring could be removed intact would be by detaching the finger close to the knuckle. My theory is that the finger was detached so that the ring could be removed."

Paula offered a theory.

"Whoever did this – and I guess there must have been two people at least to hold her down – were after the ring. I'm assuming it was a wedding ring, and probably the only thing of value she had. I think someone was collecting a debt."
"That's a sound theory. Let's try to speak to her when she turns up."
"Let's try the house again."
"OK. While we're on the way, ring Teresa and see if she can give us an address for her husband."

Eileen Davies let them in. The house was a tip, with empty beer cans littering the carpet and overflowing ashtrays.

"So, this is where you had the party?"
"Yes."
"So, where did he cut off your finger?"
"Kitchen."
"Shall we go and have a look?"
"Nothing to see. I've cleaned up."
"But you didn't get round to cleaning in here?"
"No."
"So, tell us what happened in the kitchen."
"He got a hammer and chisel and chopped it off."

"How did he manage to hold you down while he needed both hands to cut your finger off?"

"I can't remember. I was dazed. He'd hit me a lot. I was probably out cold."

"OK, what did he do with the finger?"

"Don't know. He must have taken it with him."

"What about the ring?"

"What?"

"Your wedding ring. What did he do with that?"

"Must have taken it."

"We don't believe you."

"It's true."

"We've spoken to your boyfriend. He was at work."

"He's lying."

"His boss corroborated his alibi. So, who cut off your finger and took your wedding ring?"

"My boyfriend."

"Why did you put your finger in the bin? If you'd taken it to hospital with you, it's possible they could have re-attached it."

"I thought he'd taken it. I didn't know it was in the bin."

"How much debt are you in?"

"I don't have any debt."

"We don't believe you. We think they came to clear your debt and the only thing they could find of any value was your wedding ring. So, they took it. If you tell us who did this, we can catch them and charge them. So, how about it? We might even get your wedding ring back."

"If I told you, they'd kill me."

"You'll only be safe if they're in jail."

She hesitated before speaking; then gave a sigh.

"Mullinder."

"Joe Mullinder? I thought he was still inside. He got seven years!"

"Well, he's out."

"Any idea where we can find him?"

"No. But he's never far away."

"OK. Let us know if you see him or hear about him."

"I never want to see that bastard again."

****

Teresa discovered that Joe Mullinder had made a deal. He got eighteen months knocked off his sentence in return for information which led to the arrest and prosecution of a rival criminal gang. And he was back on his old patch. It was made clear to all officers that he should be arrested on sight and brought in for questioning. DI Peters had no intention of allowing him to work on *his* patch.

Mullinder's name was mentioned in team meetings, in connection with the murders of the rough sleepers, but was dismissed as a person of interest due to the victims having no money, and therefore would be of no use to Mullinder, who only lent to those who could pay back by whatever means. Still, they hoped to nail him for something, just to get him off the streets.

Back at his desk, Brian read Jo-Jo and Paula's report. The mention of Mullinder's name worried him. He had ruled in the years before Brian joined CID, but he had heard of his exploits and was determined to stop him before he regained his previous influence over the criminal fraternity in the area. He sent Paula and Jo-Jo to interview Mrs Davies again in the hope she knew any of the other local people in debt to him. Meanwhile, he was reading Mullinder's criminal history, carefully compiled for him by Teresa.

****

The call came through at 9.15am.

"There's a dead body in my allotment."
"What's your location, sir?"
"Stanley Street allotments, at Greengates, near the junction."
"Just a moment, sir. Right, now which allotment is it?"
"Far right, at the back."
"Thank you. Now, could I have your name, please, sir?"
"Martin Steele."
"Thank you. Will you please stay where you are until we get someone there? Should only be a few minutes."
"Yes, I'll wait."
"And, please don't touch anything, sir."
"I won't."

Martin waited nervously in his car by the entrance to the allotments, thankful that the body could not be seen from there. Soon, a police car appeared with two uniformed officers who quickly confirmed the report was valid and required the support of the Forensics team and CID. In the meantime, they cordoned off the area.

At HQ, Teresa picked up the call and passed the information to Brian, who despatched Lynn and Andy to the scene. They arrived before Forensics and took a statement from Martin Steele, who was asked to remain at the scene until the preliminary investigation was concluded. He agreed and accompanied them to the scene, describing what he'd found when he arrived.

"I got out of the car by the gates and walked over to my patch. I headed straight for the shed, where all my stuff is kept, locked securely. It was only when I got to the shed door that I noticed some of the stuff I keep stacked at the side had been disturbed. These canes are normally stacked in the gap between the shed and the hedge, out of the way, but they'd been pulled out and strewn on the ground. And a body had been stuffed into the gap. I nearly fainted when I saw it, then I threw up when I saw all the blood."

"Did you touch anything, sir?"

"Are you kidding? I couldn't get away fast enough. I phoned 999, and then sat in the car until the policemen turned up."

"Did you notice anything out of the ordinary, apart from the body, that is?"

"No. It's not visible until you get to the shed."

"There was nobody else about?"

"No."

"And what time was it when you found the body?"

"Just after nine."

"OK, thanks, Mr Steele. If you don't mind, could you please hang around until Forensics get here. They won't be long. They may have some more questions for you."

"OK. I hope they'll be careful if they have to do any digging."

"Why's that, sir?"

"Well, I've just planted all down this side. The ground on the other side of the path could do with a bit of digging over, though."

"We'll bear that in mind, sir."

Forensics were soon on the scene and Allen had a quick chat with Martin Steele before allowing him to leave. They erected screens around the crime scene before commencing their examination of the body. Lynn and Andy went door-knocking and questioning the local residents. Nobody had seen or heard anything unusual.

"Nothing else we can do today, Andy. We'll call back this evening to see if anyone we've missed knows anything. Let's have a quick word with SOCO to see if they can give us time of death."

Forensics were on the point of packing up when Lynn spoke to Allen Greaves.

"Only five or six hours, I would say. Between 4 and 5am."
"Cause of death?"
"Stab wounds. Three to the stomach, one to the heart. She bled out. From the trail of blood, she must have been attacked at the end of this narrow path which runs through to Haigh Hall Road and dragged into the allotment to finish her off. She'd also been beaten quite savagely and kicked in the head and ribs. Whoever did this is a very angry man. We've picked up some cigarette butts from the ground by this end of the path. It's possible they were dropped by the killer, so we'll see if we can get usable DNA. Of course, it's possible that someone other than the killer dropped them. We believe they approached the site from Haigh Hall Road. It's possible he knew her, otherwise, why would she walk with him? By the same token, why would she walk up a dark, narrow footpath on her own?"
"OK, Allen. Thanks. We need to find out who she is, where she'd been and who she'd been with."
"I'll send the report as soon as we've examined the body on the slab. Oh, we couldn't find any ID on her. You may have to put out an appeal for missing persons. She'll be difficult to recognise after the beating she's taken. But, then again, if she has a criminal record, her DNA will identify her."

They drove in silence back to HQ, each wondering what sort of man – they were both certain it was a man – could inflict wounds like that on a defenceless person. They were both also wondering if there might be a connection with the murder of the schoolgirls.

67

They would write up their notes, grab a sandwich and go back to Greengates to question more of the locals.

****

Stephen Marks was proofreading the text he'd just typed about the latest murder. It excited him, from the moment he'd met the young female drug addict and offered her a hit, to the disposal of her body. From his window he occasionally saw or heard the police vehicles driving towards the scene, lights flashing, and then, later, leaving quietly. He was satisfied with his script but felt the need to go over it again and again, changing the odd word. In truth, he was not trying to improve it; he merely got his satisfaction from replaying the scene in his head while he read.

He looked at the time, and, realising he'd been awake for more than twenty-four hours, shut down his laptop and went to bed, waking regularly as his memory of the night's events would not leave him and caused a constant erection. He got up and switched the laptop on once again to add to the story the fact that it caused a sleepless night due to a repeated erection. Having typed the additional text, he re-read his version of the night's action.

LATEST VICTIM

He saw her seated on a bench in Greengates Park in the early hours of the morning. She was shivering, although wearing a thick overcoat and jogging bottoms. He approached her.

"Are you OK?"

She looked up, startled.

"Who are you?"
"Just walking home when I saw you. You look cold. Would you like a cig?"
"Please."

She took one and smiled,

"Thanks."

He sat down beside her and asked again.

"Are you OK?"
"I've been better."
"You shouldn't be out here in the cold. Why don't you go home?"
"He threw me out."
"What for?"
"We had an argument."
"What about?"

There was a moment's hesitation before she replied.

"Weed."
"What about it?"
"We ran out. He said I'd used it all."
"And you hadn't?"
"No more than my share. But our delivery never turned up."
"So, he threw you out?"
"Yeah. The bastard."
"Don't you have anywhere to go?"
"No."
"Well, you can't sleep out here all night. Apart from the cold, it's not safe. Come back with me. You can sleep on the couch. I promise you'll be safe. And warm."
"I'm not sure."
"It's up to you. I won't harm you. And I've got some coke."

Again, she hesitated before replying.

"OK."

He led her through the park and down to his house near New Line, opening the door and motioning for her to enter. She could feel the warmth radiating from the living room as she walked in.

"Sit down. Would you like a vodka first to warm you up?"
"Please."

He smiled. It was all going to plan. He went through to the kitchen, poured her a large glass of vodka and a glass of water for himself, and returned to the front room, handing the glass to his guest.

"What's your name?"

"Mandy. What's yours?"

"Steve."

"Thanks for the drink, Steve. What about the coke?"

"You can have that, no problem. But there's a price."

She was expecting as much.

"What do you want me to do?"

"A blow-job."

"OK. Give me the coke first."

"No."

"Come on. I promise I'll do it afterwards."

"It's not that I don't trust you, but that's the deal. Blow-job first. Coke later."

She sighed.

"OK. Get it out."

Five minutes later, it was over. She passed him a tissue and downed the rest of her vodka while he cleaned himself up.

"So, where's the coke?"

"I'll text him now."

"You haven't got any?"

"He'll bring it straight away."

"You've tricked me, you bastard."

"Look, it will only take a couple of minutes. I'll get you another vodka while I sort it out."

"OK. But get the coke. That was the deal."

He went into the kitchen and planned what he needed to do, rehearsing what he'd say and trying to anticipate how she'd react. Confident his plan would work, he strolled back into the room, smiling.

"We can meet him on Stanley Street in a couple of minutes. Get your coat on."

"Can't I wait here?"

"Sorry, I don't know you well enough to leave you alone in my house. You'll have to come with me. It'll be worth it for the coke."

"OK. But no more tricks. Just get the coke."
"Yeah. That's the deal. Let's go."

He took her up Haigh Hall Road and they turned left towards Stanley Street, accessed by a narrow, poorly lit path at the end of which, on the right, were the allotments. As soon as they reached that point, he suddenly pulled out a knife and stabbed her in the stomach, putting his hand over her mouth to stifle her screams while he stabbed her again, in the stomach and the chest as she slumped to the ground. He caught his breath and listened. The night was silent; nobody heard the disturbance. He dragged the body through the entrance to the allotments, to the plot he'd earmarked previously because it had a shed at the back behind which he would dump the body. He dragged out the lengths of cane and timber which were stored there and placed them out of the way before returning to kick the corpse savagely about the head and body. Just for fun. Then, he bundled it into the space behind the shed and left quietly, smiling.

****

He sat back in his chair, gazing at the text on the screen, happy with what he'd written and not in the least surprised that he had an erection. Opening the file containing the 'crime scene' photos he had taken previously, he checked them once again. Perfect! At least one of them would be perfect for the book cover. He shut down the laptop and went back to bed, soon falling asleep and dreaming about his next killing.

CHAPTER 5

Lynn and Andy were door-knocking in Greengates in the hope that they'd gain some useful information regarding the Stanley Street allotments incident when a call came through from Brian.

"Lynn, we've just received a call regarding body parts discovered close to where you are. Forensics are on their way. Will you attend the scene, please?"
"OK. Let's have the address."
"Kipling Court. It's only a few yards from where you are."
"I know it. Retirement housing."
"OK. Get down there. The manager is waiting for you."

It took longer to drive to the scene than it would to have walked, but Lynn wasn't keen on leaving the car unguarded on a back street. However, they were able to park in the visitors' car park where the manager was waiting for them and walked with them around the back of the buildings to an open garden where a compost bin stood, its lid lying on the ground beside it. Sitting on a bench was a distraught-looking man. The manager, Mrs Craig, explained.

"This is John Starkey. He lives here and he's the one who looks after the compost bin. He keeps the garden tidy round the front."
"Hello, John. Can you tell us what's happened?"
"I opened the bin this morning to put some more gardening waste in. The bin's full to the brim now, so I thought I'd take some out to spread on the roses. So, I opened the hatch at the bottom and started to dig out some compost. At first it was fine, but then my shovel met some resistance. It's not unusual. Some rubbish takes longer to degrade. So, I kept prodding to loosen it and that's when the hand fell out."
"The hand? A human hand?"
"Yes, I think so. It's over there, on the path."

Andy walked across to look at it, immediately noticing that the ends of the fingers had been removed. He mentioned it to Lynn and asked.

"Is the hand exactly how you found it?"

"What do you mean.?"

"The ends of the fingers are missing."

"I haven't done that. As soon as I picked it up and realised what it was, I threw it over there."

"OK. And are you the only person who puts waste into the compost bin?"

"Yes. At first it was used by everybody, but they were throwing all sorts of rubbish into it. Stuff which doesn't degrade. So, I stopped it. I paid for the damn thing, so now I'm the only one who uses it."

"How often do you take compost out?"

"This is the first time in over a year. I like to leave it as long as I can. But it was overflowing so I had to dig some out from the bottom."

"So, when you put garden waste and stuff in the top, you've never noticed a hand in it?"

"No. I'd have reported it if I had. No, whoever put it in must have buried it further down."

"OK, thanks. I'm afraid you won't be able to use the compost bin for a while. Forensics will have to empty it. There may be other surprises in store."

"That's fine. I don't really want to dig any more out until I know it's just compost."

They were interrupted by Allen Greaves and a couple of his Forensics team walking up the path towards them.

"Morning Lynn, Andy. I understand you've found something unusual in the compost bin?"

"Over on the path, Allen. Mr Starkey discovered it and threw it on the path over there. He was digging some compost out of the bottom of the bin, met with some resistance, but kept prodding until the hand fell out."

"So, it wasn't on top. It had been concealed?"

"Yes. I was hoping you'd be able to tell us how long. Apparently, nothing has been removed for about a year. But more waste has been added to the top."

"Any sign of the rest of the body?"

"No. We thought your lads might want to dig it all up."

"We will, once we're certain the owner of the hand is dead."

"I think it's fair to assume the owner is dead. Otherwise, why would the ends of the fingers have been removed?"

"Point taken. OK, we'll take the hand and the compost bin back to the lab after we've done what we can here."

Lynn and Andy went to the office for another conversation with Mrs Craig, the manager.

"Could you tell us, please, if any of your residents have disappeared without warning?"
"No, they have to give notice."
"And all those who've moved out have done so?"
"Yes. I've been here for twelve years and nothing like this has happened before."
"What about visitors?"
"What about them?"
"Do you know if any of your residents had visitors who stopped visiting suddenly, without explanation?"
"None that I know of."
"Do you mind if we talk to your residents?"
"No. By all means. If you give me five minutes, I'll print you a list."
"That would be very useful, thanks."

They went door-to-door without much success. One of the residents took the opportunity to tell them how disgusted she was that her next-door neighbour regularly had female visitors at night.

"It was obvious just from looking at them what they came for. It shouldn't be allowed. Once, one of them knocked on my door by mistake. I could tell as soon as I looked through the peephole what her occupation was. She was obviously a tart! I didn't answer the door. I don't want people like *that* round here. It used to be respectable until people like him next door moved in."
"Thank you. We'll have a word."

Over the course of the week, they visited all the residents and drew a blank, but at least they were able to narrow their search, Forensics having concluded that the hand was that of an adult male, it had been severed by a sharp instrument and death occurred between twelve and eighteen months ago. They went back to have a further chat with the manager, while the rest of the team used any spare time to search the records of persons reported missing from the area during the timeframe in question.

During their chat with Mrs Craig, they learnt that it was not uncommon for a resident to leave without giving their new address. She explained.

"It's their choice. If they refuse, there's nothing we can do as long as they don't owe any rent. Some are happy just to fill out a change of address form for their post. In that case, after the notification of change has lapsed, any mail is returned to sender."

They returned to HQ to follow up on residents who had left in the previous eighteen months, and armed with a long list, they set out the next day to interview them.

****

Brian pulled up outside the neat suburban semi and checked the address before getting out and walking up the path. He rang the doorbell and waited patiently until it opened.

"Good morning, Gary. I hope I'm not disturbing you."
"You surprised me, boss. I didn't expect to see you. Is there something I can help you with?"
"Can I come in? I'd like a chat."
"Of course."

He followed Gary into the living room where they sat facing each other. Brian broke the silence.

"Gary, I have to say I was surprised to hear you'd given notice. Are you sure it's the right thing to do?"
"Absolutely, boss."
"Call me Brian."
"Sorry, Brian. Habit."
"So, can we talk about it?"
"There's not much to say. I couldn't handle the pressure. I don't know how you managed, particularly after what happened."
"I couldn't manage, Gary. I fell to pieces. But, given time, and the support of my colleagues, I'm now in a position to get on with my life. What's happened has happened, and I'll never forget it, but at least I can deal with it. Anyway, I'd like to thank you for holding the fort while I was absent."

"That was the problem, Brian. I was just holding the fort, while the team were wishing you were back in charge. I couldn't handle it."

"OK, but that's no reason why you should quit. You were perfectly capable of working to the highest standards and you've done some great work while I've been here. But now I'm back, the pressure is off."

"I've lost the respect of the team."

"I don't agree. The problem was, they had become used to working for me. Playing by my rules. You were different and they struggled to adapt. But don't forget you were a very good DS, and I'd like you back in my team at that level. What do you think?"

"I'll give it some consideration, Brian. Let me talk to my husband."

"By all means. If you decide it's not the right thing for you, I'll accept it and wish you all the best for the future. And I'd like to thank you for the sterling work you did for me prior to my breakdown."

"Thank you. I'll give it some thought."

They shook hands and Brian left. Driving back, he knew Gary was unlikely to change his mind, but at least he'd tried. Just because he was not a good leader didn't mean he wasn't a highly capable DS.

****

After a week, Lynn and Andy had exhausted their list without having a suspect. They went back to speak to Mrs Craig.

"Last time we spoke, Mrs Craig, you said there were some leavers who didn't provide contact details."

"That's right."

"Surely you maintain a record of previous tenants. Names, date of birth, that sort of thing."

"I have names, date of birth, national insurance number, if that's any use."

"Perfect. We can trace them with that information."

"I'll just print it for you."

"Thank you."

While they waited, they exchanged small talk.

"I bet you meet some weird people in this job, Mrs Craig."

"Oh, absolutely. Some are right wankers, if you'll excuse the terminology. Most of them just get on with their life. Others can't resist being nosey about their neighbours. One of our tenants had a blazing row in the lounge once at a coffee morning, when another tenant asked where she got her woodworking skills. And from that point they referred to her as 'the lumberjack.' So, she stopped doing little jobs for them and eventually left."

"What sort of jobs?"

"DIY. Little gardening jobs and that. She made the planters in the garden over by the lounge."

"She used power tools?"

"Oh yes."

"Print out all you've got on her, please. Quickly."

"You don't think it's anything to do with her, do you?"

"It's possible. It's worth looking into."

"There you are then."

"Thank you. One final question. When did this lady leave?"

"Fifteen months or so ago."

"Do you happen to have a photograph of her?"

"Possibly. Wait a minute."

She opened a photo album on her PC and scanned quickly through the folders until she found 'Xmas 2020'. She opened it, paging down through the images until she found what she was looking for. It was a snap taken at the Residents' Party. She enlarged it for the officers' benefit.

"There. Second from the left. Front row. That's Ellen Sturgess, AKA the lumberjack."

"Could you please send a copy to my phone?"

"Just give me the number."

Seconds later, they were ready to leave with all the information they required, apart from Mrs Sturgess's address.

"Thanks for your help."

In the car, Andy started looking through the information they'd been given on the suspect. Ellen Sturgess, aged 63. No forwarding address. That wasn't a problem. Teresa would be able to trace her. They were both agreed Mrs Sturgess was a strong suspect. According to a couple of residents they'd spoken to, she had a relationship with a man who visited her at night. Nobody knew his name, but he stopped visiting, or rather nobody saw him visiting, in the weeks before she moved out. The nature of their relationship was assumed to be sexual, as he arrived after dark and left before dawn.

Teresa had located an address for Mrs Sturgess in Keighley; a flat run by a housing association. This time, however, she shared it with her husband, whom she married after meeting him there. Lynn and Andy went directly to the address, but received no answer to their knock, so went to the manager's office. This, too, was unattended, as a note on the door advised that the manager visited the court twice a week, Mondays and Thursdays. Unfortunately, this particular day was a Wednesday. They were about to leave when they were stopped by an elderly gentleman in the car park, who asked if he could help.

"Can you tell me where we might find Mrs Sturgess?"
"We don't have anybody called Sturgess here, I'm afraid."
"We were told she lived here. Number 34."
"Oh, wait a minute. You're looking for Mrs Nugent. Sorry, I'd forgotten. Sturgess was her name before she married Bob. She's in the Lounge. She'll be playing bingo. It's bingo morning."
"I don't suppose you could tell her someone is looking for her, could you?"
"I'd rather not. She doesn't take too kindly to being disturbed during bingo. It'll be finished in about half an hour if you'd like to wait."
"OK, we'll do that. Thanks."

They sat in the car until they saw residents beginning to emerge from the Lounge. Seeing Mrs Sturgess/Nugent, they approached her as she walked with a man, presumably her husband, and showed their IDs.

"Could we have a word, Mrs Nugent?"
"What about?"
"We'd like your help to identify a man who seems to have experienced a suspicious death."

"What makes you think I can help you?"
"We believe you may know him."

She turned to her partner.

"Bob, can you give me some time to speak to these officers in private, please?"
"OK. I'll have a walk into town."

She looked around, nervously, before asking the officers.

"Do you mind if we speak in my flat? Otherwise, the gossipmongers will have a field day."
"By all means. After you."

It was a small, one-bedroomed flat, clean and tidy. They were offered a cup of tea, but declined, citing the need to conduct their business as quickly as possible. Ellen sat opposite them in an armchair.

"So, would you like to tell me what this visit is all about? Have the neighbours been complaining again?"
"Again? Have they complained before?"
"No. Not exactly. Once we had a small party which got a bit noisy and upset a neighbour. She was only upset because we didn't invite her."
"Don't you get along with your neighbours?"
"Oh, yes. It's just the nosey old bugger next door. She doesn't like to see people enjoying themselves. She's a widow. Her husband had a heart attack."
"She's not blaming you, is she?"
"She's blaming everybody."
"OK. Can we get to the point of the visit?"
"Oh, yes. Please do."
"OK. Why did you leave the place in Greengates?"
"Needed a change. I got fed up."
"Didn't you have friends?"
"Yes. Until I stopped helping them with the gardens. They were an ungrateful lot."
"I understand you are quite handy with power tools."
"I was, before arthritis kicked in."

"You don't use them any longer?"

"No. I couldn't hold them with my hands aching. So, I got rid of them."

"Did you sell them?"

"No. I took them to the tip. They were just about worn out."

"Which tip?"

"The council one, on Midland Road."

"OK. What about your boyfriend at the time. Didn't he want them?"

"Boyfriend? I didn't have one."

"That's odd. We've been told you regularly entertained a man in your flat at night."

"Oh, him. He was just a friend who called in for a chat."

"Could we have his name?"

"I don't know his name. He just called himself Charlie."

"How long did you know him?"

"Only a couple of weeks. We had sex a few times, then decided to call it a draw."

"Where did he live?"

"No idea. I just met him in the Hog's Head in Greengates one night and took it from there."

"Can you describe him?"

"Average height. Average build. Short dark hair. 50ish."

"Do you have any photos?"

"No."

"None?"

"None. Look, what's this all about?"

"We've found a severed human hand where you previously lived."

"And you think I have something to do with it?"

"We're just talking to all those who lived there at the time it happened."

"Good, because it's got nothing to do with me."

"You're saying you don't know anything about it."

"Correct. I'm saying I don't know anything at all about it."

"Thanks for your time. We'll see ourselves out."

They walked back to the car, considering their next move. Andy suggested they call in the Hog's Head to see if anybody knew 'Charlie'. They were lucky. The lady behind the bar was able to help.

"We used to have a customer called Charlie. Mind you, he hasn't been in for a while."

"Approximately how long since you saw him?"

"Maybe eighteen months. I'm not sure."

"Do you recognise this woman?"

He showed her the photo of Ellen.

"Yes. She used to come in fairly regularly. Lived across the road, I think. Ellen. I don't know her surname."

"Did you ever see her with Charlie?"

"Yes. For a while they seemed quite close."

"You're certain?"

"Yes. They didn't arrive together, but often left together."

"Did Charlie have any other friends in here?"

"Yes. He talked with a few customers. I don't think he had any close friends, but he was a sociable type."

"Any of his acquaintances in now?"

"John, over in the corner. They used to talk to each other often."

"Thank you. You've been a great help."

They approached John, showing their IDs.

"Mind if we have a word, John?"

"What have I done?"

"Nothing, sir. The lady behind the bar said you used to talk with a man called Charlie in here. Is that correct?"

"Well, yes. Haven't seen him for a while, though."

"What can you tell us about him?"

"He lived up in Idle, I think. I don't know a great deal about him. We mainly talked about sport. He was a City fan. I support Leeds. We got on OK."

"Do you happen to know his surname?"

"Wallace, I think. Yes, Wallace."

"Anything else you can tell us?"

"Not really. We used to meet regularly, but then he suddenly stopped coming in."

"Can you remember when, roughly?"

"Fifteen – eighteen months, maybe."

"Did you ever see him with anyone else?"

"He met a woman in here. I don't know her name."

"Is this her?"

He showed her the photograph.

"Yes."
"Ever see them arguing?"
"No. They always seemed happy enough."
"Thanks for your time."

Walking back to the car, they were pleased with their progress. Now, they had to find out as much as they could about Charlie Wallace. First stop, Teresa, who, although up to her neck in outstanding work, was more than happy to accept more.

****

Lynn and Andy were on their way to Idle to interview a man whom Teresa had identified as the landlord of the address she believed to be the home of Charlie Wallace. Lynn had phoned him in advance of their visit and he was waiting for them outside the property.

"Come in. I'm just doing it up after the damage he left."

The house was a mess. Doors had been damaged and were hanging loosely in their frames. There was water damage in the bathroom, where fittings had been broken. Furniture was damaged beyond repair.

"This is the mess he left me. I've only just got the money together to fix it and put it back on the market. And on top of that, when he did a runner, he was three months behind with his rent. He's cost me a fortune."
"Did you know he was leaving?"
"No. I'd confronted him about his rent arrears but he promised me he had a load of money coming his way. An inheritance, he said, and promised to pay 'shortly'. He kept stalling until I gave him an ultimatum. Then, next time I called, I discovered he'd gone and left all this mess. Have you found him? I'd like to speak to him."
"I'm afraid that may not be an option. We believe he may be dead."
"Tell me where he's buried and I'll spit on his grave."

"That's the problem. We haven't found his body yet. We believe we have a part of it, but we're still investigating the case. So, can you tell me the date you last saw him?"

"September 17th, 2021. That was when I threatened him with the bailiffs."

"And you've no idea where he went?"

"No. But if you find him alive, I'd like a word with him, in private."

"Did he take anything with him?"

"No. He just took the clothes he brought with him in a suitcase. And wrecked everything he couldn't carry."

"Well, we're sorry about the damage he's done, but I'm afraid it's unlikely he'll ever pay it back. You are insured?"

"Yes, so at least that helps. But I've still lost income over the last year or so."

"Well, thanks for your time. I hope you get sorted."

"I hope he's not dead and I can meet him some dark night."

"I'll disregard that statement, sir. But I understand how you feel. If you like, I'll let you know the outcome when we close this case."

"Thanks. I'd appreciate that."

Back in the car, they discussed the case.

"As I see it, Andy, he couldn't or wouldn't pay his rent and was facing eviction, so he turned to Ellen Nugent to put him up. I'm guessing the relationship turned sour and she killed him and disposed of the body, probably after cutting it up into small parts, one of which ended up in the compost bin."

"Now, all we have to do is prove it. Let's go and write up what we've got and decide where we go from here."

"We've missed something!"

"What's that, Lynn?"

"We didn't check his rented property for his DNA. It's a long shot, but we might get something. Call the landlord and ask if we can have another look around. I'll see if Forensics can oblige."

They were lucky. There were still usable prints on glassware and other items, but no DNA traces. Still, it was possible they could get permission to check Mrs Nugent's house for matching evidence. They decided to call on her again in the morning. It had been a long day.

****

Things brightened up the moment they arrived at work. A message from the Forensics lab stated they'd managed to extract usable DNA from the severed hand. Now, they needed another sample to compare it with. With Teresa's help they searched Charlie Wallace's family tree, discovering that he had a brother and sister, and soon found their last known addresses, one of which, his sister's, was in Keighley. They phoned to confirm she was at home and set off immediately.

"They tell me Keighley's nice at this time of year."
"Would you choose it for a holiday?"
"Nah."
"Me neither. Bet you it's raining when we get there."

It was indeed lashing it down as they pulled up outside the house in Exley Head. Charlie's sister, Margaret, was waiting for them and ushered them into the lounge.

"Thank you for seeing us, Mrs Walmsley."
"The lady who phoned said it was important. What's it about?"
"When did you last see Charlie, your brother?"
"I haven't seen him for a couple of years. Why? What's he done?"
"I'm sorry to have to tell you this, but we believe he's dead."
"But you don't know for certain?"
"Were you close?"
"Never. He raped me when I was sixteen."
"I'm so sorry to hear that, Mrs Walmsley. Did you report it?"
"I told my parents, but they didn't believe me. So, I went to the police, but they didn't believe me at first."
"Please tell us what happened."
"He came into my bedroom one evening when I was reading. Mam and dad were out and out of the blue he asked me for sex. I refused, but he held me down and pulled my pants down and forced himself inside me. I was crying and it was all over very quickly. He zipped himself up and went out after warning me not to say anything. So, I kept it to myself till the next day, then told my mam. She told dad and he came to see me and told me he thought I was lying. Charlie was always the favourite. In their eyes he could do nothing wrong. So, for a day or two I kept it to myself. Then I

told a school friend, and she told me to go to the police. She believed me and went with me. But the police weren't interested. They spoke to my parents, and to Charlie. He denied it and my parents backed him up. That was it. So, if Charlie's dead, all I can say is good riddance."

"I can only apologise for the way you were treated, Mrs Walmsley, but the reason we're here is because we believe Charlie's been murdered, but we don't have his body, only a hand we think belonged to him. We have extracted DNA but need to compare it to a sample from a close family member. Would you be able to provide us with a sample of your DNA for analysis?"

"You said you've got his hand? Which one?"

"His right hand."

"His wanking hand. Serves him right. Yes, I'll give you a sample, if it proves the bastard's dead."

"We'll arrange for someone to call on you this afternoon, if that's convenient."

"That's fine. The sooner, the better. Will you please let me know when you're certain he's dead? I'd like to celebrate."

"I promise I'll let you know as soon as we have the results."

"Just one thing. My husband doesn't know anything about Charlie. Please make sure he doesn't find out."

"I promise it will remain between us."

When the results came through the following afternoon, they confirmed with almost 100% certainty that the hand belonged to Charlie Wallace. They discussed the situation with Brian.

"We intend to confront her with the evidence, boss. We think she'll confess."

"OK. Just don't put words into her mouth."

"We know what we're doing, boss. You taught us, remember?"

"Of course. OK, get to it."

They spent the rest of the afternoon working out their strategy for the confrontation with Mrs Nugent due to take place next morning as soon as they'd collected a search warrant.

****

CHAPTER 6

They rang the doorbell and waited until they heard the sound of the key turning in the lock. A tired-looking Mr Nugent opened it.

"Good morning, sir. We'd like a word with Mrs Nugent."

They both held out their IDs for his scrutiny.

"You'd better come in before the neighbours start talking. Ellen's through in the lounge."

They followed him. Her face dropped when she saw the officers.

"Bob, why don't you go for a walk while I speak to these officers?"
"If it's all the same to you, I'd rather know the reason for the visit."
"Suit yourself."

Lynn started the conversation.

"You may be interested to know that we've extracted usable DNA from the severed hand we spoke about. It belonged to a man called Charlie Wallace, who, we understand, you were having a relationship with around the time he disappeared."
"We were friendly. I wouldn't call it a relationship."
"Do you want your husband to hear all this?"
"I've nothing to hide."
"Very well. You say you were friends. According to others, he often stayed overnight."
"OK. He occasionally stayed overnight, but I soon ended the relationship. I realised we weren't compatible."
"Is that why you killed him? Because you weren't compatible?"
"I didn't kill him."
"We believe you did."
"Then prove it."
"We intend to. Here's a search warrant. The team will be arriving shortly."

Bob just sat there, aghast, speechless, until finally he found his voice.

"What the hell is going on here? Are you accusing my wife of killing a man?" What evidence have you got?"
"Enough to warrant searching the premises and taking Mrs Nugent in for quoctioning."

He turned to his wife, puzzled.

"Ellen, surely this is some mistake. Why are they accusing you of murder?"
"Don't worry, Bob. I'll get it sorted, and I'll be suing the police."
"Good luck with that."

The doorbell rang.

"That will be the forensics team. Let them in, please."

Three officers entered and performed a systematic search. It wasn't long before they found the carrier bag in a cupboard at the back of the kitchen. They dragged it into the lounge before opening it and taking out the contents. Power tools, including a saw.

"This is what we were looking for. I thought you said you took them to the tip. You couldn't use them due to your arthritis."
"I must have missed these. I didn't realise I still had them."
"More likely you kept them to dismember your next victim."
"You can't prove any of this."
"I think you'll find that the lads in Forensics will find some trace evidence on these tools. So, would you like to make things easier by telling us exactly what happened."
"I'm saying nothing until I've spoken to my solicitor."
"Call him now. I'm arresting you on suspicion of murder. I'll save you the embarrassment of having your rights read in the presence of your husband, but if you'd like him to hear the entire process, I'll read them now."
"Do it now. I've nothing to hide. I want my husband to witness everything so I can sue you."
"Good luck with that. Now, will you come quietly, or do you want your neighbours to see you in handcuffs?"

The news from Forensics was bad. No trace of blood, nor any other substance which could be traced back to Charlie Wallace, could be found on the tools. Still, Lynn remained positive.

"We still have other options available. First, we go back to her previous address and search the flat she occupied there. There may be residual blood stains somewhere. And while we're there, we'll ask if any of the grounds were ever dug up while she lived there. Maybe check the flowerbeds with the ground-penetrating radar."

****

They found nothing. Even the carpets had been removed before she left. The floors beneath had been scrubbed and treated with various detergents and cleaners, so no trace of blood remained anywhere in the flat. They queried whether any landscaping of the grounds had taken place, and checked the flowerbeds with help from Forensics, but drew a blank. Ellen Nugent was released on bail.

They were at a loose end, until Teresa phoned, asking Lynn and Andy to come up to her desk. They were intrigued to be met by the biggest smile they'd ever seen on her face.

"I thought you might be interested. I've done some research on other addresses where Mrs Nugent lived, and I've found something interesting."
"Well, don't keep us in suspense. Share it."
"OK. I checked with the housing association which owned the two addresses prior to the ones we already knew about. In both cases they confirmed that a male resident disappeared without notice. Neither could be traced. They both vanished off the face of the earth. How interesting is that?"
"Well done, Teresa. We'll call and arrange to visit the sites. Where are they?"
"East Midlands. One in Nottingham, the other in Mansfield."
"Good. We should be able to call at both on the same day."

The Nottingham site, a few miles from the city centre in the suburb of Beeston, had been re-developed. The council officer they contacted explained,

"Some years ago, part of the site was bulldozed so that a tram route could be constructed running thorough Beeston into the city centre. The rest of the site was more recently cleared and sold to a developer for the construction of new homes. I've just looked back at all the records, and nothing unusual was excavated during the redevelopments. Mind you, sometimes, they're like a bull at a gate. They just bulldoze the site and level it. It's not exactly a site of ancient architectural interest. They don't sift through every shovelful of soil they turn over."

"OK. Thanks for your time."

They travelled to the Mansfield address where the manager was unable to help them, having only been there for a couple of years, but referred them to her Head Office. They dutifully followed the lead and made an appointment for the same afternoon where they were referred to a member of staff who managed the area at the time the resident disappeared.

"Nobody knows what happened to him. He gave no indication he was leaving. No notice or anything. And the strange thing was, he didn't take anything. He just disappeared. The local police investigated but since there was no evidence of any criminal activity, they just logged him as a missing person."

"Did he have any close friends here at the time?"

"The residents were interviewed. It seems he spent some time with one of them. Apparently, they'd become quite close. The police interviewed her but didn't think she had anything to do with it."

"The resident wasn't called Sturgess, Ellen Sturgess, by any chance?"

"Yes. That's her."

"Thanks for your time."

They discussed the situation as they walked back to the car.

"I'm beginning to think we may have a serial killer at large, Andy."

"Me too. So, next move?"

"Call Teresa. See if she can get a full life history for Mrs Sturgess/Nugent. It wouldn't surprise me if she has more skeletons in the closet, so to speak."

"You call her, I'll drive."

****

Brian had a meeting with Lynn and Andy where they expressed their opinion that they felt unable to manage the two recent murder cases at the same time. Both seemed to have wider implications, in that neither seemed to be isolated incidents.

"You think we may have two serial killers at large?"

"We think it's possible, boss. There's been a series of seemingly random murders where the victims were all vulnerable people. The rough-sleepers, a heroin addict, two OAPs on a barge, two schoolgirls on a quiet lane, a jogger, and even the young boy asphyxiated could all be linked. And then we have Mrs Nugent who seems to have moved around the country leaving missing persons, or body parts in her wake. We're struggling to keep on top of both cases."

"OK. I'm glad you've brought it to my attention. Have you a preference which case you'd like to pursue?"

"No, boss. They're both equally complex. We'll go with your decision."

"OK. Stay with the local one. If you need more people on it, just let me know."

"Thanks, boss. We can manage if we're just focussed on the one case."

"OK. I'll sort out the workload with the rest of the team."

After studying the whiteboards and looking at the individual cases, he decided to call a meeting in the Conference Room. He'd prepared a whiteboard with a list of the ongoing cases before speaking to the assembled officers.

"We need to reassign our work, so here are my proposals. We have a number of murders, but I believe we can split them into two groups as discussions have indicated we probably have two distinct serial killers at large. I intend to go with the theory that one person is responsible for the local murders and another is responsible for a series of murders around the country where the victims have been dismembered. We also have the drugs cases. Again, these are possibly linked. We have the takeaway trade, and also the direct collection at different sites. So, here is my suggestion. Lynn and Andy are already working the local murders and will continue to do so. Scoffer and Ruth will continue working the drugs cases. However, I need at least two of you to take over the body parts murders. Paula and Jo-Jo are pencilled in for that. I'll help out in any of those areas if need be. Is everybody OK with that?"

There were nods of approval all round.

"At the moment, there's nothing happening concerning the moneylender, but if that emerges again, we'll have to deploy whatever resources we have at the time. OK, get yourselves up to date with your cases and let me know how you wish to proceed and if we need more manpower, I can always borrow from local areas, if necessary, but I've got total faith in all of you. And, for your information, I've spoken to Gary and it seems unlikely he'll re-join us. So, I know some of you were of the opinion you were being micro-managed, but you can rest assured you are in control of your cases. By all means, discuss them with me, but you are all capable of making the right decisions. Prove to me how good you are at your job."

****

By the time Paula and Jo-Jo arrived at HQ the next morning, Teresa had already left them some notes, promising a more detailed history by lunchtime. They left her to it and discussed the information they'd already received, setting up a whiteboard to log all the relevant facts.

With regular input from Teresa, they'd soon set up a picture of their suspect, Mrs Nugent, from her early years. She was fostered shortly after her unmarried mother died in childbirth. She was sexually abused by her foster father.
All victims were comfortably well-off widowers. She stole debit cards from the first two victims after they were dead. She entered their flats and took details of passwords from retail sites, using them for purchases she then collected at drop sites. She used the cards only for a couple of weeks before destroying them. She used VPN when ordering.
They sat for a while discussing how best to bring their investigation to a successful conclusion.

****

Brian shifted his attention back to Mullinder, the money-lender. They still had no address for him; they knew he was highly mobile, working mainly on ex-council housing estates. On a whim, he phoned the local Citizens Advice Bureau and asked if he could have a chat with the staff to discuss debt in general without breaking rules of confidentiality. He was given an appointment for the following morning.

They had assembled in the Rest Room before the office opened to the public. Brian thanked them for coming in early and explained the reason for his visit.

"We have a man on our patch who is a violent criminal who acts as the friendly local moneylender, until, that is, his victim is unable to repay the loan on time. Then, he can be very violent, recently severing a woman's finger to take her wedding ring in payment. He is a vicious criminal who should be jailed. I want to catch him, and I need your help. I understand you have confidentiality rules but am appealing for information to help me find him. Can you please help me?"

There was a marked reluctance to speak out, until the manager spoke.

"Please give the inspector as much information as you can. This man needs to be caught. He is a violent criminal. You don't have to speak in front of the group. One-to-one interviews will be arranged and whatever you tell DI Peters will be strictly confidential. He will be given the use of my office and you will be asked to tell him whatever you think may help his inquiry. This is really important. Please help."

They entered the office one at a time and were asked to give their Christian name only if they were comfortable doing so. Brian recorded and took careful notes of each interview and thanked the group, and their manager, when he'd seen them all. He returned to HQ to analyse the information he'd gathered.

He was able to ascertain that Mullinder was frequently seen in a black Mercedes, but nobody had taken note of the registration. He occasionally visited his clients alone, but was often accompanied by two heavies, one of whom was shaven-headed. He often arrived unannounced, used violence if necessary and occasionally demanded sex in lieu of payment. If sex was provided, the debtor was then informed the debt still remained outstanding. He also used different names, and Brian had already noted he was known by the names Mullinder, Miller, Mellor, Mallory, Marley, Malton and Morley. He made a note of the customers he intended to interview initially and set off with Ruth next morning to tour the Ravenscliffe estate, armed with a list of addresses to visit.

At the first address, the curtains were drawn and they could hear music from within, but nobody answered their repeated knocking. Brian asked Ruth to shout through the letterbox to announce they were police. Eventually, a voice asked her to show her ID at the window, where the curtains had been pulled back a little. She complied, and the door was opened by a middle-aged, toothless woman in a dressing gown.

"What do you want?"
"We'd like to talk to you about a visitor you don't want to let in, Mrs Gibson. You are Mrs Gibson?"
"Yes."
"Your visitor, the moneylender, Mrs Gibson, is he due to call?"
"Yes. That's why I don't want anyone to know I'm in."
"It might help if you turned the radio off. So, how much do you owe him?"
"£50 last week, but I didn't have it, so he'll want £60 this week."
"Do you have it for him?"
"No. I've got £30. He'll take that and slap me around a bit and leave me with nothing for food again."
"How did you get to know him, Mrs Gibson?"
"A neighbour told me about him. I was desperate so I called him, and he gave me £30 on the spot. But ever since, I've had to pay what he calls 'interest'. And if I don't or can't pay, he beats me up or sends someone round to shag me while they hold me down. I know you won't believe this, but I used to be a respectable woman. Now I have to shag everyone he sends round, and all because he got me started on drugs and now I can't get off them."
"What drugs are you taking, Mrs Gibson?"
"I don't know. Whatever they bring. They're all the same to me now. I just take them, or they beat me up. It's just a game to them."

"Will you help us put a stop to it?"

"Depends. If they find I've been helping the police, they'll kill me."

"We can protect you if you'll help us catch them."

"I don't know. They're probably watching us now."

"I'll check."

Brian peeped through a gap in the curtains and could see a black Mercedes parked fifty yards up the road. He carefully closed the curtains.

"What sort of car do they use, Mrs Gibson?"

"A big black one. I don't know what sort. Expensive looking."

"Mrs Gibson, I think your visitor is here. If you come with us, we'll take you somewhere safe. Do you want to pack some things?"

"No. He'll find me and give me a proper hammering. He likes to teach people a lesson. He's shown me pictures of people who haven't paid up."

"We can't make you come, but I'd recommend it."

"No."

"OK. Is there a back door we can leave by. I don't want him to know we've called. He'll take it out on you if he thinks you've called us. Take my card and put it away somewhere safe."

They left by the back door and by the time they'd reached the end of the row and turned back towards their car, the Mercedes had driven away. They got in the car and drove to the next address on their list.

There was no reply at the next address, and while Ruth was looking at the quickest route to the next on the list, Brian suggested they drive back past Mrs Gibson's.

"I just want to make sure the Merc hasn't come back. I've got a bad feeling."

As they turned on to the road, in the distance they could just make out a black Merc pulling away from the house.

"Follow them, Ruth."

As they drove past the house, they could see the curtains were in flames.

"Stop, Ruth. Stop!"

The car screeched to a skidding halt. Brian threw the door open and raced back to the house, trying the front door and finding it locked. He stood back and aimed a kick at it. Then another, and another until he felt the wood splinter. He put a shoulder to it, and it swung open as flames shot through the opening. He pulled his jacket over his head and felt his way forward through the flames into the front room until his foot brushed against the body on the floor. Coughing, he lifted the body and dragged it backwards to the doorway, where Ruth helped him drag Mrs Gibson out into the road.

"The fire brigade is on its way, boss. An ambulance as well. Are you OK?"
"I think so. I'm not sure about Mrs Gibson."

He checked. She was still conscious but had suffered significant burns. Brian put his jacket around her and attempted to console her, keeping her talking and conscious until the ambulance arrived to whisk her away. The two officers knocked on the neighbours' doors, to ensure they left their homes and stood well away until the firemen had pronounced the area safe, and once other officers had arrived at the scene, Ruth drove Brian to hospital to be checked.

He was soon discharged, his scalp covered in a cotton mesh cap, and with a bag containing some tubes of lotion and a pack of painkillers. He was advised to go straight home and rest. He did so, once he'd established that Mrs Gibson was alive and recovering.

CHAPTER 7

Even while resting at home, his mind was still on the case. He called Teresa.

"Teresa, can you ask around if anyone has talked to Mrs Gibson's neighbours. Perhaps one of them has seen the Merc and noted the number. It's a long shot, but worth checking."
"Already done, Brian. Scoffer went up with Ruth and they found a neighbour who'd seen the car driving off and got a partial plate. So, I'm running it through the DVLA database. Since it's only a partial plate, YO18, and we've only got the model and colour, I've started a local check, and we'll extend it if nothing turns up."
"I should have known you'd be on top of things. Thanks, Teresa. Keep me briefed if anything turns up before I get back to work."
"Will do. Get some rest. It's all in hand."

After two days, Brian was back at work, but they still hadn't found a match on the car's plate, though Scoffer had an idea which he took to his boss.

"Boss, I know this is clutching at straws, but it's possible the car and the number plate belongs to one of his henchmen. If we have a chat with some of his customers, maybe they've heard some names."
"Worth a try, Scoffer. You and Ruth see what you can find and feed the names to Teresa."
"Will do, boss."

They struck lucky with the third customer. She told them Mullinder had called one of his henchmen 'Smithy'. Scoffer immediately called Teresa and within fifteen minutes, she had the owner of the car and his address and passed the news to Brian.

"It may just be coincidence, Brian, but I doubt it. This 'Smithy' has got form for GBH."
"We'll take backup with us."

****

Later that evening, the officers and armed backup sat in two separate cars at either end of the terrace of houses, watching for movement. Eventually, the Merc drove up, stopping outside number 34. The driver and three passengers got out and walked to the house which they all entered.

Brian thought about the situation, before urging caution.

"There are eight of us. We know there are four of them, but we don't know how many are inside. Let's think for a moment before we act."
"Can't we call for reinforcements, boss?"
"I've got a better idea. We split them up. Give me a minute to phone base."

He called Teresa who in turn passed his instructions to a mobile unit in the vicinity, explaining exactly what they had to do. The police car carrying two officers turned up within ten minutes, drove slowly past the house and stopped at the kerb close by. Both officers got out and walked to the house, knocking on the door. When it was opened, he spoke to the gentleman.

"Sorry for bothering you, sir, but does this car belong to you?"
"No. It's my mate's. Why?"
"Someone's slashed your tyres, sir."
"What?"
"And scratched the paintwork. Come round to the other side and take a look for yourself."

The man shouted to his mates inside, swearing and telling them to come and look. In all, there were five of them. Brian gave the 'go' signal as soon as they were all walking to the car, unaware the officers were approaching fast, so intent were they on examining the damage to the car.

Within seconds, the men were surrounded by armed officers, outnumbered, and advised to surrender. They were handcuffed and a van quickly arrived to take them in. Brian called Forensics to come to search the house and waited at the premises while the armed team checked the house was empty. He was aware that Mullinder was not among those arrested and may possibly still be in the area. Nevertheless, he couldn't resist the temptation to take a look around, so, donning gloves, he opened the top drawer of the filing cabinet in an alcove. In it were bundles of banknotes. He could only hazard a guess at the value, but it was substantial. He left it for Forensics and went upstairs out of curiosity. There was hardly any furniture; every room was full of boxes. Only one of the rooms was used as a bedroom, with one sleeping bag on the floor. It was clear the house was being used as a store rather than a dwelling. He climbed a further flight of stairs into the attic which was an open space used for storage, and lit only by the presence of a skylight. On a long trellis table were items of jewellery. It was possible that Mrs Davies' wedding ring was among them. At that moment, he heard the front door open, breathing a sigh of relief when he realised it was the Forensics team.

He escorted them round the house, watching as they pulled away the plywood cladding covering an alcove in the attic to reveal a stash of money and high-end jewellery. A further search revealed a large amount of cocaine and other Class A drugs. Finally, when they'd finished, he locked up and returned to base, wondering where Mullinder might be hiding. He called Teresa, requesting that she instigate a BOLO, noting that Mullinder should be considered armed and dangerous. He completed his report of the day's incidents, switched off his PC, locked his desk and left the office. He couldn't get Mullinder out of his head, yet knew it was essential that he maintained focus on all the other open crimes at the same time.

****

They were gathered in the Conference Room. Brian had been thinking about the spate of murders and had a theory he wanted to present and hopefully prove.

"Teresa, will you please project a map of Greengates on the big screen, please."

She did as requested.

"Now, expand it to include, say, five miles in each direction. OK, thank you. Now, I'm going to pin the sites of the recent murders on the map. Here's the one on the canal at Rodley. Next, the jogger on the towpath. Next, the rough sleeper at the back of the Greengates store. And close by, the body in the allotment, again at

Greengates. Now, on to Idle, again a store. Then to Thorpe Edge, where the boy whose body was dumped at the BRI lived. And, finally, the path behind the school at Thackley, where the two girls were murdered. The Forensics lab has kindly calculated the time of death for each victim. We have checked traffic cameras around all the areas and followed up on all traffic captured in the attack areas at the indicated times. We have no probable culprits. So, let's assume the culprit is on foot. Right, if we assume these murders were all committed by the same person, then the spread of the locations would suggest he is based in or close to Greengates junction. That's the epicentre."

There was murmured agreement. They all knew what was coming next.

"So, I suggest we go door-to-door. Speak to everyone. We're looking for a male with access to a vehicle, which he would need to take the boy's body to the BRI. I want each of you to use this weekend to check all properties on the areas covered by the street maps Teresa will hand out. You will each be accompanied by a uniformed officer, or PCSO, so that we can visit more addresses. So, sorry, everybody, but whatever plans you have for the weekend, cancel them. I want to catch this bugger."

Scoffer spoke up.

"Can I make a comment, boss?"
"Go ahead, Scoffer."
"Well, we're assuming these murders are the work of one serial killer, but I think we should keep an open mind."
"What's the basis of this theory, Scoffer?"
"Well, most of them are vulnerable people. I believe they were targeted because they were vulnerable. But that assumption doesn't fit all the murders. The two schoolgirls, the jogger, for instance. Even the young boy, maybe. How would the killer know he was vulnerable? Did he know the boy had asthma? I think we should keep an open mind that these cases have a different perpetrator."
"That's a valid point, Scoffer. You're right. But there are other similarities. All the murders were opportunistic, and even though there may be more than one killer involved, I think it makes sense

to lump them together until we uncover some concrete evidence to disprove the 'mass killer' theory. Another possibility we haven't explored is that we may have two killers who work in tandem, possibly competing with each other for victims."

"So, how about if we use one board to map all the incidents, and separate boards for each individual one? If we have them side by side, we can more easily determine where the similarities and differences lie."

"OK. Do the same digitally. Spreadsheets. Note every similarity and every variation. I'll ask Teresa to set it up. In the meantime, it's door-to-door. And, I'm sorry, but we need all of you on this, as a priority."

It was a long slog, taking several days. Teresa had printed out a list of addresses for each pair to visit, with each visit taking around ten minutes. Several of the properties visited had to be re-visited, as there was nobody at home at the time. Some had nothing to say regarding the murders, but took the opportunity to report other grievances, such as loud music from the neighbours, or offensive behaviour by the neighbourhood kids. Overall, though, they had few comments worthy of following up. Largely, it was a waste of time, and at the end of the following week, Brian gathered all the officers together to issue his apologies for wasting their time. However, he felt there was still a glimmer of hope as altogether there were still a couple of dozen properties to visit.

Alone in the office at the end of the day, Brian looked through the mass of information they'd gathered. They'd missed something. He was still sure the perpetrator lived within the Greengates area, so why hadn't their search indicated any evidence? Then, it clicked. Their search was too wide. The officers were too stretched and were only able to conduct a cursory meeting with the householder. He'd missed a trick. He stood in front of the whiteboard, looking at the blank space until he realised what was missing and wrote in capital letter just two words – SINGLE OCCUPANT. They were looking for a serial killer, and, disregarding the Yorkshire Ripper, most were likely to be single. On top of that, he'd re-read the post-mortem report on the asphyxia victim, paying particular attention to the fact that fibre was found in his lungs. He'd checked with Forensics, and they'd concurred with Brian's theory that he'd probably been held in an environment where cavity wall, or loft insulation, or similar, was present. He made a note to speak to Teresa in the morning.

****

Brian was at Teresa's desk when she arrived at work and asked the question immediately after they'd exchanged greeting.

"Teresa, how do we find which of these properties in Greengates are occupied by only one person, a male, presumably. Electoral roll?"
"That's a possibility, but there are also others which are held by the council. They have a register for Council tax which may help. There are others, not so obvious, which hold that kind of information too. Any company which sells direct through mail shots keeps demographic data. I can do a quick scan through those, but it will take time."
"Will you get me the ones the Council have first, please?"
"Of course. You'll have something to work on by lunchtime."
"Thank you."

He briefed his team as they arrived, advising them they would be going door-to-door once again, but with a reduced number of properties, and apologising for not realising initially he had made an error of judgment.

"And this time, you will ask the occupier if you can inspect the property for insulation. If they decline, we'll get warrants and go back."
"How can we check for cavity wall insulation, boss?"
"Ask the question. Have they had any fitted? If you've any suspicion, we'll go back with someone who installs it. They'll be able to take a sample. Look, I know this is a long shot, but it's all we've got at the moment. We need also to ensure we maintain a presence in the area, even if we're not making any progress. The public needs to see we're actively investigating."

It soon became apparent that the majority of houses in the area had insulation of some sort. Progress on the case was grinding to a halt, and the team returned to pick up their previous investigations.

****

Two days later, Stephen Marks was queueing in the Post Office in Idle when he overheard a conversation between two old ladies in the queue in front of him.

"... and they're asking everybody if they've got loft insulation."

"What for?"

"No idea. My next-door neighbour told me. When they asked her, she said, 'why, are you selling it?' She thought they were door-to-door salesmen!"

"I wonder what that's all about?"

They got the answer that evening, when the story was all over Facebook. DI Peters was incensed!

So was Stephen Marks. That night he began to strip out all the insulation he'd fitted, shoving it into sacks which he put in the boot of his car before driving out of town to dump it all on the moors above Ilkley. He made several trips over the next few nights until the house was clean. Eventually, though, he began to relax and started to plan the next chapter of his story, opening a map of the area on his laptop. Buck Wood caught his attention and looked more appealing the more he read. He pulled on his outdoor coat and a pair of stout boots and set off on foot down to the canal bank walking at a good pace until he reached the swing bridge by the Water Treatment Works, where he crossed the canal and made his way up the steep Ainsbury Avenue before turning off into Buck Wood on the right.

Patiently, he made his way back and forth along the tracks through the woods, writing his observations in his notepad. Eventually, he reached a clearance where a plaque informed him of the previous existence of a bronze age enclosure and, further along, the site of a former open-air school. He criss-crossed the area, ensuring he would be able to find his way in the dark before leaving the wood and calling into the Commercial for a pint while he plotted his next venture.

He sat quietly in a corner of the bar, nursing his pint when a scruffily-dressed woman, probably in her late forties but looking much older, staggered through the door and made her way to the bar. Immediately, the barman came round the bar and confronted her.

"You know you're not welcome here. Out!"
"Just a drink. A small drink. A quick one."
"No chance. You're barred. You've been told every time you've come in here. So, get out. Go home and sober up."
"Just a quick whisky?"
"Out! Or else, I'll throw you out."

She cursed him under her breath and turned to the door, before unleashing a torrent of foul language aimed at the barman. She slammed the door behind her as she left. Stephen waited for a minute, considering his options and formulating his plan before draining his pint, buying a quarter bottle of whisky, and leaving the pub. He could see the woman staggering down the road, and followed her, carefully thinking through his intended actions.

He increased his pace and caught up with the woman, waving the bottle in front of her face. She stopped.

"Hi. I saw that bastard refusing to serve you. Would you like a swig of this?"
"Oh, yes."
"OK. Not by the road, though. Let's walk up to the football ground where we can have a bit of privacy and you can tell me all about yourself."

He smiled his best disarming smile, and she agreed, lured by the expectation of alcohol. They walked along, making small talk as he dangled the bottle in front of her. She was impatient for a drink but he had something quite different in mind, but finally, he coaxed her off the road and into the woods, steering her to the secluded glade he'd earmarked earlier. They sat on a tree stump. He smiled at her and handed her the bottle. As she threw her head back to take a long swig, he slit her throat. She kept her grip on the bottle as she fell, and died quickly as he watched, a wide smile on his face. He extracted the bottle from her hand and put it in his pocket, leaving the scene immediately and walking through the cover of the woods down to the canal, from where he walked briskly back to Greengates.

By the end of that evening, he had completed writing another chapter of his novel. He held up the remains of the whisky bottle with the toast; "Here's to you, you drunken old whore!", and drank it.

****

The body was found by two young boys riding their bikes along the paths of the wood. They pedalled furiously back to Ainsbury Avenue where they approached a parked car in which a young couple were engaged in some heavy petting and hammered on the window. Having listened to their story, the driver called the police.

SOCO were called to attend the scene, along with a patrol car, and a message was passed to Brian, since he lived close by. He pulled on his coat and hurried to the scene. His first question was,

"Who found the body?"
"Those two kids. They were riding their bikes through the wood, so they knocked on the window of a parked car in which a couple were having sex."
"Coitus interruptus."
"Yep."
"OK. Any ID on the woman?"
"No. The lads say she's a local. The local drunk."
"OK. Cause of death?"
"Her throat was slashed by a sharp blade. Not self-inflicted."
"Time of death?"
"Early evening is our best estimate at the moment. We'll have a better idea when we've got her on the slab."
"No witnesses?"
"No."
"I smell alcohol."
"Yes. She's been drinking."
"OK. I'll call in at the local pubs. Maybe she's been in one earlier."
"Good luck."

He'd never seen her in the Ainsbury, which was the nearest pub, so instead called first at the Commercial, showing an image on his phone to the barman, who confirmed she was in earlier.

"Yes. I recognise her. She looks exactly the same as when she was alive. She was in earlier. I refused to serve her. She was an alcoholic, a tart and a nuisance. She'd go with anyone who offered her a drink."
"Did she talk to any of your customers when she was in?"
"No. I refused to serve her and told her to leave. Then she gave me a load of foul language."
"What did she say?"
"No idea. It sounded foreign."
"So, how do you know it was bad language?"
"I could tell from her tone of voice."
"OK. Thank you for your time."

As he was leaving, he turned and asked the barman another question.

"Did anybody follow her out?"
"Come to think of it, a man left just after she did."
"A regular?"
"Never seen him before. He just had a pint, and then bought a drink to take home."
"What did he buy?"
"A quarter bottle of whisky."
"Can you describe him?"
"Mid-fifties. Slim. Clean-shaven. Dark hair. Medium height."
"What was he wearing?"
"Lace-up boots. Dark, winter coat, buttoned up to the throat."
"Was he on foot?"
"I don't know."
"Can you tell me what time she left?"
"Five-fifteen, five-thirty. Around that time."
"OK, thanks. By the way, do you know if she has any family?"
"No idea. I don't know anything about her, to be honest. I just know she's a pisshead and a nuisance."
"Well, to me, she's a murder victim. Just bear that in mind. We may need to speak to you again."

Outside, he tried to imagine what had taken place. Had he just followed the woman into the woods? Or had he approached the woman and enticed her into the woods with the offer of whisky? It was immaterial, unless someone had seen the two of them walking down the street together. He went door-knocking on the road leading to the wood. No-one admitted to having seen them together. A waste of an evening, he thought. He called into the Ainsbury for a quick one, and not surprisingly, Teresa had already asked Nicky to only serve him with one. She advised him.

"Be grateful someone's looking out for you, Brian."

CHAPTER 8

At his desk the next morning, he tried to find out about the woman's background. So far, all they knew was her name and address, which they found on an envelope in her pocket. Brian had already called at her neighbour's to verify her address, and Forensics were presently at her home, with Scoffer and Ruth on their way. They returned to HQ early in the afternoon with some unexpected news.

"The first thing we noticed in her house was a framed photo. It was Carole Knight's graduation from Cambridge University!"
"She's a graduate?"
"Classical studies. She then continued to get a post-graduate degree and a job as a lecturer at York University."
"So, how did she get to the state she was in when she was murdered?"
"Teresa's looking into her background now."

The news from Teresa was startling.

"She had a successful career at York and loved the job. Then, one day, during a one-to-one session with an undergraduate, he raped her. She reported it and there was an inquiry. It turned out the rapist's father was a member of the House of Lords, very wealthy, and had the entire affair hushed up and swept under the carpet. After that, Carole Knight was broken, her life was in ruins and she started drinking, eventually losing her job and her residence and reputation. She rented a small house in Thackley and lived alone until her death. It's a really sad story. Oh, and by the way, she had a habit of swearing at people in Latin."

Shortly afterwards, Brian took a call from Forensics.

"The post-mortem examination is complete. Apart from the expected damage to her liver through excessive abuse of alcohol, and other alcohol-related problems, she was reasonably well, although she did have syphilis. I guess she needed the income from sex to pay for the alcohol. Death was caused by her jugular vein being severed by a sharp blade. She bled out and died quickly. We were unable to find any foreign DNA on her skin or clothing, and there was no attempt at intercourse on this occasion. Her attacker took her to Buck Wood solely to murder her. It was premeditated and clinical."

Brian immediately added it to his whiteboard listing his serial killer's crimes. He had no doubt the same person had committed all those murders.

****

Back home in Greengates, Stephen Marks had finalised the rental of a small property in Eccleshill and cancelled his contract on his Greengates home. He was due to move in a week or so. He was becoming uneasy about the amount of police activity in his area, and although nobody had been able to inspect his house yet, he was sure it was bound to happen eventually. It made sense for him to move on and he looked forward to it. It would give him some breathing space while he worked on his novel. It would also expand his target area for potential victims, and with that in mind, he pulled on his coat and boots and went for a walk around Eccleshill and Undercliffe. What he had in mind was a departure from his normal methods; he didn't want to become typecast in his choice of victim or location, or weapon. He thought back to his first two murders and smiled.

He soon found what he thought was a suitable location. It was a block of flats owned by a Housing Association in Undercliffe. He walked around the perimeter before presenting himself at the door and calling for the manager. He spoke over the intercom.

"Good morning. I'm looking for a flat to rent, and someone said I should try here. He praised you very highly. I wonder if I could have a quick look around."
"I'm sorry. I'm very busy this morning. Is it possible for you to come back this afternoon? Say, 2.30?"
"Yes. That would be OK."
"Could I have your name, please?"
"Gerald Drinkwater."
"OK, Mr Drinkwater. I'll see you at 2.30."
"Thank you. 'Bye."

He walked around the area, making a mental note of places of interest to him personally before calling into Morrisons for a snack, while he wrote the outline of his planned action in a notebook as he killed time before his appointment. That task completed, he walked back to the flats to meet the manager, Mrs Caldwell.

She showed him around and allowed him to view one of the flats which was currently vacant. He'd spun his well-rehearsed tale that his wife died six months previously and he needed to move on and reluctantly sell the house they'd called 'home' for almost twenty years. Before he left, she handed him an application form and explained he would have to go on a 'waiting list' until something suitable became available. He left in the knowledge that several flats could become available in the very near future.

Over the course of the next few days, he honed his plan and sourced the necessary goods to execute it. He had initially been dismayed to discover that the entire site had been fitted with double glazing, but, having looked at the weather forecast indicating a period of unseasonally warm weather for the following weekend, he cheered up immediately, knowing his plan would still work as long as he lowered his sights. He earmarked Sunday night for the operation and looked forward to it immensely.

****

Shortly before midnight on Sunday, he left home in his car and drove towards Five Lane Ends before taking Idle Road until its junction with Northcote Road, which he followed to the traffic lights at the junction with Otley Road. Just past the lights, he parked in the small car park on the right, behind the shops. From there it was a short walk down the track to Hatfield Road, where the entrance to the flats was located. His rucksack over his shoulder, he walked into the car park and squatted in the bushes for a while until he felt safe. He was sure nobody had seen him, and no lights were showing from the flats. As predicted, it was a relatively warm night and as he'd half-expected, he spotted two ground floor windows which had been left open. He took two litre bottles from his rucksack and placed them on the ground while he unwrapped the paper covering them and exposed the cloth wicks he'd shoved into their necks. Taking a deep breath, he took a final look around, and, certain nobody had seen him, lit the wicks, stepped forward and pushed a bottle through the open window from where it fell to the floor dislodging the cap causing the contents to spill and catch fire rapidly engulfing the room in flames. He moved quickly to the second open window and repeated the action immediately illuminating the room behind it with fire. He ran as fast as he could back to the car and drove off down to Greengates, taking a different route and using secondary roads wherever possible. Minutes later he sat at his computer, watching as news came through of a fire at some flats in Undercliffe. He followed the breaking news for ten minutes, glass of whisky in hand, before going to bed with a wide grin on his face. He would write his story in the morning when more details would be available.

He woke at eight o'clock having slept well. He made himself a cup of coffee and took it to his desk, sipping while he waited for his laptop to load. First, he read the local news, focusing on the report of a fire at a block of retirement flats in Undercliffe which resulted in four deaths and a number of residents treated for smoke inhalation. He smiled when he read that the police were treating it as an arson attack. Immediately, he began to write his version of the incident in his novel.

****

Brian, along with Ruth, was already at the scene, talking to members of the Forensics team.

"So, there's no doubt it was arson?"
"None at all. The fire was started at two different points within seconds. Two windows were left slightly open, and bottles of incendiary liquid were pushed through the gaps. Fragments of the bottles were found inside on the floor at both locations. Someone pushed home-made firebombs through open windows to start the blaze. We haven't yet identified the liquid used as the catalyst, but it is an off-the-shelf product, probably the same as that which was used in the murder of the homeless men a while ago."
"So, he's at it again?"
"Looks like it."
"OK, thanks. Are there any witnesses we can talk to?"

"There was a man on his way home, quite drunk, who'd stopped to use the cash machine at the Tesco opposite. He was the one who called 999."

"Name and address?"

"I don't have it. I'm not sure whether the incident has been written up yet, but the Call Centre will have the details."

"OK, thanks."

They got the details and walked over to the man's house on nearby Vernon Place. It took a while before their knocking was answered by a woman, the witness's wife, who explained her husband had gone to work. He was drunk the previous night and told her only that there was a fire near the junction. She didn't know any details. They arranged to call in the evening, before they went door-knocking to see if there were any other witnesses. Nobody had anything to offer. The incident had taken place after midnight, before a working day. Most of the local people were already asleep and were only woken by the noise and lights when the emergency services arrived. At the back of his mind, Brian thought whoever committed this arson attack was the same person who had previously murdered the rough sleepers. If he was wrong, they had another murderer on their patch. He arranged for traffic camera images to be made available in the hope they would show some activity.

That evening, they returned to Undercliffe to interview the man who'd alerted the emergency services about the fire. He could tell them nothing of any use, apart from seeing flames coming from the flats and calling 999. He saw nobody else in the area. Ruth felt compelled to comment.

"About as much use as a chocolate fireguard, that one."

An appropriate analogy, Brian thought.

However, the following day yielded a result. The camera footage showed only one car in the area at the time, although the number plate was not clear, at least they had the model – a dark-coloured Ford Fiesta Hatchback, post 2017. Little did they know, it had already been sold for cash to a scrapyard in Doncaster and was in the process of being broken up for parts.

****

Brian called a meeting the following morning, commencing by asking for opinions about the latest case.

"Can I have a show of hands from those who think we have one mass murderer at large, apart from the 'body parts' killer, that is?"

Only one officer failed to raise a hand. Lynn.

"Would you please explain your reasoning, Lynn?"
"The geographical area has increased. We made the assumption that since no vehicles were identified in the areas of the crimes, they must all be in walking distance of the killer's base. This one seems a little out of range."
"Just because we were unable to identify the use of a vehicle in the earlier crimes doesn't mean he doesn't have a car, only that he didn't need it previously. And, let's not forget, the boy's body was transported to the grounds of the BRI by a vehicle. I doubt it was a taxi!"
"You're right, Scoffer. There's another possibility, of course. He may have moved home. Our doorstepping in the Greengates area may have spooked him into moving elsewhere."
"That's a good theory, boss. We could check estate agents for rentals, and private landlords as well."
"OK. Let's get to it, then. Decide amongst yourselves how you intend to assign the tasks, bearing in mind we still have properties to visit in the Greengates area. Let's see some results."

****

Stephen Marks wrote the chapter concerning the arson attack and the protagonist's subsequent disposal of the car. Satisfied with his work and with one eye on the time, he shut down his laptop and set about preparing his worldly goods for transportation to his new address in Eccleshill. He still had to find time to inspect thoroughly the house he was leaving to ensure he'd removed all trace of the insulation he'd previously installed.

A week later, settled in his new home, Stephen quickly established a routine whereby he went for a walk, morning and afternoon, taking in his new neighbourhood, checking out the lie of the land. He quickly identified opportunities to provide material for his book.

There seemed to be a disproportionate number of bungalows in the area, many of them occupied by retired couples. Easy pickings? He would do his homework before making a decision but was clearly looking forward to the opportunities and the challenge.

The following day, he again patrolled the area on foot. It was warm and sunny, and he hoped that a large number of the inhabitants would be out in their garden so that he could weigh up the possibility of breaking in and murdering the occupants. He was looking for an elderly couple or single person, possibly someone disabled, someone incapable of fighting back. He made a mental note of a few of those who seemed to be contenders and decided to come back at another time for a second look. He went home and started to write a new storyline.

'It was dark, and the street was quiet. There were lights on in a few of the properties, but the only noise seemed to come from TVs which would explain why the lighting changed every few seconds. He reasoned that other rooms would most likely be empty so it would be possible to get in through the back door without disturbing the occupants. He chose Number 47. His notes taken during the day indicated that it was likely only one person lived there. He only saw an old lady tending the garden during the day. Of course, it was possible she had a husband or partner, but he would go with the logical conclusion that she lived alone. He walked slowly and quietly round to the back of the house, down a narrow alley, counting the houses as he passed them until he arrived outside the back gate of Number 47. He put on his gloves and pulled the roll neck of his sweater over the lower half of his face, took a deep breath and walked up the path to the back door. He tried the handle. The door was locked. He stood for a few seconds listening. The area was deathly silent as he knocked on the door. There was no response. He knocked harder and waited. There was still no response from within. It occurred to him that the occupant may be deaf, but he was unable to hear the TV, so it was more likely she was asleep. He walked back around the block to the front door and rang the bell. There was still no answer. He knocked hard, but not hard enough, he hoped, to disturb the

113

neighbours, but still he had no response. Becoming frustrated, he walked back to the rear and knocked once again on the back door. Again nothing. He stepped back and ran at the door, putting his shoulder hard against it. He could feel it give just a little, so went hard at it again. This time it definitely moved, and third time lucky, it flew wide open. He pulled it closed behind him and stood quietly, listening. All was silent except for the faint sound of the TV in the front room. He approached the door quietly and turned the doorknob, opening the door slowly until he could see the occupant seemingly dozing in front of the TV. He walked right up to her and shouted 'Wakey, wakey!', at the same time shaking her by the shoulder. Her lack of a response disappointed him. She was cold. Dead cold. He walked around the house quickly, opening drawers and cupboards until he found what he wanted, a laptop, her bank card and a large wad of cash, seemingly several thousand pounds worth. He put everything into a carrier bag and left the house by the back door and disappeared into the dark.'

He saved the file, read it through and poured himself a large vodka while he mentally replayed the event to ensure everything would be credible. Even though no murder was committed, he liked the story and decided to use it. It would confuse the reader.

****

Barry Ramsden finally had a few days free to visit his recently-vacated rental in Greengates, so that he could check it was in sufficiently good condition to go back on the rental market. After breakfast on the Tuesday morning, he drove to the property, parking outside and letting himself in through the back door into the kitchen. It looked in reasonable order, needing perhaps a good clean, but acceptable. He made a note of things which needed doing before advertising the property. However, when he went down to the cellar, he was surprised to find bolts on the door and fittings for a padlock. He switched on the light as he entered and saw a stack of sawn timber with nails sticking out as if they'd been wrenched apart. A closer look at the walls enlightened him. There were holes with wall plugs inserted at regular intervals, indicating that the walls had been covered with sheets of timber for some reason. There was also a great deal of dust on every surface. He sighed and went back to the car for a brush and a bucket of warm water. As he reached the car, he was stopped by two women.

"Excuse me, sir. Is this your house?"
"I own it, yes."
"Do you mind if we look inside?"
"You might want to wait until I've cleaned it."
"Actually, sir, we'd like to look around *before* you clean it."

They showed their ID and a puzzled Mr Ramsden let them in.

"Are you interested in renting or buying?"
"Neither, sir. We're looking for evidence of criminal activity."
"I don't know anything about that. I own the house and it's been rented out for the last nine months or so. I just got the keys back a couple of days ago. I'm just seeing what I have to do before I can rent it out again."
"Can you tell us, please, if the house has been modified in any way without your knowledge?"
"Certainly. The cellar for a start. There are planks of wood all over the place. It's full of dust. Like a factory."
"We need to look at this, sir."

He showed them down the stairs and opened the door.

"It wasn't like this when he moved in. It was clean and tidy. Just a store."

They were amazed at what they saw. Paula took photos while Jo-Jo called HQ.

"Teresa, we think we've found a crime scene. Remember the kid whose body was found in the grounds of the BRI? I think we may have discovered where he died. It's a cellar. The window's been blocked up and it looks as if all the walls have been boarded over. The door has had extra bolts fitted. It's really dusty! It looks like a cell, not a cellar."
"I'll pass it to Brian. He'll decide whether SOCO should attend."

They went back up the steps and outside for some fresh air. Paula quizzed the landlord until Brian arrived.

"So, tell me about your tenant."

"Well, he was never any bother. Never complained. Always paid on time."

"His name?"

"Drinkwater. Gerald."

"How did he pay his rent?"

"Well, that was a funny thing. He paid in cash. He pushed it through my letter-box in a sealed envelope every month."

"Wasn't that a bit odd?"

"He said all his business was in cash, so it was easier for him."

"What did he do for a living?

"A market stall. In Otley, he said."

"Did you ever see proof of his identity?"

"I saw a letter addressed to him. From the council."

"Do you remember the address on it?"

"No. I remember it was Rawdon."

"And that was the only proof of ID you saw?"

"Yes. He seemed genuine enough."

Meanwhile, Jo-Jo had called Teresa, asking her to run a trace on 'Gerald Drinkwater'. She was surprised when the result came through a few minutes later. She interrupted Paula's questioning of the landlord.

"You've got to hear this. Gerald Drinkwater died about three years ago. In suspicious circumstances."

"Don't tell me. He had a market stall in in Otley."

"Yep."

She turned back to Barry Ramsden.

"OK. What else do you know about Mr Drinkwater?"

"I bought the house a couple of years ago and spruced it up a bit so I could put it out to rent. I advertised it in the paper and this Drinkwater, or whatever his name is, called and asked to have a look at it. So, I showed him round and he said he'd take it. He seemed like a nice, honest, straightforward bloke, so we agreed a deal, and he moved in a week later."

"Do you know his previous address?"

"It was on the letter from the council."

"We need to see it."

"It's at home, but you're welcome to it."
"OK. I'll drive you home while Paula waits for the boss. Then, I'll have to bring you back here to speak to the boss."

They drove away; Brian arrived five minutes later. Paula quickly brought him up to date and showed him the cellar. He agreed with Paula's describing it as a cell and called Forensics immediately.

"Allan, I think we've found the place where that young kid picked up the fibre in his lungs. Can you get over to Greengates? Fast!"

Allen took only a few minutes to agree that the cellar was most likely the source of the fibre but took samples back to the lab to compare before issuing a statement that the tests he ran to compare the samples were positive. The cellar was pronounced a crime scene and was cordoned off, with a police guard outside while the Forensics team searched the property from top to bottom.

Meanwhile, Teresa had been looking into the circumstances of the real Gerald Drinkwater's death and was preparing a report for Brian. She sent what she'd discovered to Brian's phone. He read it as soon as he'd parked up outside his destination.

Brian,
The story so far.
Gerald Drinkwater was a market stallholder in Otley. He sold fruit and vegetables and was popular and well-liked. He was homosexual, but discreet about his private life. When he failed to appear one Saturday at market, his customers were a little worried. He never missed a day, so one of them who knew his address went to his house to see if he was OK. There was no answer although all the lights were on in broad daylight. She asked neighbours if they'd seen him, but nobody had. Becoming apprehensive, she eventually called the police who were reluctant to act and decided to wait twenty-four hours to see if he turned up, reasoning he may have gone away as his van was missing. They alerted local forces to keep an eye out for it. The following day it was found burnt out on the moors above Haworth. Mr Drinkwater's body was in the driver's seat. A postmortem examination indicated he may have died before his body was set alight, due to a number

of injuries (broken arm, broken nose, fractured skull) which, since the van was undamaged, were not due to an RTA, and also his lungs did not show signs of smoke inhalation to the extent typical in those who died in a fire.

He was still thinking about this discovery when Jo-Jo returned with Barry Ramsden. She introduced him to DI Peters and handed over the letter showing the real Drinkwater's address in Otley.

"So, it looks like our serial killer murdered the stall holder and adopted his identity to rent this flat. I wonder what identity he's using now."
"Why don't we ask Teresa to check? Maybe it's still Drinkwater. Maybe he's taken the identity of someone else he's killed."
"Good idea, Jo-Jo. Follow it up with Teresa. You get the credit if you're right."
"I'll do that. If you don't mind, I'll pop up to the Undercliffe flats and talk to the manager. It's quite possible our serial killer had a look around before deciding how to set fire to it. The manager may even have shown him around. Maybe he used the Drinkwater alias. Maybe she remembers him. Maybe she can give a description."
"OK, Jo-Jo. Go see what she remembers. Good luck. Take Paula with you. I'll wrap things up here.

The two drove up to Undercliffe after checking the manager was on duty. She was there and invited them into her office as workmen were busy making good the damage done in the fire. Paula explained the purpose of their visit.

"We were wondering if you'd maybe shown someone around in the last couple of weeks before the fire. Workmen, or prospective tenants, possibly."
"Actually, yes, I did show a gentleman round with a view to putting him on our waiting list. Just a second while I consult my diary. Yes, here it is. A Mr Drinkwater. 2.30 last Wednesday."
"Did he fill in an application form?"
"No. He took it with him."
"So, you don't have his address?"
"No. Sorry."
"Could you describe him?"

"Mid 50s, I guess. Short dark hair. Quite tall, maybe six feet. Slim build."

"Any distinguishing features you can remember?"

"No, not really. Sorry."

"Would it help if we brought a police sketch artist to help you remember what he looked like?"

"I don't think so. There was nothing about him which made him stand out. He was just so normal."

"Mr Average?"

"Well, yes."

"Did he arrive in a car?"

"I don't think so. If he did, he parked it off site somewhere."

"OK, anything at all about him which made him stand out from the crowd?"

"He spoke very well. I imagine he was well-educated. He was very confident."

"Anything else you can tell us which might help us catch him?"

"Sorry, no. I'll get in touch if I think of anything."

"Thank you."

Walking back to the car, Paula made the suggestion.

"So, what do we do now? Arrest everyone who looks normal?"

****

CHAPTER 9

Scoffer and Ruth were now working mostly nights, handling reports of drug dealing and distribution. They had made themselves known on social media platforms and had managed to identify a number of small-time distributors. They were biding their time, working their way up the chain until they could build a case against the men at the top. Ruth had managed to convince a dealer she wanted to play a part in the distribution chain. She had money and access to many vulnerable young people who were ripe for exploitation as potential users in her role as a school dinner lady. He believed her and gave her a selection of drugs at a little over cost price to establish whether she could create a market for their merchandise. Within a week she had sold out and wanted more, including Class A. Her dealer told her he would arrange a special delivery for her if she would meet the price. She said she'd talk it over with her boyfriend, as he was the one who handled the money, and give her answer the following day.

They went immediately to Brian to discuss the situation. He listened attentively to their plan.

"So, we were thinking, we'd arrange to pick it up from their warehouse, so that we could raid it later."
"And if they don't agree to that?"
"We'll ask for a massive amount to be delivered. They'll use someone fairly high up the chain to do that, I would imagine. Then, we'll make an arrest and threaten the delivery boy with a long sentence unless he cooperates."
"OK. I suggest you ask someone from Forensics to be with you to test the substances for purity. They may be setting you up."
"Do you have anyone in mind?"
"No, but Allen will know someone who will fancy the challenge. Ask him. And don't forget to tell us the time and place so we can be ready and in position to arrest the lot of 'em."

Delivery was arranged for 9pm the following night in the car park on the left of Hawksworth Road on Baildon Moor, in a white Transit. Cash only – £20,000. No haggling. The purchase price ensured at least a 50% profit. Brian was a little concerned with the arrangement.

"It's very open up there. I don't see how we can keep our officers hidden."

"We could take our female officers and pretend to be courting couples, maybe."

"And take a couple of people with drones. That would be a bonus. We can follow and film their progress while pretending to be amateur enthusiasts. Forensics staff would like that."

"OK. Set it up. And count me in."

"OK. We'll take some dog walkers, too. Police dog walkers."

"Take them up for a walk this afternoon, just to check the lie of the land. See if there are any hollows where officers could hide out of sight. We need to get this right. If they're carrying such a large quantity of drugs, they'll want to ensure the site's safe."

The CID team, along with assorted members of Forensics and police officers in plain clothes were in position by 8pm. There were also 'spotters' monitoring traffic heading towards the site and relaying messages to CID. Shortly before 9pm they spotted a white Transit heading for the site and notified Brian who was watching the action from a nearby trench. Brian relayed the information to the other concealed officers. As it came closer, they noticed the company name printed on the bonnet. However, it drove straight past them. Brian called the officers parked at the beginning of the moor to intercept it. The stop-and-search proved it to be a parcel delivery van on legitimate business.

They waited until 10pm before calling a halt and disbanding. Brian had a feeling there had been a tip-off, but that was, he thought, highly unlikely because he trusted all those who took part. But he couldn't get it out of his head.

Over the next few days, it was a common topic of conversation among the team, but nobody believed any member of the team would be stupid enough to talk about something so important outside work. Gradually, it dawned on one member of the team that she may inadvertently have disclosed information which wrecked the operation. Whatever the consequences, she felt obliged to come clean and face the music. The following morning, she presented herself at Brian's desk.

"Could I have a word in private, boss?"

"Of course, Ruth. We'll use one of the Interview Rooms."

In silence, they walked downstairs and entered Interview Room 1.

"Sit down Ruth and tell me what's on your mind."
"I think I may have been the cause of the Baildon Moor operation failing."
"Tell me the whole story. Leave nothing out. You realise there may be consequences?"
"Yes, of course. And whatever the consequences are, I'll accept them."
"OK. I'm listening."
"I have an older sister. She's married but we occasionally meet up for a natter. Anyway, she called me at about five o'clock on the day of the operation and asked if I'd meet her for a drink. I said, sorry, I can't. I'm working. She said we could meet later. I told her I'd be working until about 10pm. She asked what on earth I'd be doing until then. I told her it was a special job. She said something like 'it sounds interesting'. I told her it was just routine. She said if I was anywhere near her house, to just call in before I went home. Just for a natter. I said I was miles away."
"Is that it?"

Ruth hesitated before replying.

"I was trying to focus on the operation and couldn't seem to be able to get her off the line, and I just said 'we're in Baildon'".
"So, you think your sister has warned off the dealers?"
"Initially, yes. But my sister's not like that. Then, I remember her husband. He's OK, but his brother is a bit of a crook. He's done time and knows a lot of criminals. So, I called my sister last night and asked her if she'd told her husband anything about the operation. Eventually, she told me that she'd let slip I was working on something in Baildon that evening. Later he went out to meet his brother for a pint. I believe he told his brother. He said he didn't, but I don't believe him. He probably let it slip out without thinking. That's it. I'm sorry."

Brian was quiet for a moment before he let out a sigh.

"I'm sorry, Ruth, but you're suspended with immediate effect. Leave your ID and sign yourself out. We'll be in touch in a couple of days before we call you in for another chat. In the meantime, think long and hard about what's happened here, and the consequences. I'll see you out."

Ruth was devastated. She went home and wept. She decided not to mention it to anybody. If her sister asked, she'd simply tell her she'd taken a few days off sick.

****

'That night, he was checking out the row of bungalows again. As before, the area was quiet, with many of the buildings standing silent and dark. This time, he decided to try one of those where it seemed the occupants were already asleep. From his research, he had established which of the houses had old or infirm occupants who would most likely have an early night. One on his short list had, he believed, a single occupant, an old lady with limited mobility. She was tonight's target.

He crept round to the back door which, to his surprise was unlocked. He smiled to himself and walked through the kitchen and quietly down the dark hall. Suddenly he heard the noise of a flushing toilet and stopped dead, his back tight to the wall as an old lady came out of the toilet and walked away back towards her bedroom. He came up behind her, his hands tight to her throat as she struggled furiously. Luckily for her, she still had many of her own teeth and managed to bite his hand. He winced in pain and slapped her hard, so she fell to the floor. He was quickly on her and strangled her until she was dead. He searched the house, finding where she kept her money and took it all, nearly £6000 in total. He crept out of the house and made his way home.'

He read the story, making minor corrections, before saving the file and closing his laptop. He marked in his diary the date he planned to carry out the murder.

****

Ruth spent most of her time indoors, watching TV and having the odd drink. She'd heard nothing by Friday lunchtime so walked down to the off-licence to buy a couple of bottles of wine to keep her going over the weekend. She was still distressed and spent her time wondering how her future would pan out.

As she approached her house, a man she hadn't seen before was in the garden next door. He introduced himself.

"Hello. I'm Mike, your next-door neighbour. And you are?"
"Ruth."
"Pleased to meet you, Ruth. I've seen you through the window occasionally. Aren't you working today?"
"No. I'm off for a few days."
"What do you do?"
"Admin. What about you?"
"I'm a writer."
"Interesting. What genre?"
"Adult fiction. Light comedy."
"What's your surname?"
"Thomas. That's the name I write under."
"I'll look you up."
"Please do."
"Anyway. I'm a bit busy. Nice to meet you."
"You, too. Have a good day."

He seems nice, she thought, and then promptly forgot all about him, instead having a snack and watching daytime TV.

Next door, 'Mike' was thinking about his neighbour. She was attractive and seemed to live alone. He started to wonder what might happen if he got to know her better. Learn her routine. Plan how to make her his next victim. The very thought excited him and brought on an immediate erection.

At home, Ruth received a phone call. Brian asked her to attend a meeting on Monday morning to discuss her future. She agreed, then opened a bottle of wine and poured herself a glass. She relaxed, glass in hand, watching a film on TV when her doorbell rang. She put down the glass and went to the door, unlocking it to find her neighbour, Mike, a bottle of wine in his hand.

"Sorry to bother you, but I was sat next door all on my own with this bottle of wine and I thought I'd be neighbourly and ask if you'd like to share it."

She thought for a short while, as he smiled at her, pleadingly, before answering.

"Why not? Come in."

He grinned and stepped into the hallway closing the door behind him as she motioned him to follow her into the lounge. She turned her back on him just long enough for him the lock the door and remove the key, slipping it into his pocket, before following her.

"OK if I sit over here?"

He motioned towards the armchair.

"Please yourself. I'll get a glass for your wine."

She went into the kitchen, returning with a glass to find him on the settee, next to where she had been seated.

"I thought I'd move a bit closer. My hearing's not too good."
"I'd rather you moved back. Give us time to get to know one another."
"I already know you well enough, I think."
"What makes you think that?"
"You invited me into your house. That tells me you're up for it."

By now, it was apparent to Ruth exactly what he expected once she'd invited him into her house. She'd acted in all innocence but had been stupid and now she had to think hard before the situation escalated. Then, he said something which terrified her.

"You'll remember this for the rest of your life. Your short life."

The statement hit her like a hammer, but she gathered her wits, and though terrified, smiled and spoke calmly.

"You're in my home. *My rules.* I'm going upstairs to take all my clothes off and lie on the bed. I'll call you when I'm ready. I have to get all my sex toys out first. You sit there, finish your glass and

125

stroke yourself. If it's not big enough, it's not good enough. I'll be five minutes. Wait there."

She squeezed his thigh, stood up, picked up her handbag and calmly walked out of the room and up the stairs. She stepped into the bathroom, bolting the door behind her before taking out her phone and dialling Brian. She cancelled the call before it connected, reasoning that her visitor may be outside, listening. Instead, she messaged Brian, switching on the shower as she stood behind the door.

"Intruder in my house. May be killer. I'm locked in bathroom for safety but hurry. I'm scared."

While waiting for a reply, she took a pepper spray from her bag, clutching it tightly.

Brian was writing on the whiteboard when he heard his phone buzzing. He picked it up and displayed the call, replying immediately.

"On our way. Stay calm. Try not to act frightened."

Brian called Scoffer and Andy from their desks.

"Come with me. Now. Ruth's in trouble. Grab a stab vest and a taser."

They raced to the car park and set off at speed while Scoffer called for armed backup. As they drove, Brian realised how little they knew about the situation, but feared the worst.

The arrived on the road where Ruth lived, parking a short distance away. As they got out, four armed officers arrived in a van, and after a quick discussion the two groups split up, three armed officers accompanying Scoffer to the back door, the other one with Brian and Andy approaching the front. They swapped cryptic messages to ensure their actions were synchronised before battering open the doors and rushing in. They surprised Mike who was halfway up the stairs with a kitchen knife in his hand.

"FREEZE!"

Mike saw the handgun pointed at his chest and the tasers in the hands of the other officers. He immodiately ran away up the stairs and round the corner, out of their sight."

"Careful, lads, it's likely he's hiding, ready to jump out and try to stab as many of us as he can. I'll go first. I want the bastard alive."

They inched their way up the stairs until they reached the corner. Brian counted silently to three before launching his body in a crouching position. Immediately he saw the figure running towards him, brandishing his knife, screaming. Brian shot his taser, stopping his adversary in his tracks as the other officers followed him and discharged their tasers, while the armed officers watched intently, handguns cocked and ready if required.

Mike was screaming in agony and frustration as he writhed on the carpet where he was subdued while Brian rapped on the bathroom door, shouting.

"Ruth. It's Brian. You're safe now. Open the door. It's OK. It's over."

The door opened slightly, showing Ruth's worried, tear-stained face and the pepper spray in her hand.

"Come on, love. It's OK. He can't hurt you now."

She embraced him, her face buried against his chest as he comforted her.

"Well done, Ruth. It's possible you've just caught our serial killer."

Over Brian's shoulder, she caught sight of Scoffer, smiling. She returned the smile. They would talk later.

****

CHAPTER 10

On Monday morning, Ruth reported at Reception, stating she had an appointment with DI Peters. The receptionist called him, then informed Ruth she was free to go upstairs and speak to him at his desk. She immediately felt that good news was in the offing.

Brian met her at the top of the stairs and gave her a welcoming hug, before ushering her into an Interview Room and motioning her to take a seat.

"How are you, Ruth?"

"OK, sir. I feel much calmer than I'd expected."

"Less of the 'sir', please, Ruth. You can call me 'boss', since you're back in the team."

Her face lit up.

"Does that mean....?"

"You're reinstated, Ruth. Your record is clean and unblemished. I'm delighted to have you back."

"I'm delighted to be back, sir. Sorry, *boss*."

"Are you ready to return to duty? I'm quite happy to allow you to have time off, fully paid, if you feel you need time to get over the trauma."

"I'm fine, boss. Honestly."

"Then, are you ready to face your attacker? I'd like you to assist with the interviews, if you're up to it."

"I'd love to do that, boss. I want to see him squirm."

"I don't think we'll ever see that, Ruth. He's a psychopath. He feels nothing apart from the pleasure he gets from murdering innocent people."

"The experience will be good for me, boss. I'd love to be part of the process that sees him locked up for a long, long time."

"That's fine, then. You can have the rest of the day off, to celebrate."

"I'd rather start now, boss. I've had enough to drink while I was suspended."

"OK. Back to your desk. And thank you."

****

Ruth was immediately brought up to date with progress on the drugs case. Nothing had happened, It seemed all communication had been severed by the drugs gang and the officers were desperately trying to find a way back on to their customer list. As usual, Teresa came up with the solution. Instead of posing as buyers, Teresa would make contact on the pretext that her company were wholesale importers looking for distributors in the North of England. She made a pitch, explaining how she became aware of them and promising them good terms if they would become regular customers and as a result a meeting was arranged. In turn, Brian called a meeting to discuss ideas how to proceed.

Teresa, as usual, was the fulcrum of the operation, naming herself The Hood, and all communications were fed through her. Almost every day, she received emails asking questions about the organisation, its prices, delivery, terms and conditions. She ensured they were answered professionally and were consistent. Eventually she gained sufficient trust for small orders to be placed, and as they grew, the NSA became involved. It seemed that Bradford CID now had some international dealers on its books, but not the resources or manpower to bring them to justice. Gradually, most of the larger customers were handed over to the NCA so that Bradford CID could concentrate their efforts on local trade.

****

After weeks of planning and hard work, Teresa finally managed to set up a large delivery with the distributors they'd previously failed to nail on Baildon Moor. This time there would be no mistakes.

On the Friday night, Ruth, as agreed with Brian, called her sister for a chat and accidentally let slip the fact that the entire CID department were having a party on the Saturday night in Halifax to celebrate catching the serial killer. Ruth made a big play about how excited everyone was about it and how everyone looked forward to it. Finally, when her sister said how jealous she was and how her husband rarely took her out, Ruth made the suggestion.

"Why not mention it to him and ask him why he never treats you to a good night out?"

She'd sown the seed, and ended the call, hoping her sister would act accordingly. As expected, her sister told her husband, who in turn told his brother that CID would be out of town on the Saturday night. He, in turn, told the distributors, as expected.

During the course of the day, officers drove up to Baildon Moor in small numbers and built hides in the vicinity of the drop site. By five o'clock, preparations were complete and a meeting was held at HQ to finalise details and ensure everyone was comfortable with his or her role. Before leaving to prepare for the evening's operation, Brian re-emphasised the importance of the operation and wished everybody good luck before they dispersed to relax for a couple of hours.

From eight o'clock onwards, officers were ferried up to the drop site in small numbers in unmarked cars, and made their way, unnoticed, to their allotted hides. Text communication was established between all those involved as the clock ticked towards ten, when a message was sent to all officers that a large lorry was on its way towards them. It approached slowly and parked at the roadside. Two passengers got out and walked carefully around the car park, looking for any signs of life. They neither saw nor heard anything. The site was clear.

At the same time, the lorry containing armed officers was approaching from Baildon, slowing as it neared the car park, and stopping alongside the criminals' lorry. The driver got out and approached the newcomers as they climbed out of the cab. As he put out his hand in greeting, he immediately found a handcuff snapped round it. Simultaneously, armed officers emerged in number, surrounding the vehicle and ordering the criminals out into the road where they were handcuffed and made to kneel. They were outnumbered and offered no resistance as they were escorted into the back of the police vehicle under armed guard, and driven to HQ, where they were charged and led to the cells. Less than an hour later, police officers knocked on a door in Allerton and took Ruth's sister's brother-in-law in for questioning. He was placed in a cell opposite those brought in earlier and had to endure their jibes and threats of retribution.

At the party in the Conference Room two flights above, Ruth heard the news and burst out laughing, before walking down to gloat on her relative's misfortune. She spoke just a few words before returning to the party.

"Serves you right, you arsehole."

****

Teresa took the call on Monday morning.

"Oh, good morning. My name is Julie Hughes. I work for Nottingham Council. Some months ago, I spoke to two of your staff who were investigating a possible murder, out at Beeston."
"Just let me look at the files, please. It will only take a moment. Ah, yes. Here we are. The area had been re-developed, and they could find no evidence, so the case is still open. Do you have some news for me?"
"Yes. Some more re-development is due to start tomorrow, and a cycle lane is being created. It means a long stretch of ground will be dug up and from the notes I have, it seems to pass over the area you were interested in."
"Any chance of the work being postponed?"
"No. I'm sorry. It's already overdue and they want to start ASAP."
"OK. Thanks for the heads-up. I'll pass it on, and I expect we'll be sending a couple of officers down. If anything turns up we *WILL* order work to stop."
"I understand. I imagine you'll want to liaise with the local police, so I'll send you the contact's name and number."
"Thank you. Will you also send contact information for your SOCO team?
"I will. Anything else?"
"Yes. Do you still have plans of the area before the redevelopment?"
"Where the Housing Association flats were?"
"Yes."
"Yes, we have them."
"Could you please send me a copy, along with a schematic of the area as it is now? I want to overlay them to highlight possible areas of interest."
"I'll do that now. Anything else?"

"No. Thank you very much for your help. It's very much appreciated."

Teresa called Brian immediately.

"This may be some good news, Brian. There's been a development in the body parts case. The Council are having to excavate some of the Beeston site again, to construct a cycle path, starting tomorrow. That's Beeston, Nottingham, by the way. Not Leeds."
"Yes, I realise that. Just give me a second to check. OK, yes, some of our team can look forward to an early start in the morning."

He ended the call and rang Paula.

"Paula, we may have some good news on the body parts cases. There's an area in Nottingham where a man disappeared without trace. We thought at the time he may have been buried, or parts of him at least, in the gardens around the flats. However, when Lynn and Scoffer went down, they found that much of the area had been redeveloped. Now, some of it is being dug up again, to make a cycle path. It's possible that something may emerge during the excavation. Can you and Jo-Jo go down first thing in the morning and see if anything turns up?"
"When you say 'first thing', what time do you mean?"
"I'd like you there for nine. You can finish early today."
"OK. I'll pass on the good news to Jo-Jo."
"Thank you. You can collect all the info from Teresa."

Teresa had prepared a folder of information for them. It included a site map of the area where the flats were, and a corresponding overlay of the site at present, as well as how it will look when the cycle path is completed. She had highlighted areas of shrubbery and hedges on the map of the flats so that it was clear where the new excavations crossed areas which may have been accessible prior to the initial redevelopment yet partially hidden by shrubbery. These were the areas of particular interest to the officers.

On arrival at the site, they introduced themselves to the person in charge. He had already been notified and had commenced work away from the areas of interest so that they would be present to advise should anything emerge.

Early in the afternoon, they began tearing up the tarmac in one of the areas marked as being of interest. The officers, wearing hi-vis jackets and helmets, watched closely as the diggers tore up the earth, pushing it into a mound before loading it onto an open-backed lorry. Suddenly, Paula yelled.

"Stop! Stop! There's something."

She was right. Although covered in soil and mud, it was unmistakeably a Sainsbury's carrier bag tied at the neck. The driver leapt down from the digger and brought the bag to her. She carefully untied the knot and opened the bag, backing away from the stench. It was the remains of a severed head. They waited until the digger was moved away and the area cordoned off before moving forward to inspect the area more closely. Jo-Jo borrowed a shovel and a trowel and began to break up clods of mud. She soon found more of the skeleton, the bones roughly severed. Paula notified the local Forensics team who were quickly on the scene as the area was cordoned off and the Council's work abandoned for the day. It was not long before the trunk was unearthed, wrapped in a beach towel with 'Benidorm' printed on it. Jo-Jo called the council officer before he left the site.

"I'm surprised you didn't find these when you knocked the buildings down and cleared the site."
"We employ demolition men, not archaeologists."

The officers remained on site until they were satisfied with their finds. They thanked the Forensics team and drove back to Bradford, calling Brian on the way to update him on their day's work. He was pleased and stopped at the Ainsbury for a quick pint on the way home so that he could think about the status of the various ongoing cases. He had one pint before going home, taking two bottles of non-alcoholic beer with him.

****

Next morning, he was at his desk early, planning the team's tasks. He also called the Forensics team in Nottingham for an update but was disappointed at the progress made. The evidence his team had found was as yet unexamined, due to a backlog of work, but he extracted a promise that it would be next in the queue. There was nothing he could do apart from finding out whether his suspected killer, or the victim, possessed a 'Benidorm' beach towel.

Soon he was on the phone to the housing association which owned the original site in Beeston. He was passed from pillar to post before finally getting the name of the missing person, Alex Simpson, which was only flagged because his rent was overdue. He was given contact details of his next-of-kin, his daughter, whom Brian eventually managed to contact with help from Nottingham Council by checking her council tax information. It was an awkward conversation which left the woman in floods of tears as Brian explained what had happened. However, he managed to persuade her to send him photos of her father, which he forwarded to the Forensics team in Nottingham. They came back with a 95% match. He made an awkward call to the daughter, expressing his sympathy while hoping she would cooperate with his enquiry.

"Could you please tell me, to the best of your knowledge, did your father by any chance have a beach towel with 'Benidorm' on it?"
"I can't say for sure, but it's possible. He had a flat in Benidorm. He went to stay three or four times a year."
"You don't happen to have a set of keys for the flat, do you?"
"No, sorry. I never even went there. I have the address, though, if that's any use."
"Yes. That would be very useful. Thank you."
"One other thing, did he ever mention a woman called Ellen Sturgess, or Ellen Nugent?"
"No, I don't remember hearing either of those names."
"OK. Thank you."

He sent Paula and Jo-Jo to pick up Mrs Sturgess/Nugent and bring her in for questioning. They soon came back empty-handed. Her flat had been emptied.

"OK, check local airlines to see if Ellen Sturgess/Nugent has recently booked a flight to Alicante airport."

They soon verified that she'd left the country the previous day and gave the bad news to Brian.

"OK, how do the two of you fancy a couple of days in the sunshine? Get yourself booked on a flight as soon as you can. I'll ask Teresa to get an arrest warrant sorted, and to liaise with the Spanish authorities to agree extradition. Bring her home."
"OK, boss."
"And if you have to stay overnight for some reason, book yourselves into a hotel. It's on us. Just don't tell anyone about it, OK?"
"Thanks, boss."

****

They flew out on the first flight the following morning and were met by a local police officer who took them to his HQ where they met two officers who had been assigned to assist them. They were taken first to the block of flats where Alex Simpson owned an apartment and sat in the police car across the road, watching.

After an hour, Jo-Jo had had enough.

"We could be here all day. I think we should go to the flat and knock on the door."
"OK. Let's do it."

They left the Spanish officers in the car and crossed the road, taking the lift to the third floor. They knocked on the door but received no answer.

"What now, Paula?"
"Should we try the neighbours?"
"I don't know. What if they tip her off?"
"That's a good point. Better go back to the car."
"We could sit outside the bar across the road from the entrance. We'd get a good view from there."
"What about our escort?"
"They'd probably get into trouble if their boss found out."
"You're right. Back to the car, then."

As they walked across the lobby to the main entrance, a woman entered the building. They recognised her immediately and strode towards her. Paula stopped her.

"Excuse me; I wonder if you could help us."
"What is it you want?"
"Would you confirm your name, please?"
"Certainly not! That's none of your business."

They pulled out their ID cards and held them in front of her face. Jo-Jo issued the statement.

"Ellen Sturgess or Nugent, or whatever else you call yourself at the moment, I'm arresting you on suspicion of murder...."

Her jaw dropped, but she remained defiant.

"I don't know what you're on about. There's obviously been a mistake."
"Well, not to worry. We'll sort it out back home. Turn around, please, so I can put the cuffs on. We'll take you down to the police station and process the paperwork for your trip home. Then you can relax in a cell while we check out your flat. Then we fly home. OK?"

She nodded and gave a long sigh. The officers merely smiled.

They left her languishing in a cell while they went to check out the flat, piling what were obviously the tenant's belongings into her suitcase, before locking up and taking the case with them to the police station. Their next stop was at the nearest bar for a celebration, from where they sent a message to Brian, stating 'Mission accomplished. Just paperwork to do. It will probably take all night.' The reply soon came from Brian.

"Well done. Relax and have a drink. See you tomorrow with your guest."

****

While the officers were flying back to Leeds/Bradford Airport with their prisoner, Brian finally got the call from Nottingham's Forensic

Unit. Their examination of the body believed to be that of Alex Simpson indicated that the probable cause of death was a fracture of the skull. The indentation in the back of the skull was the size and shape of a claw hammer. Now, all that remained to be done was to interview the prisoner when she landed, and then prepare a report for the DPP.

He put aside the files when the phone rang.

"Sorry to bother you, sir. We've got a lady in Reception who says she's been raped."
"OK. I'll send someone down in a minute."

He looked at his staff's workload before asking Lynn to perform the interview. She agreed, happy to get a break from the cases she was currently involved in. She took the victim to an Interview Room.

"OK, Miss Hallam. Tell me what happened."
"I was raped last night."
"Where?"
"In my house. On Ravenscliffe."
"Do you know your attacker?"
"Yes."
"Can I have his name, please?"
"David Allcock. He was quite proud of his name. He's a bit of a boaster."
"Did you invite him into your house?"
"He just turned up."
"But you let him in?"
"Yes."
"Did you know he intended to rape you?"
"No. Not really."
"So, what exactly was your relationship with Mr Allcock?"
"We were friends, I suppose."
"Friends? In what sense?"
"We went to the same pub. We'd spoken to each other and met up occasionally."
"You say he just turned up at your house. How did he know where you live?"
"He's been before."

"You've invited him?"

"Yes."

"For what purpose?"

"A drink, and a chat."

"Have you had sex with him before?"

"Well, yes."

"Regularly?"

"On and off."

"So, you had a sexual relationship with him?"

"Well, yes. But this time I said 'no'."

"Any particular reason?"

"I was tired."

"OK. So, he forcibly raped you?"

"Yes."

"Why didn't you report it last night?"

"I was tired. I thought I'd get some sleep and report it this morning. Then I slept in."

"So, you have no evidence?"

"I've got a durex in my handbag. It's got his cum in it."

"Have you showered since the event?"

"Yes."

"So, there's no point having an inspection at the hospital?"

"No."

"Ok. Anything else you'd like to tell me?"

"No."

"I'll leave you to fill in this form. Write down exactly what happened. What time. Everything you remember. And your attacker's address, if you know it."

"Yes, I know it. It's just round the corner from where I live."

"Have you been there?"

"Occasionally. Parties, and that."

"OK. I'll pay him a visit as soon as you've finished."

"Can you give me a lift home?"

"Sorry. No. I'll talk to you later when I've seen Mr Allcock."

Lynn had her doubts about Christine Hallam, so she took a look at the criminal database where she found Miss Hallam had a record. Prostitution, shoplifting, drunk and disorderly, receiving stolen goods. Armed with that knowledge, she took Andy with her to visit Mr Allcock.

When they pulled up outside his house, they noticed immediately all the curtains were closed. Andy commented.

"Looks like someone's had a late night."
"Or sleeping off a hangover."
"Or both."
"Let's go and wake him up."

They hammered on the door until finally they heard someone coming down the stairs and fumbling with the keys, cursing when he dropped them. Eventually, an unshaven, sleepy-looking face appeared.

"What do you want?"
"Mr Allcock?"
"Who's asking?"
"Police, sir. We've had a report that you raped a woman last night."
"Bollocks! I paid for it. More than it was worth, as well."
"Well, sir, she's accused you of rape. Can we come in and discuss what happened, sir?"
"Please yourselves."

They walked into a living room which smelt heavily of smoke and rotting takeaway curry.

"Sit down", he motioned towards a stained settee.

"We'd rather stand if it's alright with you."
"Suit yourselves."
"So, tell us what happened last night."
"I was in the pub, having a few pints and minding my own business when she walked in. We know each other, so she joined me at a table and told me she needed some money. She had bills to pay, and asked if I could lend her thirty quid. I knew what she wanted it for."
"What was that?"
"Drugs. Heroin. She was an addict."
"So, what happened next?"
"I told her I didn't have the money. Then she said she'd let me shag her for thirty quid. I said I'd give her fifteen. She said it had to be thirty. I told her to eff off. Then she said she'd take fifteen if I

bought her a vodka as well. So, that's what happened. We went back to hers and I shagged her, paid, and walked home. I watched TV and had a few more drinks, and then I heard someone knocking on the door. It was her. She was high. She asked for more money. I told her to eff off and shut the door. She stood outside swearing for a while, but I just ignored it and eventually she went. I went to bed, and then you lot turned up."

"So, you're saying she's a prostitute?"

"Yes. Ask anybody. She's always propositioning somebody. Schoolkids, even. They come round at dinner time, and she sucks 'em off or gives 'em a hand job."

"Can anybody validate your story?"

"You can ask at the pub at the end of the road. They heard her proposition me."

"Ok. We may have to talk to you again, but in the meantime, I'd advise you to keep your distance from Christine Hallam."

"Don't worry. I wouldn't touch her with a bargepole. I've been itching like buggery since last night."

"If I were you, I'd see a doctor."

They drove away wondering what to do next. The only course of action was to discuss it with the boss.

Brian was immersed in his Outlook calendar, trying to juggle upcoming conferences while on his phone to Teresa.

"The only day I have free at the moment is 4th May, but I need to leave that free."

"Why can't you attend the Manchester conference then?"

"Because it's a special day."

"What's so special about it?"

"It's Star Wars Day."

"What are you on about, Brian?"

"May 4th. Star Wars Day. May the fourth be with you!"

They could hear Teresa groaning. Lynn did the same, while Andy just laughed. Brian grinned.

"I got caught out with that one in the Ainsbury recently. Now, what can I do for you two?"

"We've been interviewing a woman who alleges she was raped. The accused insists he paid her, though less than she asked for, because he insists she spends it on drugs. He says she's a heroin addict and she offers sex to local schoolkids to pay for her habit. We need to get her off the street, I think."

"I agree, but I think we need to find out who her supplier is. It may be Mullinder. Go talk to her again."

****

They drove back to Christine Hallam's house and arrived just as a heavily-built man was leaving. Andy decided to speak to him.

"Excuse me, sir. Can we have a word?"
"I'm busy. Who are you anyway?"
"Police, sir. May I ask what your business is here?"
"What do you think? She's a whore."
"What I want to know is, are you paying her or is she paying you?"
"Are you arresting me?"
"No, sir."
"Then I'm off. I've work to do."

They had no choice but to let him leave but noted his car's number plate as he drove away.

"Let's have a chat with Mrs Hallam."

Their first question was, did he pay her, or did she pay him.

"Neither. He's a friend. He just called for a chat."
"We don't believe you, Mrs Hallam. He either paid you for sex, or you paid him for drugs. Or have we got it wrong? Did he just come to collect money you'd borrowed previously?"
"He just came for a chat. He's a friend."
"Really? What's his name?"
"Gerry."
"And how do you know him?"
"He comes for a chat now and again."
"Look, Mrs Hallam. We can't help you unless you're honest with us. Just tell us who this guy is. We believe he's either a dealer, or a collector for a money-lender, or both. Which is it?"
"OK. Look, I had to borrow some money a while ago, to pay bills."

141

"Bills for heroin?"

"OK, yes."

"Who did you borrow from?"

"I swore I wouldn't tell anybody."

"Mullinder?"

There was a pause before she answered.

"Yes. He helped me out once when I needed quick cash, but the interest rate goes up all the time. I'll never be able to pay it off. That's why I have men coming to the house. I have to get money from somewhere to pay Mullinder."

"And to pay for the heroin as well?"

"Yes."

"We may be able to help you, but only if you'll help us."

She sighed.

"What do I have to do?"

"Do you have a phone number for Mullinder?"

No. But I have one for Gerry."

"OK. It's a start. We'll take that. Then, I suggest you come with us and we'll find you a safe house for a while, but only if you co-operate fully."

"Give me half an hour to pack some things."

"OK. We'll wait in the car outside."

They sat in the car, talking to Teresa while she took the details and attempted to organise safe accommodation for Mrs Hallam. Andy looked at his watch.

"She's taking her time. I'll see if I can speed her up a bit."

He knocked on the door and rang the bell but got no response. The door was locked. Panicking, he ran around to the back and hammered on the door. Again, there was no response, and the door was locked. A neighbour, hearing the noise, came out into the yard.

"She's just gone out."

"Where?

"I don't know. She got in a taxi."

"Did you notice what firm the taxi was from?"
"No. Sorry."
"OK, thanks."

He dashed back to the front and got in the car.

"She's done a runner. A taxi's just taken her away. Her neighbour saw her go but didn't see where the taxi was from."
"So, what next? Tell the boss?"
"I don't think he'll be too pleased."
"*You* can tell him, then."

They were dismayed to hear later in the day that her body had been fished out of the river Wharfe near Otley. She had been brutally beaten.

****

Brian was at his desk when Teresa phoned him. She sounded agitated.

"Brian, Forensics have just sent me some files they copied from Stephen Marks' computer. You'll be horrified when I tell you."
"Go on, then."
"Well, it appears he's created a record of his murders. It reads like a crime horror story. It's very detailed, but the thing is, he describes murders we don't know about. It's possibly fiction, or acts he was planning, but it may be a record of crimes he has committed that we're not yet aware of."
"Christ, that's all we need. Send me a copy, please."
"I'll copy it to a USB stick and bring it down."
"Thanks. I'll read it and then have a word with him."
"Oh, and by the way, as you asked, I sent a photo of Marks to both his ex-landlord and the Retirement Housing scheme in Undercliffe. Both identified him."

****

CHAPTER 11

He took Ruth with him to interview Marks, who was on remand in Armley prison. On the way there, he explained why he'd asked her to accompany him.

"He's a real cold-blooded murderer, Ruth. A psychopath. During your time in CID, you'll meet a few of these animals so I think it's important for you at this stage in your career to know what you're going to be confronted with and learn to come to terms with it. Only by experiencing monsters like Marks will you learn about yourself and whether you can handle it. Let me say now that there is no shame in deciding this career is not for you, and it's better to find out now rather than years down the line when you realise your life is a mess. Now, if you wish, I'll take you back to HQ."

"Thanks, boss, but I need to face this. I need to know if I'm up to it. As you say, there's no point in finding out what I'm made of in years to come. I'd rather know now."

"Good for you. I'll always be there if you want to discuss anything, or simply vent your rage, or even burst into tears. Just remember, all the officers in CID have had to learn to live with it."

The Interview room was ready for them when Marks was brought down. He stared at Ruth, and said,

"Morning, gorgeous. We've met before. I'm Stephen. And you are?"

Ruth looked him straight in the eye.

"I know your name. The last time we met you told me it was Mike. Don't you remember?"

"Ah, yes. My neighbour. The beautiful woman who was aching to have sex with me."

"In your dreams. Come to think of it, you seem to have a lot of erotic dreams, judging by what I've read on your laptop. I bet you wish it was real and not fiction."

Brian decided to allow Ruth some latitude, so rather than control the direction of the interview, he sat back and took notes.

"How do you know it's not real?"

"Tell me. Is it?"

"That's for you to find out. That's what you're paid for."

"Yes. That's right. We get paid for putting arseholes like you in prison. So, tell me, is it real?"

"Some of it is. The rest was still in the planning stage when you arrested me. And, of course, there are other chapters I haven't written up yet. But, of course, you don't know about them yet."

"No. So, why don't you tell us about them?"

"I don't want to forewarn you. After all, I haven't been to trial yet. They might let me off."

"In your dreams."

"Mmm. You'll be glad to know you're in my dreams."

"And you're in mine. I dream about you languishing in jail until you die."

Brian was impressed with the way Ruth had coped up to that point, but he felt he had to intervene to discuss some of Marks's stories.

"OK, that's the introductions over. Now, let's talk about your writing. It's certainly horrific. Do you hope to get any of it published?"

"I'd love to. I'm sure there's a market for this sort of true crime."

"Nobody would believe it. They'd think you were demented. Nobody could imagine the things you seem to have done were real. We'll certainly be keeping a lid on it. You're not going to achieve the sort of notoriety you crave. You're no master criminal. You were caught by a novice DC who hadn't even completed her training. Your victims were all disadvantaged to some degree. You never came up against a real adversary. Just social inadequates. People with problems. You really were useless, so don't try to build yourself up into some sort of master criminal. As soon as you came up against someone with a brain, like my colleague here, your criminal life was over. So, is there anything else you'd like to boast about?"

"I don't think there's any point, do you? You're clearly not interested."

"Oh, we are. You're just a long way down the list of serial killers. You're way short of the Yorkshire Ripper's total. How many was it? 13. Yes, that's right, isn't it? 13 kills. And how many have you?"

"I'm not saying any more. This interview is over."

"No, it isn't. I'm still listening."

There was silence for a moment until Marks spoke again.

"Walls have ears."

"Why do you say that?"

"I have nothing more to say."

"Why not? I'm still listening even if nobody else is."

"Walls have ears."

"OK. This is pointless. This interview is over. The next time I see your face will be across a courtroom."

On the drive back to HQ, Brian asked Ruth for her opinion.

"He's still trying to maintain he's the world's best serial killer. He's very haughty."

"Did he frighten you?"

"No. Probably because he was handcuffed and you were there."

"What did you make of his final comment – 'walls have ears'?"

"I don't know. It was an odd thing to say. Did he suspect the interview was being recorded?"

"It was."

"Oh. I didn't know."

"Yes. You never know when something useful might be mentioned, then quickly forgotten. Still, it was an odd thing to say. Give it some thought, will you?"

"Of course. By the way, will I still be involved in this case, or was today just part of my training?"

"Would you like to be involved?"

"Yes."

"OK, then. I'll give you access to all the files. You can start by reading the stories he's written on his laptop. If at any time you think it's too much for you, just tell me. It's no admission of weakness, but it is hard going and will show you the sort of thing you can expect from a career in CID."

"I'll give it my best, boss. At least no two days are the same. There's no way boredom will ever set in."

"You're right. Every day is a new challenge. And don't forget, there's always someone to turn to if you need advice or support. Welcome to the team, Ruth."

"Thanks, boss."

Ruth was happy to work on her own. She felt that her boss trusted her and for that reason alone she would do her very best. It was her chance to stand out. She was determined not to let anybody down.

She started by asking Teresa to give her access to everything they knew about Stephen Marks. Teresa had pre-empted her request and dug deep into Marks's past, providing previous addresses, work experience, and family history. There were inevitably gaps, but it was enough to start with. She began by reading his version of his recent crimes which was an emotional and exhausting experience, leading to a dilemma: did he write the book to record his crimes, or did he commit the crimes to provide the storylines for the book. A further thought entered her head. Are there any undocumented murders? She decided to go as far back into his history as possible, finding that he had underachieved at school and left with few qualifications, eventually finding a job with a company which provided maintenance work for council properties. There he learnt the basics of carpentry, bricklaying, plastering, painting and decorating at which he became no more than competent. She traced his addresses, trying to match his whereabouts with unsolved crimes in the area. Most of her leads brought no joy, but finally she came across a missing person case in Halifax. Her eyes lit up when she realised the missing person lived next door to Marks. Immediately, she went to Brian.

"Boss, I've discovered something new relating to Marks. I think it could be important."
"Pull up a chair and tell me about it, Ruth."
"Well, about ten years ago, he lived alone in a small terraced house in Halifax. He'd bought it and was doing it up. He fancied himself as an all-round tradesman. Anyway, a couple in their thirties lived next door, and the husband one day reported his wife had gone missing. She was never located. Initially, her husband was suspected of killing her, but that was soon dropped. Everybody the police spoke to said what a lovely, close couple they were. Nobody had ever heard them arguing, they went everywhere together, and then, she just disappeared. Her husband actually hired a private investigator to try to find her, but he had no luck."
"Was Marks a suspect?"

"Not really. He was interviewed but it seemed they were just neighbours. There was no evidence of a relationship between them, in fact, the wife had told her husband more than once she felt uncomfortable in his presence. She thought he was 'a bit creepy'. So, it's a cold case."

"I take it you'd like to re-open it."

"I think it's worth looking into."

"OK. Go for it. If you need any help, just ask. We'll support you as much as possible. Keep me informed."

"Thanks, boss. I will."

"There's another thing which might be worth looking into. When you first met Marks, he introduced himself as Mike Thomas. Now, we know that once previously he took the name of a victim, when he looked around the flats in Undercliffe. Then, he introduced himself as Gerald Drinkwater. So, it's possible that someone called Mike Thomas may also have been one of his victims. Look into that as well, please."

"Mind if I ask Teresa?"

"Good idea. I think you've enough on your plate at the moment."

She turned her attention to locating John Sanderson, the husband of the missing woman, and called him to ask to speak to him. He agreed she could call the following morning at his home. Surprisingly, she felt, he still lived in the same house he occupied with his late wife, a point she raised with him when she arrived.

"Thank you for seeing me, Mr Sanderson. I had rather expected you would have moved away from the memories this house must have for you."

"I'm always hoping she'll turn up one day, with an explanation of some kind. Even if she said she'd been abducted by aliens, I'd take her back. She was my *life*."

"I'm sorry, sir. I realise this must bring back some awful memories for you, but I'm doing some research into a neighbour you once had. Stephen Marks. I'd like to know what you thought of him."

"Not much, really. Elaine and I both thought he was a bit odd. We said 'hello' and that, but we were never friends. He kept very much to himself."

"Did you notice anything unusual about him? His habits? The way he looked at women?"

"What's this about?"

"Your ex-neighbour is awaiting trial for a series of murders, sir. I've been asked to look into his past to see if he may have been active a lot earlier than we suspected."

"You think he may be responsible for Elaine's disappearance?"

"We're not ruling it out until we're fully satisfied he had nothing to do with it. We're just gathering evidence of his past before he goes to court."

"Well, I can assure you Elaine would never willingly be alone with him. She thought he was creepy."

"What can you remember about the last time you saw Elaine? Did she seem agitated, or anything?"

"No. She was a 'morning' person. Always bright and breezy. We had breakfast together as usual. Then I went to work. We kissed at the door before I drove off. She would then take the bus into town for her job. But she never arrived…."

"Did any of the neighbours see her that morning?"

"No. She got the same bus every morning, but nobody remembers seeing her that morning. She just disappeared."

"What about your next-door neighbour?"

"He was still in bed, apparently. He called in sick that morning."

"When did you report Elaine missing?"

"About eight o'clock that evening."

"Why so late?"

"On Wednesdays, she used to go to her mother's straight from work. Her father had died a year earlier, and she'd call on her mother once a week to spend some time with her. When she hadn't arrived home at the usual time, I called her mother. She said she'd never arrived. The police said they'd send someone to talk to me in the morning and to let them know if she turned up. Anyway, she never did and when I phoned her work next morning, they told me she'd never arrived the previous day."

"Can you remember, when you came home from work that first day, was there anything unusual about the house?"

"Not that I remember."

"She hadn't left a note or anything?"

"No."

"Were any of her clothes missing? A suitcase missing?"

"No. The only thing missing was Elaine."

"What about cash in the house? Did she take any?"

"No. We always had a kitty for housekeeping. There was a fair amount in it, probably £50. She didn't take any."

"What about her bank account?"

"Not touched since the day she disappeared. Although her bank card was missing."

"OK. How did your neighbours react?"

"They were sympathetic, mostly. Apart from him next door. He just carried on with his life."

"Was he ever a suspect?"

"The police interviewed him, but nothing came of it. I hope you have better luck."

"We'll do our very best, Mr Sanderson. One more question. When did Marks move out?"

"About six months later."

"And the people who moved in, are they still there?"

"No. They moved about a year ago. There's a young couple with a baby there now."

"Thank you for seeing me, Mr Sanderson. I hope I can bring you some news eventually. I'll carry on until I bring this to a conclusion."

"Thank you. I just want closure. Elaine would never have walked out on me without saying goodbye."

Ruth called next door and spoke to the young woman who was at home with her young child. She confirmed that they'd made no alterations to the house since they'd move in, apart from painting and decorating. Ruth asked her to ensure they left the structure as it was.

"It's nothing to worry about. We think an offence may have taken place here some years ago, and we may need to look into it forensically."

****

She couldn't wait to report back to Brian.

"Can we get Forensics to check out a house in Halifax? A woman named Elaine Sanderson went missing from home about ten years ago. Her husband refuses to believe she would ever have left him. They were a very close couple, very happy together. None of her belongings were missing. No money was taken. She simply disappeared. And guess what? She and her husband lived next door to Stephen Marks."

"What makes you think we may find her body? Surely if someone's been living there all these years since…"

"It was something Marks said. It's been bothering me ever since. 'Walls have ears', he said. Maybe walls have complete bodies."

"OK. I'll talk to Allen."

He immediately authorised a search of the property by Forensics, with scanning equipment required.

****

Ruth met the Forensics team at the premises and introduced them to the residents at the property, explaining what they had to do, and that any subsequent damage would be made good at public expense. Mr Sanderson declined the offer to be present during the examination.

They started in the cellar, which had some cladding on one of the walls, but found nothing. They worked their way upwards, floor by floor until they reached the attic. Here, they discovered that the floor area was less than shown on the plans. It seemed an area a metre deep had been covered by a false wall which had then been plastered over and wallpapered. The area was scanned by the technicians who were absolutely certain all was not well.

"There's a body behind this wall. It's quite clear. It's female and it appears she's had her throat cut. We'll have to remove the body and take it back for analysis."

Mr Sanderson was informed and collapsed in tears, having to be comforted and given assistance before an ambulance took him to hospital. After the SOCO team had finished and photos had been taken, arrangements were made for the damage to be made good. The householders were offered counselling but declined. Ruth was visibly distressed but called Brian to update him and ask if she could finish for the day.

"Absolutely, Ruth. Go home and relax. Switch off, come in tomorrow if you feel like it, otherwise call me and we'll discuss some appropriate therapy."

"I feel like I'm letting the side down."

"Not at all, Ruth. You've been through a traumatic experience and seen it to conclusion. You deserve to take a break to recover. Call me when you feel back to normal. No rush. Take it easy, and well done, by the way."

The call from Forensics came only minutes later.

"The body belongs to the neighbour, Brian. It's definitely Elaine Sanderson. Her throat was cut with a sharp knife. There is no sign of sexual or physical assault. It seems to have been premeditated. Blood spatter indicates she died where she was found and was hidden with hastily-erected plasterboard which was then papered over. A callous murder."

"Thanks. I'll pass the news to Mr Sanderson after I've had a word with Stephen Marks."

****

He sat for a while, pondering his next move, before plugging in the USB stick and carefully reading the killer's manuscript, making notes and ticking off the murders as he identified the victims. At one point he came across an incident he didn't recognise. He read through it again, making notes as he did so, trying to decide whether the incident had already taken place or was still in the planning phase. He read it again.

NEXT ONE

"She heard the doorbell and opened the door to find a man smiling at her.

"Mornin', love. I've been given a report that you've got a problem with your heating. Just come to check it for you."

"I haven't reported a problem."

"Well, someone has, love. Number 46. That's you."

"Oh, it was probably my son. He always says it's cold in here. Well, you'd better come in, then."

"It won't take long, love."

"Would you like a cup of tea while you're here."
"That'd be nice, love. Two sugars, please."

She was standing at the sink, filling the kettle, her back to him. She never heard him creeping up behind her, but suddenly felt his gloved hands tighten around her throat. She offered no resistance, simply feeling the life draining from her body as she slumped to the floor. He smiled.

"Job done."

He moved the curtain slightly so he could check if anybody was outside. It was clear. He took a deep breath, opened the door, closing it quietly behind him and walked up the street and round the corner to where he'd parked his car. He got in, started the engine, put on his belt and drove away. As far as he was aware he'd gone unnoticed. All he had to do now was call back in the middle of the night to dispose of the body."

Brian shook his head in wonder. Was this a record of an event which had already taken place, or one still to occur. He picked up the phone.

"Teresa, can you do a search for me, please. Any open cases concerning incidents of a woman – I'm assuming an old woman – being strangled to death in her home by someone she'd apparently invited in?"
"Give me ten minutes and I'll get back to you."

Brian sighed. Marks was already getting closer to the Ripper's tally.

CHAPTER 12

Paula and Jo-Jo had been gathering together all the evidence they had concerning Ellen Nugent's criminal activities and were finally ready to interview her at her temporary home in New Hall prison in Wakefield. They were hoping she would admit to all her crimes, so they could wrap the case up quickly and present their report to the DPP. They were not disappointed. She co-operated right from the beginning of the interview.

"Let's get it over with. I'm guilty. But don't try to pin every outstanding crime you've got on your books on me. I'll admit to all those I've committed, so go ahead."

"OK, let's start with Charlie Wallace. You knew him when you lived at Kipling Court?

"Yes. We had a relationship for a while."

"So, what went wrong?"

"He turned up at my door with a suitcase demanding to move in with me. I said 'no'. We had an argument and I killed him. Then I got my power tools out and sawed him up in pieces and disposed of them all over."

"You left a hand in the compost bin?"

"Yes. I thought it might be a memorable gesture. I never liked the place. Some of the residents were rude to me."

"OK, what came next?"

"I moved to Keighley."

"Have you killed anyone while you've been there?"

"No. I'm happily married."

"So, Charlie Wallace was your last victim?"

"Yes."

"So, let's go back to where you lived before Kipling Court. Mansfield. Did you commit any murders there?"

"You tell me."

"We think so. We have a report of a man going missing while you were there. A Mr Tony Jackson. Tell us about your relationship with him."

"He was friendly. Probably too friendly. He was always at my door with some excuses, such as he'd bought too many strawberries at the supermarket and would I like some. He was becoming a real pest."

"Did you ask him to leave you alone?"

"Yes. Several times."

"Did you have sex with him?"

"A couple of times, but he wasn't very good. So, I ended it."

"And how did he react?"

"He was upset."

"So, how did you stop him from pestering you?"

"Easy. I invited him in one night and had sex with him. When he fell asleep, I got the power drill out and drilled a hole in his temple, right through into his brain."

"Go on, what next?"

"I dragged his body onto some plastic sheet and cut it into pieces. I bagged them all up separately and over the next week or so, I drove out into the countryside and dumped them in rivers, weighted down."

"Could you identify the sites for us?"

"No. I can't remember, to be honest."

"OK. Then you moved?"

"Yes, to Beeston."

"And you continued your games there?"

"Yes. There must be something about these places. They all seem to have at least one dirty old man who wants a shag and won't let you have any peace."

"What was his name?"

"Alex. Alex Simpson."

"Tell us about your relationship with him."

"He was quite nice to start with. He had a flat in Benidorn and invited me to go there with him."

"And you went?"

"Of course."

"And?"

"I enjoyed it. I went twice with him."

"So, what went wrong?"

"He asked me to marry him."

"You declined?"

"Absolutely, but he kept pestering me, saying I'd had two free holidays at his expense, and he wanted something in return. Well, he got something."

"A hammer to the skull?"

"Yes, that's right. How did you know that?"

"We investigated. It's what we get paid to do. So, carry on."

155

"I cut him up and buried the lot under some bushes. Then, I gave notice and moved on."

"Any other offences we should know about?"

"No, although you've probably saved Bob's life. I'm getting a little tired of him. He's very demanding."

"OK. Well, I guess the next time we see you will be in court. You'll face a very long sentence."

"I suppose I deserve it. If only men had stopped demanding sex all the time, life could have been so different."

Driving back to HQ, both officers were unable to understand Ellen Nugent's attitude to her actions.

"She's a real psychopath. If she didn't want sex, why not just say 'no'?"

"I agree. It's not as if she'd been raped by her victims. If she had, I'd possibly have understood her actions."

"Well, let's get the report completed and move on to the next maniac."

****

Mullinder smiled as he read the Telegraph & Argus, whose front-page headline stated "Three bodies discovered after house fire". Beneath, it told the story about how the Fire Brigade was called out to a report of a fire in a boarded-up house on the Holme Wood estate. By the time they arrived, the building was engulfed in flames, and it was only after the fire was extinguished that the bodies of three adult males were found. They were as yet unidentified but were thought to be homeless men seeking shelter. The paper promised more news in the later edition with a statement to be issued by police in due course.

They had become a liability; they had to go. He was always worried that they knew too much about his business and that one day, one or more of them would spill the beans in return for cash, or even a reduced sentence. It made no difference now. He could start again with a clean sheet. He had the contacts and knew the game well enough.

He pulled out his laptop and searched the Dark Web. He was looking for opportunities in drug distribution. He posted his 'qualifications' and waited for replies.

He'd been staying in a B & B on the outskirts of Skipton, using the name Jim Mullins. He'd already rented a unit on the nearby industrial estate which would be his base for operations and had begun the task of recruiting workers who would be prepared to work on such an illegal enterprise. He knew some of them from his time in prison; others had been recommended. They knew the score. Toe the line and be well rewarded; otherwise, you could be eliminated. For most of them it was a risk worth taking. Their criminal records meant most other jobs were unavailable to them. He sat back, basking in the knowledge that if his new venture didn't work out, there were still many people in Bradford who owed him money. The interest on those debts would be collected in due course. They would fund his retirement in Spain.

The 'ping' indicated a message had arrived. He opened it and read,

"Interested in your proposition. Can we meet? Just us two. No heavies."

He replied,

"Red Lion, Skipton. Tonight, 7.30pm?"
"OK. How will I recognise you?"
"Ask for half of lager. I'll watch for you."
"OK."

He was in position, early, seated at the end of the bar, and reading the late edition of the T & A where an update on the story of the dead bodies found in a blazing house in Holme Wood was featured. He smiled as he read the victims had been shot and were almost certainly dead before the fire was started. They had not yet been identified.

****

Teresa's search had drawn a blank. Brian was unsure whether the story he'd read had actually already taken place, or was still at the

157

planning stage, or whether it was simply fiction. He decided to quiz Stephen Marks about it and made an appointment to speak to him in Armley Jail. He'd already told Mr Sanderson the truth about his wife's disappearance and wanted to see Marks's reaction to that while he was there. They met in an Interview Room.

"How are they treating you?"
"It's not the most hospitable place I've stayed in, but better than some. But never mind that. What can I do for you?"
"We found the woman's body. Your neighbour in Halifax. Remember, Mrs Sanderson? The one you guided one of my team towards."
"Clever woman, your detective. Sexy, as well."
"I've been reading your stories. The ones we found on your computer."
"What do you think?"
"Interesting, but far-fetched."
"Really? You don't think they're true?"
"A figment of your warped imagination."
"Well, I'll tell you. They are all true! Every word."
"I don't believe you. So, they won't be considered among your tally of victims. You're still a long way behind the Ripper."
"I'm telling you, they're all true!"

He banged his fist on the table in his fury. Brian smiled.

"Prove it. This one about pretending to strangle a woman when you went to see her about a problem with her heating. When was this supposed to have happened? And where? There's no record of it anywhere."
"It's all true."
"Well, it won't count towards your tally of victims, I'm afraid. As far as I'm concerned, it never happened."
"Oh, it happened, all right. I remember every detail about it."
"Well, if it's true, give me an address, and the date."

There was silence as Brian sat back, arms folded, waiting for Marks as he deliberated. Finally, he told the story.

"The reason you haven't a record of this death, is that you haven't been doing your job properly."
"So, the crime has been reported?"

"She was reported as a missing person. Obviously, nobody's done enough searching."

"So, why don't you tell me where her body is?"

"I buried her. In her back garden."

"If you give me the address, I'll check."

"I can't remember exactly. It was one of the streets off Great Horton Road. Rugby Place."

"The number?"

"I can't remember."

"The date."

"Last year. September? Round about September."

"Do you know her name?"

"No."

"Well, unless we find a body, we don't count it."

"I could take you there."

"Not a chance. We'll have a look. If we find anything, I'll talk to you again. In the meantime, have a think about any other murders you might have committed. Unless we confirm them, they don't count."

"I'd love to help you, but I don't want to make your job easier than it already is. We can't have you taking all the glory for solving crimes, when I'm the one who's put in all the effort and had to tell you about murders you weren't even aware of!"

There was silence as Brian considered his strategy. He needed to encourage Marks to open up. He tried a different approach.

"Why did you start killing people?"

"I wanted to be a writer. Most of the crime books I've read were pretty crap. I always thought I could do better, but I needed first-hand experience. I needed to sound realistic."

"From what I've read so far, your writing is pretty crap. Did you do any research before the killings?"

"'Course. I visited every site. Everything was planned to the finest detail."

"Did you feel any emotion when you were killing someone?"

"'Course. Occasionally."

"Did you feel any emotion when you were writing about your killings?"

"Yes."

"Which gave you the biggest hard-on? Killing or writing about it?"

"Killing."

"I thought so. There's no emotion in your writing."

"It's supposed to be cold-blooded."

"But you just said it gave you a hard-on."

"It did."

"Well, did any agents think it had any promise?"

"No. But what do they know? Have they ever killed anyone?"

"Well, reading your tales makes me think you just wrote how you *think* you should have felt. Because you didn't actually *feel* anything. That's why your writing is so crap. The reader can't engage with it. It's just so matter of fact. Believe me, none of this stuff will ever sell. So, any more victims?"

"Maybe."

"OK, let's change the focus. Why did you kill? What made you kill the first time?"

"Grandad. He told me about a Summer School he attended in Buck Wood in the 1950s. Told me all about it. He loved it, apart from one kid he hated. A clever kid who couldn't do wrong in the eyes of the teachers. He killed him."

"How?"

"He led him into the woods on some pretext, then bashed his head in. He hid his body in undergrowth. He said he hadn't seen him that day. Nobody saw him and the other boy slip away after dinner. Nobody suspected him. He told me all about it on his deathbed."

"Why?"

"I guess he was proud that nobody found out."

"Was the body ever found?"

"I don't know. He didn't say."

"So, there's no evidence he actually killed someone?" How do you know he didn't make it up? Like you did with some of your stories."

Marks banged the table in anger.

"It was true!"

"Show me the proof!"

Marks was silent.

"I'll tell you what I'm going to do. I'm going to get one of my team to research what you've told me. And I guarantee it's all bullshit! Your grandad, your hero. He's full of shit. You're going back in your cell to give you time to think about things you want to tell me. And separate the truth from the lies. I just want the truth from you."

He drove back to HQ in silence and went straight to Teresa's desk.

"I've another job for you, Teresa. It's important."

"Go on."

"Apparently there used to be a Summer School in Buck Wood in Thackley back in the 1950's. According to Marks, his grandad killed another boy and buried the body which has never been found. Can you find out if there's a report of a boy going missing? Sorry, I can't be more specific."

"I'll see what I can find."

"Thanks."

Back at his desk, he opened a map of the area around Thackley on his PC and read all he could find about the history of the school in the woods. He would visit the site on his way home after work.

****

It took a week before Teresa made a breakthrough. She called Brian to her desk immediately where all the information was laid out on her console and printed copy.

"Here. 1956. At that time, what used to be a school in Buck Wood before the 2nd World War re-opened for use by community groups like the Scouts and also became a base for summer holidays for local children whose parents worked in Bradford factories. There's a report of a child going missing during the day when the kids were engaged in one of the outdoor activities which were part of the schedule. The head count when they returned to class late one afternoon showed that a nine-year-old boy couldn't be accounted for. A search of the area was made. The police and local volunteers were drafted in to make a thorough search, but the boy was never found. All the children were interviewed but nothing explained what happened to the boy. There was a rumour that he'd been taken by a tramp who frequented the woods, but nothing came of that either. In the end, it was just filed and forgotten."

"Thanks, Teresa. Could you tell me where you got this information?"

"Google mostly, but a local group published a history of the area as well."

"OK. I wonder if Mr Marks got the story from there."

"It's possible. Why don't you ask him?"

"Is there any point? I wouldn't expect him to tell the truth."

Brian was back at Armley the following morning, in the Interview Room with Marks. He glared at the prisoner.

"It was all bullshit, wasn't it?"

"What?"

"What you told me about your grandad."

"He told me, and I believed him."

"Well, let me tell you there's no record of any child going missing from the school. No body has ever turned up. It's all in your imagination."

"No! It happened."

"Your grandad made it up. Either that, or you made it up."

"It's true! You lot just haven't searched properly."

"So, where exactly should we search?"

"Away from the school."

"Would you be prepared to take us to the site?"

"No. I'm not doing your job for you."

"In that case, it never happened. Your grandad was a fantasist, just like you."

"I'm not a fantasist! I'll prove it. Take me to the wood. I'll show you!"

"I'll make the arrangements. See you soon."

The following morning, Stephen Marks was escorted to Buck Wood, where the Forensics team were assembled and ready. Brian pulled Marks aside and, uncharacteristically, issued a threat Marks had no option but to believe.

"If you think you're leading us on a wild goose chase, think again. If we don't find a body today, they'll find one tomorrow, and it will be yours. I'll make sure of that. I'm sick of your games. I want proof before I believe any more of your stories."

"Follow me. Just down here."

He took them off the path into an area barely accessible due to the unrestricted growth of thick foliage.

"Here. Dig here. Go carefully. You don't want to harm the poor kid."

Brian dragged him away so he couldn't watch progress, and led him back to the path, tripping him so that he fell face first into brambles. His hands cuffed behind him, Marks was unable to shield his face from damage.

"Sorry, pal. You need to watch where you put your feet. Accidents easily happen in places like this."

"My lawyer will hear about this."

"Sue me."

He was called back by Forensics.

"Brian, you need to see this."

They had uncovered the naked body of a young boy. His skull was fractured into pieces behind his right ear. Marks's face broke into a huge grin.

"Told you."

****

The report from Forensics came through the following morning.

"The body was that of a male child, approximately nine years old. Death was caused by a single blow to the skull which fractured the occipital bone and caused severe bleeding to the brain. Death would occur in minutes.
Examination of the condition of tissues of the body and its surroundings lead me to conclude death occurred no more than five years ago."

Attached was a drawing by a forensics artist who had attempted to reconstruct the appearance of the boy's face from the information provided. It was fairly generic in appearance and could be a basic likeness of a fair proportion of boys of that age. However, it at least established the boy was of European ethnic origin.

Brian again asked Teresa to perform a search for missing white male children aged eight to ten, reported in the last eight years, in the area. She replied within hours.

"Paul Bastow was reported missing in September 2018. Last seen at Thackley Corner talking to an adult male at around 4pm. Address of parents attached, along with photo of their son. Good luck."

He asked Ruth to accompany him and the two of them drove to the address in Wrose and stopped outside a semi-detached house. He checked the address before walking up the drive and pressing the bell. A slim blonde-haired woman in her late thirties opened the door.

"Mrs Bastow?"
"Yes."

"Mrs Bastow, I'm Detective Inspector Peters from Bradford CID. This is DC Crawford. I wonder if we could have a word, please. Inside, preferably."
"What's it about?"
"You reported your son missing in 2018."
"Oh, my God! Have you found him?"
"Can we speak inside, please?"
"Yes. Yes, come in."

They settled in the lounge, where Brian began a difficult conversation.

"Is your husband available, Mrs Bastow?"
"No. We divorced a couple of years ago. Will you please tell me what this is about?"
"OK. I'm afraid there's no easy way to say this, but yesterday we found the body of a young male, believed to have died around that time. Do you have a photo of your son, please?"
"Yes. Just give me a second."

Brian looked at the photo and compared it with the artist's impression. It was a good match.

"Mrs Bastow, I believe the body we found is that of your son. Would you please come with me to the mortuary to identify the body. Bring someone with you if you wish."
"I'll phone my sister."

She burst into tears. Ruth did all she could to comfort her while she made the call.

"She'll be here in a few minutes."
"Is there anyone else you wish to notify?"
"No. Not until it's confirmed."
"Of course."

When her sister arrived, they all went together in Brian's car to the mortuary. Brian issued a note of caution before they entered.

"When we go in, we'll stand in a room adjacent to where the body is laid on a table. You will be able to see him through a glass partition when you are ready. I must caution you that many people find it a very disturbing process, but as soon as you've made the identification the blind will be drawn, and we'll go into another room. OK?"

She nodded and they moved to the viewing area.

"Are you ready, Mrs Bastow?"

Again, she nodded. The body was revealed laid on a table. Mrs Bastow gasped, and nodded, before being ushered away by her sister. Brian followed them to a comfortable lounge.

"I'm sorry, Mrs Bastow. I have to ask. Can you please confirm the body you've just seen is that of your son, Paul Bastow?"

She nodded and said 'yes' as her sister comforted her.

"We'll leave you for five minutes and then there will be some paperwork to complete. Can we get you anything?"

She shook her head. Brian left the room to join the Forensics team before arranging to interview Stephen Marks once more.

****

The formalities completed, they drove the tearful Mrs Bastow and her sister home before driving back to Armley where Marks was waiting in an Interview Room.

"OK, Marks. We've identified the body. Tell me about it."
"I already did."
"No. You told me your grandad told you about it. We know that's not true because your grandad was dead before this boy was even born. So, how did you know it was there?"
"Somebody told me."
"Who?"
"Some paedo guy."
"Give me his name."
"I don't know his name."
"Where and when did he tell you about it?"
"We had a chat online. I never met him. I don't know his real name. He just told me about it."
"I want the name of the site you used and his online identity."
"It's on my laptop. I'm surprised you haven't found it yet."
"Give me the details. Now."
"I'll write them down for you."

Brian immediately sent the details to Teresa. She replied within minutes.

"Brian, you need to see this. It's mind-blowing stuff."

"OK. We'll be straight back."

He turned to Marks.

"We'll talk again soon. Don't go anywhere."

Back at HQ, they were reading in disbelief the stories which were discussed during the online conversation. It consisted of a catalogue of tales of debauchery and paedophilia committed in Buck Wood and dating back to the late 1950s.

"This is dynamite. We need to identify the culprits hiding behind these pseudonyms. Some of them will still be alive. They need to be punished."

The response to such an explosion of crime was well-rehearsed and immediate. As soon as Teresa identified a lead, it was passed to Brian who would allocate officers to follow up and investigate. The Conference Room was set up with whiteboards and IT equipment necessary to co-ordinate their response. Everybody knew the drill and would immediately cancel all other engagements in order to provide a rapid and efficient response to the crisis. There would be no holding back.

DCI Gardner sought, and was granted, permission for Stephen Marks to be transferred from Armley and held in custody in the cells at Bradford HQ, so that he could be grilled the moment a lead emerged.

By midway through the next morning, Teresa had identified one of those involved in the online conversation with Marks about the death of Paul Bastow. His name was Harold Stackpole; he lived in Eccleshill. Lynn and Scoffer were despatched to arrest him.

****

CHAPTER 13

Scoffer rang the doorbell and was surprised when an old man answered.

"Good morning, sir. We're from Bradford CID. Here are our IDs. We'd like to talk to Harold Stackpole, please. Is he in?"
"Yes. You're speaking to him."

Both officers were taken aback. They expected a much younger man. Scoffer quickly recovered his composure.

"May we come in, sir. We'd like to ask you some questions."
"What about?"
"About the death of a young boy, sir. Paul Bastow."
"Sorry, I can't help you."
"We know you were involved, sir. We've been following your online conversations."
"You're mistaken."
"I don't think so, sir. We'd like you to accompany us to HQ for questioning. While you're there, we'll acquire a search warrant for this property and we'll tear it to bits, unless you'd like to show us where your PC is and give us permission to take it with us."
"Certainly not. I want a lawyer."
"You'll be able to call one from HQ, sir. Get your coat."
"Are you arresting me?"
"No, sir. You're simply assisting us with our enquiries. If you refuse, then we'll arrest you. It can be quite a harrowing and painful experience for someone your age."

In the Interview Room, with his solicitor present, they were unable to make any headway, having no real evidence apart from the fact that he'd taken part in an online discussion regarding paedophilia. His solicitor stated his client was writing a novel about child molesters and was simply doing research. In the meantime, his home was being searched and his PC taken to the Lab. His solicitor secured his release, but his freedom was short-lived as soon as hard-core child porn was found on his PC, at which point he was brought back in to share a holding cell with Stephen Marks. They were unaware that their conversation was being recorded as soon as they introduced themselves by their online ID. They were both seasoned paedophiles, from different eras, but with much in common. Eventually, Brian thought the time was right to separate them and interview them separately.

Lynn and Andy were interviewing Stephen Marks next door in Interview Room 2 while Brian and Ruth were preparing to interview Harold Stackpole in Interview Room 1 when he took a call on his mobile.

"Brian, it's Helen at the T & A. I'm sorry to disturb you but I've heard disturbing news that you're investigating a paedophile ring in the area. Can you confirm if that's true?"

"At the moment, Helen, all I can confirm is that we're looking into the possibility that a paedo group was active in the Thackley area many years ago. I'll update you in due course. But that's all I can say at the time."

"Can you confirm the focus of your investigation is Buck Wood?"

"I don't know where you've got that information from, Helen. Would you like to reveal your source?"

"It's just an unsubstantiated rumour, then?"

"Yes."

"Thank you. 'Bye."

It was bound to get out sooner or later but Brian thought, if the paper printed a story now, it might help their investigation by jolting some long-forgotten memories. They commenced the interview.

"OK, Mr Stackpole, I'd like you to cast your mind back to the 1950s and tell me about the days you spent at the Summer School in Buck Wood."

He was clearly nervous but took a deep breath and started.

"I was fourteen and a member of the Boy Scouts. Every summer we spent a week pursuing outdoor activities and volunteering at the School in Buck Wood. It was fun for us and helped us gain our badges. Our Scoutmaster kept a close eye on us and determined our daily tasks. He could be quite tough on us at times but had a soft spot for boys he thought he could exploit. Some of the kids allowed him to pursue his queer activities with them to earn their badges."

"He sexually assaulted them?"

"Only with their permission. He was never forceful. He instinctively knew who might be receptive to his approaches. He used to take groups across to the river for swimming lessons. They were all encouraged to swim naked, but he didn't force them. To most of the kids it was a bit of fun. All part of growing up. But some of them

adopted that lifestyle and went on to be perverts and child-molesters themselves."
"Could you give me some names?"
"Yes."
"OK. Let's take a short break while you write some names down for us."

As soon as they resumed, Brian looked at the list and asked Mr Stackpole,

"All of these names are the perverts?"
"Yes."
"Are you still in touch with any of these people?"
"No. Most of them are dead."
"And the others?"
"One has gone to live in Australia. I've no idea where the rest are."
"OK, note which ones are dead and the one who's in Australia. We'll see if we can locate the others."

The list was immediately passed to Teresa, who distributed them to the rest of the team as soon as she had a lead on their whereabouts. Meanwhile, the officers took a break.

Andy was puzzled.

"Do you think Marks is a paedophile?"
"I'm not sure. I think he's probably tried it, just for the experience. I think he has a number of strings to his bow, so to speak. I think he likes to be an 'outsider', a non-conformist type. He's an enigma."
"He's a cold-blooded murderer if nothing else."
"Come on. Let's see if we can pry anything else out of him."

Brian and Andy picked up where they left off while Lynn liaised with Teresa.

"So, all these murders you committed were simply material for your blockbuster novel?"
"That's right. I thought it brought some realism to the narrative."
"So, what made you think you'd be successful as a writer?"
"The realism I can bring to it. My memory is real and vivid after an attack."
"OK, tell me about the homeless man you set on fire in Greengates. Let's hear the story from your point of view."
"He was an easy target. I killed him then went home and wrote what happened while it was fresh in my memory."

"You're absolutely sure about that?"

"Yes."

"You didn't plan the murder in advance, in detail?"

"No. The opportunity was there, so I killed him and then wrote down what happened."

"You're a liar! You plotted the attack in detail. You bought the accelerant to spread the fire a couple of weeks before the attack. We found the receipt in your house."

"I bought the accelerant to burn some bushes I'd cut down at home. That's all. The murder was a spur of the moment thing. I just had the accelerant on me as I was going to dispose of it in one of the big bins. I didn't want to dump it near home."

"So, the attack was unplanned?"

"Yes."

"Spontaneous?"

"Yes."

"You just happened to be walking about near the supermarket at 2am carrying a canister of accelerant?"

"Yes."

"Are you psychic?"

"Strange question. No."

"That's odd. When we searched your laptop, we found the story of your attack on the homeless man. The first draft was saved almost three weeks before the attack. It was a detailed plan of what you intended to do, and you followed it to the letter. Spontaneous, my arse!"

Marks didn't respond. He was thinking.

"OK. It wasn't spontaneous. I wrote it because I was learning the trade of being a writer. Then, just to ensure what I'd planned was actually realistic, I went out and did it exactly as I'd imagined it. That proved I had the imagination and skills to write a credible story."

"OK, so having proved you could imagine how to carry out a crime, you wrote what you intended to happen and then carried it out exactly as you'd planned it."

"Yes."

"So, you admit to being a cold-blooded murderer."

"OK, yes."

"How did you pick your victims?"

"They were all nobodies. They were scroungers."

"Really? The two pensioners in the canal barge? What makes you think they were scroungers? They were retired. After a lifetime of hard work, they bought the boat to live on. It was their dream. They owed nothing to anybody, All their savings had gone to their kids. What they had left bought them the boat and they lived on their pensions."

"The two homeless men used to beg outside supermarkets!"

"Both of them were army veterans. Both served in Iraq. Both were discharged with PTSD. They served their country and suffered as a result."

"The kid, then. He was a menace. Trying to knock people over with his bike."

"I was wondering when you'd get to him. Is that what convinced you he had to die? Is 'riding a pushbike on the pavement' now a capital offence?"

"He could have seriously injured somebody. He did it on purpose."

"So, you're judge, jury, and executioner?"

"Somebody has to do something about menaces like him."

"That's not your job. As a citizen, you should report crime to the police and let them take care of it."

"You lot don't do anything about the kids, though, do you? They run riot and nobody cares. Well, I do."

"OK. So, is anybody safe from your wrath? You've killed kids, pensioners, homeless people, an alcoholic, a drug addict. Oh, and retired people in Retirement Housing in Undercliffe. Have we missed any category out?"

"That's for you to find out."

"Oh, yes. A Jogger. And two schoolgirls. They were easy targets, weren't they? In a quiet lane, out of sight. Just minding their own business…."

"They should have been at home, instead of hiding out of sight, having a sly fag. Waiting for boys to shag."

"OK. Let's take a break. Then we'll talk about your relationship with paedophiles."

He walked into the canteen where Scoffer was entertaining two WPCs with one of his comic tales.

"So, I was at the checkout at Aldi, watching the prices flash up on the screen as my shopping was scanned. When she'd finished, I asked the checkout assistant why toilet paper had suddenly become so expensive. She said it was just like everything else. Everything had gone up. So, I asked why toilet paper? Is there a world shortage? Has the whole world's toilet paper harvest failed? She said it was just how it was these days. So, I said I'll just have to try to cut down. Maybe try using both sides."

They were all howling with laughter. Brian too. He praised Scoffer.

"Keep it up, Scoffer. You can always fall back on a career in comedy when your crime-solving skills fail."

****

On his way back to the Interview Room, Brian took a phone call from a worried caller.

"It's PCSO Penny Marks. I've just been informed you've arrested my dad."
"Is your dad called Stephen Marks, Penny?"
"Yes. I just went to his house in Greengates, and his neighbour told me he'd moved and been arrested. What's going on?"
"Where are you now, Penny?"
"In Greengates."
"We need to talk. Can you come down to HQ?"
"Yes. I'll be there in about 30 minutes."
"OK, I'll see you then."

When PCSO Marks arrived, she was directed to an empty Interview Room where Brian was waiting. He came straight to the point.

"I'm sorry to have to break the news to you, Penny, but your father has been arrested and charged with a number of local murders. You must have read about them in the local news?"
"Yes. But are you sure it was my father?"
"Absolutely. There's no doubt. He's admitted to committing some of the murders already."
"I can't believe it."
"You'd better get used to it, Penny. It will be in the papers soon and everybody will be talking about it. Please be honest with me – did you know, or suspect, anything about this?"
"Absolutely not. All I knew is he was writing a novel, a crime novel set in Bradford."
"I think it may be in your best interests if you were taken off the streets and given leave or indoor duties for a while. Once the news breaks, you could have a hard time on street duties. And for your own sake, it may be advisable to stay away from the kill zones."

She sighed.

"I think you're right. I just can't believe this. Can I speak to him?"

"Not yet. Have you any idea why he's become a murderer? Has anything happened that could have brought this murderous instinct on?"

"Not that I can think of. How long has it been going on?"

"A number of years."

"Oh, my God. It's such a shock."

"OK. Go home. I'll talk to your boss and tell him the situation. Do you want a WPC to take you home? Maybe talk to you for a while?"

"No. I'll be fine."

"We'll keep you informed. Take care, Penny. If you need anything, just let me know. Oh, by the way, do you happen to know anybody called Mike Thomas?"

"Yes. I've heard dad talk about him. He was his best mate at school, and dad was his best man when he married."

"Is he still in touch?"

"No. I remember dad telling me he'd died."

"Any details?"

"No. Sorry."

"Can you remember when he told you he was dead?"

"A long time ago. Probably fifteen years. Something like that."

"Thanks, Penny."

He saw her out before stopping for a quick chat with Penny's father.

"Your daughter's worried about you. Did you know that?"

"Who's told her?"

"Could have been anybody. It's all over the papers. 'Deranged paedo psycho killer caught by police'. Headlines in all the papers. You're famous, but not for being a writer, just another sad arsehole!"

He returned to pick up his interview with Mr Stackpole, while Andy and Lynn continued with Marks.

Brian took his seat, placing the ream of paper on the table in front of him. He stared at it for a while, without looking at Stackpole before speaking.

"All these names. Three of them have done time for sexual assaults, against both sexes. One of them became a catholic minister before he was defrocked and imprisoned. Now, you told me these abusers never touched anyone who was an unwilling participant in the activities?"

"Yes. To the best of my knowledge."

"So, could you tell me why two of them committed suicide in their early twenties?"

Stackpole shrugged his shoulders. Brian persisted.

"I'll tell you why. They'd become disgusted at the acts they couldn't help themselves performing on young children. They couldn't help themselves! They'd been brought up to believe it was natural, but as they became adults, they realised what monsters they were, preying on innocent kids."

"I'm sorry."

"Is that it? You're sorry! You will be when you're facing the magistrate as he reads out your sentence and tells the world what you did."

Stackpole lowered his eyes and cried. Brian left the room, smiling.

****

As he walked back to his desk, his phone rang. A call from Teresa.

"You need to see the T & A, Brian. They've published an exposé about the paedo ring at Buck Wood school."

"Does it say who the source is?"

"He's not named, no. It just says he was a victim."

"OK, I'll follow it. Send me a copy."

"Already done."

He read the story Teresa had emailed to him. His first thought was Stackpole, but since he'd been in custody, it was more likely one of those on Stackpole's list which had been leaked to the press. He stood and called for attention.

"OK, everyone of you who's not up to your neck in work, get out the copy of Stackpole's list of paedos which Teresa gave you earlier and start tracking them down. This is now your top priority. I want them all in custody by this time tomorrow."

The team gathered together and between them decided which names they would take, and suddenly, apart from Brian and Teresa, the office was empty. He phoned Helen at the T & A.

174

"Helen, please tell me the name of your source for this story."

"We never got his name. Brian. I'm sorry, he just walked into the office, said he knew about the paedo ring and would we like an exclusive. We interviewed him and the editor gave approval to publish. It's in the public interest."

"Fair enough, but I'd like his name, or at least something to help us trace his identity."

"One of the staffers took his photo without his knowledge. I'll send it to you."

"Thanks."

He notified Teresa he wanted the photo running through every database she could access.

"I need to find this man immediately!"

He had the response within an hour.

"Trevor Allenby. He's already on the list that Scoffer and Ruth are checking."

"Thanks. I'll call them now."

He called Ruth's phone, as Scoffer would have been driving.

"Ruth, have you interviewed a guy on your list called Trevor Allenby?"

"Not yet, boss. He's next on the list. We'll be there shortly."

"He's been identified as the source. Bring him in."

"Will do."

They pulled up outside a semi in Clayton. A van from BBC Radio was already parked outside. Scoffer went over for a quiet word.

"Just keep out of the way. We'll give you an interview as soon as we've had a word with the occupant."

"Can you confirm his ID?"

"Not at the moment, no. Just be patient."

The officers knocked on the door which was opened by a smartly dressed lady in her late 50s.

"Can I help you?"

"We're CID, love. Can we have a word with Mr Allenby?"

"Can you tell me what it's about?"

"Are you related?"

"He's my father."

"We'd like to talk to him about an article in the T & A."

"He's very frail. Please be gentle with him."

"We just need to talk to him, love. You're welcome to sit in on it."

"I will. Please come in. He's through in the lounge."

"Thank you."

They identified themselves to Trevor Allenby and asked him to confirm his name.

"And did you give the information to the T & A in person?"

"Yes."

"And is it true?"

"Yes. Every word, I'm ashamed to say."

"Can I ask why you've waited so long?"

"I've been living with cancer for a few years. I've now been informed it's terminal. I don't want to take this secret to my grave. It's time to be honest and let God judge me. I can also implicate others."

"We'd like to take you to HQ, if that's OK."

"Can my daughter accompany me?"

"Of course."

"Then, let's go, and then at least these nosey reporters outside will clear off. Would you mind awfully if I put a coat or something over my face? I'd rather my neighbours didn't know just yet."

"OK, we'll do that. We'll make sure we keep your face out of the papers as long as we can."

Scoffer took him straight to an interview room where Brian was waiting. He read out the charges.

"Mr Allenby, these are very serious charges. Do you admit to any of them?"

"Yes. All of them. I'm guilty, I'll serve my punishment. I want to make my peace with God."

"My colleague informs me you have a terminal illness."

"Correct, and I don't want to die with this on my conscience."

"As police officers, sir, it's our duty to charge you so that a judge can decide your punishment."

"I understand perfectly. I'm guilty. I admit it. I will serve my punishment."

"You could make it a lot simpler for a judge to pass a more lenient sentence if you were to name some of your colleagues who were involved in these criminal activities."

"It's my duty to God to name them. They too will be judged by God."

"OK, sir. If you'll please write the names down. Addresses, too, if you have them."

"I'll give you everything I have."

"Thank you. We'll leave you in the company of this young lady, Ruth, while we have a chat outside. We'll be back soon."

They went for a coffee to discuss the situation. Scoffer was clearly confused about what action should be taken.

"If it was my decision, boss, I'd have him sent to a secure hospital so he can die in peace. A prison's no place for him. Someone would kill him! He's admitted his offences, hopefully named all his colleagues, and now he's dying. He could easily have taken all his crimes of the past to the grave, but he's done the right thing before he meets his maker. Let him die in peace, boss, not in a prison hospital."

Brian listened in silence before replying.

"I admire your compassion, Scoffer, but unfortunately, it's not my decision, and in all honesty, I don't know what I'd do. He's committed some serious crimes. If we let him off, in effect, we're sending out a signal that it's OK to offend as long as you're sorry. I'm not God, Scoffer. I can't make the decision. It has to go before a magistrate, but one thing we can do is delay proceedings so that he dies before he faces a court. I honestly think that's the best compromise we can offer."

"I guess he'll take that."

"OK, provided he names all his colleagues, we'll talk to the DPP and see if he's amenable. You're right, though, prison's no place for a man of his age with a terminal illness. Just one thing, Scoffer; not a word about this to DCI Gardner."

"I'm not ashamed about having this point of view."

"That's immaterial, Scoffer, but it could harm your future prospects. You can air your views when you have achieved your aims in the Force. OK, let's go back and see what he's got for us."

They compared Mr Allenby's list with the one supplied by Mr Stackpole. There were several extra names on Allenby's, some of them quite influential people who would have been considered pillars of society.

"OK, let's round them up and see about destroying their reputations."

****

It took almost a week to bring all fifteen of those named by Allenby into HQ and interview them. Most, but not all, were deeply repentant, or perhaps pretended to be repentant to preserve their reputations. Three of those arrested denied everything, regardless of the evidence. They were the ones who would appear in court first.

However, instead of celebrating the completion of another case, the group seemed muted. They were glad to put that case to bed and move on.

But that wasn't the end of it. Soon, a Facebook page had been set up – for Buck Wood Summer School Survivors, where victims were able to talk about their ordeal and meet other victims. The site featured pictures of kids from 1958, with the words,

"I'm a survivor. Are you? If your face is pictured above, private message me. We are a small but growing group who were subjected to sexual abuse during the summer of '58. We want to tell our story and exact retribution and possibly some compensation from the evil teenagers and grown men who abused us."

As the site gained more contributors - some who had moved abroad to escape the horror - even more perpetrators were named. Some had died, some had committed suicide, and in some cases, their surviving relatives were totally unaware of their past actions.

The T & A published a number of articles, causing even more people to come forward with comments such as these.

- One of my mates disappeared at school.
- 'Prefects' took a liking to some vulnerable boys and abused them. Some disappeared.
- One 'prefect' came forward.
- Dozens admitted to abusing kids. Mentored by 'teachers'.
- Seems to be a group of child molesters allowed access to vulnerable kids for payment.

- A couple of kids since committed suicide. Others became alcoholics.

Brian summoned Scoffer to his desk for a quiet word.

"Scoffer, I'm handing over this case to you. From now, you're totally in charge of it. It's been agreed by the DCI."
"OK, boss. Any particular reason?"
"I'm sick to the back teeth, Scoffer. I don't want to see or hear any more about it. You're more capable of seeing it to its conclusion than I am."
"Do you want to talk about it, boss?"
"No. The decision's made. I've had enough."
"OK, boss. No problem."

It occurred to Scoffer that Brian's reaction may have been influenced by the murder of his kids, and he totally understood. What he didn't realise, though, was that he also intended to offload his control over all the other open cases. They were draining the life out of him.

CHAPTER 14

He met with Lynn and Andy after they'd completed their interview with Marks.

"Anything new or unexpected?

"No, boss. He sees himself as some sort of vigilante. Clearing the streets of miscreants and those whose lives were not filled with joy."

"OK. How do you fancy trying to trace one of his presumed victims?"

"The woman in Great Horton?"

"Yep. Teresa may have some details. Talk to her and pick up the story, please."

"OK."

Teresa had scraped together some details, as she explained.

"It's not complete but it's the best I could do with the information I've managed to get hold of. Last September, a man, James Andrews, reported his mother missing. It was investigated, but petered out when no information could be found to class it as an abduction or a murder. It was just recorded as a missing person and filed. Even her son admitted she was prone to wandering off and just turning up again as if nothing had happened. She did have some medical issues and was very much a loner. She may be the person that Marks was referring to, or he may have heard about her and made up the story about killing her."

"OK, we'll check it out."

"Thanks. Here's the address. Her name is Patricia Andrews."

They drove up to Great Horton and parked outside the address. Their knock was answered by an Asian woman who invited them in.

"We're sorry to bother you, Mrs Khan, but we're investigating a missing person case. This is the last-known address of Mrs Patricia Andrews. She was reported missing last September. Did you ever meet her?"

"No. The house was vacant when we bought it in January this year."

"Have the neighbours ever talked to you about her?"

"No. This is the first I've heard of her."

"Were any contents left in the house when you bought it?"

"No. It had been cleared totally."

"Have you made any alterations to the house since you moved in?"
"Only decorating. Nothing structural."
"What about the garden?"
"We've put plants in the front, as you can see. The back has been tarmacked so we could park the car off the road."
"Who did the tarmacking?"
"We hired a company. I can't remember the name, but I have a receipt. Just wait a moment until I find it."

She started rummaging through paperwork she extracted from a drawer until she found it.

"Here."
"There's no company name. Who did the job?"
"Two men turned up one day. I think they were working on repairing the surface on Horton Grange Road. They asked if we wanted the back yard done. My husband agreed a price and they came back at teatime and laid the tarmac. My husband paid in cash. Very cheap."
"Mm. Cowboys. You've no idea which company they worked for?"
"No. Sorry."
"OK. I'm afraid we'll have to send someone to scan underneath the tarmac. It's possible a body is buried under it. If we find anything, we'll have to dig it up, I'm afraid."
"But you will pay for it to be re-laid?"
"I'm afraid that's not likely. However, it's highly unlikely we'll find anything. The Forensics team who come to scan it will let you know if any further action is required. Thanks for your time."

They left and called at the neighbouring addresses, talking to the occupants wherever possible. Nobody could tell them anything of any use, except that Mrs Andrews was prone to leaving the house and returning days later with no idea where she'd been.

****

Two days later, the Forensics team turned up at the Khan's house and informed Mrs Khan what they intended to do.

"First, we run our scanner over the yard. It produces an image of what's underneath this tarmac. If it indicates a body, we'll have to dig it up. If it's anything at all suspicious or even just unusual, we'll dig it up. If the scanner doesn't detect anything, we'll leave you in peace with the yard undisturbed. Are you OK with that?"
"Yes. Do what you have to do."

"Thank you. We won't take long."

Half an hour later, they had completed the scan and found nothing. They gave the news to a relieved Mrs Khan.

"There's nothing unusual there, Mrs Khan. We shouldn't need to bother you again. Thanks for your time."

They passed the news to Teresa, who in turn informed Brian. He was sanguine on hearing the outcome.

"So, we just go back to Marks and try again. Maybe massage his ego to try to squeeze something out of him."

He sat down once again in the Interview Room, facing his smiling foe.

"So, Marks, I give in. What did you do with the body?"
"Which body are you referring to?"
"Patricia Andrews. Rugby Place."
"Isn't it in the story?"
"You know damn well it isn't."
"So, perhaps it never happened. Perhaps it was just fiction. Or, perhaps, it hasn't happened yet."
"It's happened all right. Last September. Your ego wouldn't allow you to have done nothing about it in all this time. So, where's the body?"
"I took it away to give her a proper burial."
"Where?"
"Where are bodies normally buried?"
"Are you trying to tell me she's buried in a cemetery?"
"That's for you to decide."
"Aren't you going to narrow it down for me?"

Marks hesitated, smiling, before continuing.

"I'll think about it while I'm spending all that time in jail, dreaming of a holiday in Greece, or something."

Brian ended the interview and walked angrily up to his desk to think about his next move. And then it struck him. It was another one of Marks's mind games. He'd given him a clue. He called Teresa.

"Teresa, can you find me the exact date when Mr Andrews reported his mother as missing?"
"Give me five minutes."
"Thanks."

He looked for Mr Andrews' number and noted it. Teresa called back.

"14th September, Brian."
"Does the report state the date he last saw her?"
"The 9th. He'd called her several times but got no answer."
"He took a while to go check she was OK. Why was that?"
"He lives in Liverpool. He had to find a day when he wasn't working to drive over. He runs a pub."
"OK, thanks."

He called Forensics.

"A job for your lads, Allen."
"Go on."
"Looking for a body, in a graveyard."
"What's the punchline?"
"I'm serious, Allen. As soon as I've got the exact location, I'll call you back."

He called the Council offices and eventually got put through to someone who may be able to help him.

"Good afternoon, my name is Brian Peters. I'm a Detective Inspector in Bradford CID. I need some information regarding burials at Scholemoor Cemetery, between 9th and 19th September last year."
"Just burials, sir? Not cremations?"
"Just burials, please."
"What exactly do you wish to know?"
"The names, please."
"It will take a while. Can I call you back?"
"Yes. As soon as you can, please."
"Certainly, sir. Hopefully before the end of the day."
"Thank you."

The call came through within an hour.

"Sorry for the delay, DI Peters. There were eleven burials. Can I email the names to you?"

"Certainly."

When the email arrived, he made an appointment to meet the sexton the following morning and was soon looking at a list of the grave sites.

"Would you mind taking me for a quick look at them?"
"May I ask why?"
"I believe a body may have been dumped in a grave site before the coffin was lowered into it. Is that possible?"
"It's highly unlikely."
"But not impossible?"
"No. The graves are usually dug a day or so before the actual burial, and covered over with planks or tarpaulin until shortly before the ceremony takes place."
"So, in theory, someone could remove the covers in the middle of the night, for instance, dig a little deeper, and dump a body, then cover it with soil, then replace the tarpaulin before the actual official burial takes place?"
"In theory, it's possible. Who would do such a thing?"
"A murderer. Where better to hide a body than among other bodies?"
"OK, I'll show you the sites."

They toured the burial sites. Brian was looking specifically for a secluded area, not visible from the road and perhaps with extra cover from trees or bushes. He noted four of the most likely sites to focus on, before thanking the sexton for his time and informing him a Forensics team would be on site later in the day, and that they would be as discreet as possible. Next, he called Allen to make the arrangements.

On arrival, they split into two teams, concealing the sites from public view by erecting barriers around them while they attempted to identify what may lie beneath the soil. It was quickly established that they would have to lift out the coffins to check if anything suspicious lay underneath. They were into their seventh dig before they discovered the body, wrapped in a polythene sheet. They hauled it out, checked that it fit roughly the description of the woman reported missing and terminated the search. They made good the sites they'd worked on, loaded up their materials and quietly drove away, leaving Brian to thank the sexton.

Back at the lab, it was soon confirmed that the corpse was that of Patricia Andrews, and the post-mortem report confirmed that marks on the neck were consistent with manual stranqulation.

Brian called her son to inform him of the sad news.

"Mr Andrews, I'm sorry to have to give you the news that we've found your mother's body, and we have her killer under lock and key."
"Can you tell me, was it likely she suffered?"
"I would imagine so, Mr Andrews. She was strangled."
"When will she be released for burial?"
"As soon as the coroner has filed his report. It should be within a week. I'll inform you."
"Thank you. She regularly used to disappear for a few days. She'd go to the coast. She loved Filey. I remember when it became obvious that she wasn't coming back and I started clearing the house to put it up for sale. There was nothing of any value in it. No jewellery, no cash – and she always had thousands of pounds in notes in a drawer. I was always telling her to get it in the bank, but she always said she kept it for emergencies. Well, it didn't do her any good in this instance."
"If it's any comfort, Mr Andrews, she wasn't killed for her money. Her killer was a prolific murderer who preyed on the vulnerable. She was just in the wrong place at the wrong time. I'm sorry."
"Thank you, Mr Peters."

It wasn't long before Brian went back for another chat with Marks.

"I just wanted to thank you for your help in finding the body of one of your victims."
"Really! Which one?"
"The one you pointed me towards. Patricia Andrews."
"The woman from Rugby Place? So, that was her name. So, can you chalk that one up to me?"
"Yes. The body count's still rising. Any more clues for me?
"Not at the moment."
"Pity. The last one was impressive. Talking about a cemetery, then a holiday in Greece. I had to think for all of two minutes before I put them together and got Scholemoor Cemetery on Necropolis Road. OK, back to your cell. We'll talk again maybe later."

****

Mullinder's meeting with his contact in the pub in Skipton had gone well. It seemed they had much in common and the conversation flowed as soon as the word 'drugs' was mentioned. Both had done their homework in advance and knew exactly what they were looking for. As they spoke, they both realised that together they could form an effective and very lucrative partnership. At the end of the evening, having discussed at length how they envisioned their talents and skills meshing, they shook hands and parted, each with a smile on his face.

His first assignment came through on the following morning. He would make the pick-up in Wakefield and distribute the goods to four different addresses in the Bradford and Keighley area. He assembled his team in his warehouse near Skipton and informed them of their collective and individual roles in the assignment. He made it clear that there would be serious repercussions for team members should anything go wrong. They were seasoned professionals and understood what was expected of them.

At 11pm the lorry arrived at the address on a trading estate close to the M1 near Wakefield. It was rapidly loaded with sealed boxes and the bill settled before it set off back towards Skipton where it was unloaded in the warehouse. There the boxes were opened, and the contents sorted according to the quantities on the order forms for each of the four customers. Packed into smaller vans, they were soon on their way to their individual destinations, arriving before daylight and unloaded. Once contents were verified, Mullinder would receive payment. He would then pay each member of his team according to their role and responsibility. As soon as they realised how lucrative the business was, they became dedicated to providing a top-class service to the customers.

After his first month, Mullinder had made more money than he ever made as a moneylender, and his online profile became more noticeable. So noticeable, in fact, that Teresa soon picked it up and called Brian.

"An old friend has re-emerged on the Dark Web, Brian."
"Who is it, Teresa?"
"Our friend Mullinder, or Mullins, as he calls himself now."
"Do we have his location?"
"No, but I'm working on it."
"OK. Keep at it. Let me know of any progress."

"Of course."

She adopted the guise of a buyer in Shipley, making a query about prices and terms and conditions. The email reply indicated that there would be a delay of seven days while the caller's business, and identity, was checked out. Teresa had no fear of the conclusion; she'd fooled people regularly on the Dark Web when setting up 'businesses'. It was just a matter of waiting and responding to requests for references from the false identities she'd manufactured as business acquaintances.

Within a week she had been cleared to do business with Mullinder and had rented a unit on a trading estate near Shipley. It was currently being set up as a trap for Mullinders' delivery. As yet, they had no address for Mullinder's warehouse, but Teresa was sourcing a tracking device which would be fitted inside the wheel arch of the delivery vehicle while the goods were being unloaded at the bogus unit in Shipley. The only problem was Teresa was unable to get authorisation to pay for the delivery in cash, as Mullinder demanded. She informed Brian of the problem and asked for his advice.

"Can we track where his PC is located?"
"Possibly, but I'm sure he'll be blocking it. It's odds-on he'll be using VPN software and diverting the signal through different sources."
"OK, how about if we refuse the delivery on some technicality or other and while we're trying to sort it out, we fit the tracker?"
"That could work. Let me talk to Forensics. I'm sure they can test the contents of the delivery and refuse it for some reason. Say it's not pure enough. It's been diluted below the strength agreed upon. Something like that?"
"That will work. And while everybody's arguing about it, someone can attach the tracking device."
"I'll organise it."

****

They rehearsed their roles repeatedly until delivery day. They were ready. The warehouse staff were drawn from Forensics and CID. The entire team was calm and confident of a positive result. They all finished work early in the afternoon in order to relax for a while before the night's work.

The delivery vehicle arrived at 4.30am. The doors were opened to allow it access, then closed behind it. The driver jumped out and handed over the delivery note, before his two accomplices unloaded the van's contents. The warehouse staff began to inspect it immediately it was unpacked. A random selection of products was put aside for analysis, until one of the analysts called Teresa over and told her a particular package was not as described. Teresa called the driver over to discuss the matter.

"This is substandard."
"What do you mean? It was tested in our warehouse before packing."
"Well, it's under strength. I'm not paying for this."
"It's what you ordered, luv."
"I'm not paying full price for this."
"Just hang on, then. I'll ring the boss."

He walked away from the 'warehousemen', taking his team with him. At a discreet distance, he phoned his boss. So engrossed in the situation had he become, that neither he nor any of his team noticed as one of Brian's men attached the tracking device to the inside of the rear wheel arch of the delivery van.

The phone call concluded, the driver and his men came back over with their boss's decision.

"You've wasted our time, luv. We're taking it back."
"Please yourself. Don't forget to tell your boss that we'll be happy to do business once he can provide what was ordered. The specification was perfectly clear."
"Yeah, well, he says it was as described when it left our warehouse. He thinks you're trying to get a discount, but he says he won't be doing business with you."
"Tell him we feel exactly the same. We gave him the specification; he's sent us crap. You might as well try and flog that stuff at the school gates. They might not notice it's under strength, but my customers will. If he carries on like this, you lot will soon find yourself out of a job. On your bike."

They got in the cab and drove away. Once out of sight, Brian's team locked up the warehouse and went home. Brian, along with Scoffer and Teresa, returned to HQ to see if the tracker was working.

By the time they arrived, Teresa had received an email from Mullinder stating his disappointment that his order had been returned and informing her they would not be dealing with her company again. She replied, expressing her regret, but stating that she only deals in high-spec merchandise and that she would be happy to deal with them again once they'd got their quality control up to scratch. She kept the conversation going for long enough to establish the location of the supplier to within twenty yards. The tracker had been stationary for long enough for Teresa to assume it was at its depot, being unloaded. After it had been motionless for an hour, they decided the night's work was over and the operation would commence early in the afternoon. Teresa shut down the PC and they went home.

The team reconvened in the Conference Room at 1pm, when Brian outlined his plan for the afternoon's outing to Skipton.

"We're all going except Teresa, who will be tracking us from here. We meet up with an armed team on the way and go in all guns blazing. Hopefully, we'll catch them off guard, but we're prepared for eventualities with plenty backup on standby courtesy of the North Yorkshire team. We've all done this before, and we all know what to do. So, let's do it."

They drove in convoy until they reached the trading estate where they split up to attack from different directions. However, when they got to the unit, they found the doors wide open and the place empty. Pinned to a whiteboard at the back of the room was a note. Brian's face dropped when he read it.

"Sorry to disappoint you, but we had to go out and sell a consignment of merchandise which the buyer refused. We will not work with that buyer again, particularly since we discovered, thanks to some military-grade software, that she was using a false identity and is in fact on CID's payroll. Yes, you've guessed it. Our delivery van had an onboard camera. So, goodbye Teresa Shackleton. How's your girlfriend?"

He wasted no time in calling Teresa.

"Teresa, there's a problem. Do you know where your partner, Nikki, is right now?"
"Yes. She's at work. Why? What's the problem?"
"You've been identified by Mullinder. I believe Nikki may be in danger. Get somebody to collect her and take her to a safe house

for now. Hurry. I'll explain later. And don't go anywhere yourself without a guard."

"OK."

He addressed the team.

"It's possible you've all been identified, so be careful, all of you. Let's see if we can catch him before he gets any of us."

****

CHAPTER 15

Safe in her hotel room with Nikki, Teresa worked tirelessly on her laptop, remotely accessing the CID's databases, while armed guards worked in shifts patrolling the premises. All other officers who had been on duty the night when the delivery was refused were similarly watched over, all bar Brian Peters and Scoffer, who eschewed the offer, preferring to take their chances.

While mulling over the recent failed operation, it suddenly dawned on him that they may have missed a trick. He called the number.

"Teresa, it's just occurred to me that they may not have found our tracker on the van. Can you check to see if you can locate it?"
"Will do."

He got the reply within ten minutes.

"It's stationary, Brian. The location is Steeton. An industrial estate. I'll be able to give the exact unit soon."
"Thanks. We'll set off now."

He quickly assembled an armed team and set off with Scoffer. Teresa was as good as her word and had identified the exact location of the van by the time they got there. Fortunately, the unit was unmanned, and the padlock was no match for the bolt-cutters Brian had brought with him. In the far corner stood the van and they could see the camera mounted on the dashboard.

"We're in luck. Get that camera, Scoffer. Break the window if you have to."
"It's ok, boss. It's unlocked."

The camera safely in their possession, Brian raced back to Bradford to deposit it in the lab. While driving over, it occurred to him that the images may have been erased, but it was worth checking. It was more likely the footage of the delivery had simply been copied to check out the images of Teresa and others in the team.

His luck was in, and they were soon running the images of Mullinder's team through the criminal database. They got three hits and set off immediately with armed backup to their latest known addresses, and by mid-evening had two of Mullinder's team in custody. The other address was unoccupied with no forwarding address available.

The two men in custody were reluctant to talk but reminded that they would take full blame for their criminal activities regarding the sale of drugs unless they could be persuaded to divulge the identities and whereabouts of their colleagues. Eventually, one of them gave the last known address for Mullinder's right-hand man, David Sullivan, who had a long record for GBH. Brian wasted no time.

"Come on, Scoffer. We've got armed backup meeting us on the way. Better take your vest, just in case."

His vest was not required. Sullivan answered the knock on his door and was immediately grappled to the floor, cuffed and bundled into the van for the trip to the cells.

One hour later, he was with his legal representative in the Interview Room, with Brian and Scoffer opposite them.

"We're not going to beat about the bush, Mr Sullivan. You were part of the team involved in sales of consignments of Class A drugs to customers. Unknown to you and your colleagues, one such sale was a sting. The 'buyers' were police officers who later raided your warehouse and found the camera which recorded the botched transaction. The sellers were pictured, and seen by us, at the sale in Shipley. We have them on camera and arrested them soon afterwards. When questioned, they gave us your name, along with others, as being a key member of the team. Now, you could face a long prison sentence for what you've done, but we may be able to help you get a lighter sentence in return for your co-operation."
"You want me to rat on my mates?"
"That's correct."
"I won't do it."
"Really? Don't you think it's unfair that we've captured you and your mates really easily while your bosses have slipped the net? Do they pay you extra to take the fall when they take the bulk of the profit? I very much doubt it! You lot are ten a penny. So, how about we offer you a deal in return for information which leads to the capture of the slimy toad Mullinder?"
"What are you offering?"

"If what you tell us leads to Mullinder's arrest, you'll probably get a suspended sentence."

"Can you guarantee that?"

"Probably 99%. We'd have to run it past the DPP. But if you refuse, we'll throw the book at you and get you banged up for as long as possible. Somebody has to be the scapegoat. We'll have to prosecute you if we can't get your boss. You can't have been with him long. You can't possibly owe him any loyalty. He'll be happy to let you take the rap. So, what about it?"

He sat back in his chair while Sullivan held a whispered conversation with his legal representative. It was brief.

"OK. Offer me a suspended sentence and I'll give you his address."

"I'll offer once we have him in custody. That's a promise."

"OK. He lives in Skipton. He's rented a house on Lambert Street. No. 48."

"This interview is over. You'll be returned to your cell until such time as we have arrested Mullinder. Have a nice day."

****

Teams on rotation were quickly allocated to cover front and rear exits to the house over a twenty-four-hour cycle. They knew someone was inside the house; lights were switched on and off occasionally and curtains twitched, but they were unable to ascertain exactly who it was. Patience was required.

After long hours of inactivity, a car appeared at the end of the street and stopped. Its lights were switched off, but nobody got out. Scoffer, on duty in a car at the top of the street, relayed the message.

"Car arrived. Possibly waiting for instructions."

"OK, keep us informed if it moves."

Seconds later, the car, its lights still switched off, began to move slowly down the street, past number 48 and to the end of the street, where it turned right, passing the other surveillance car which notified Control and continued to relay the message as the car turned again and crept up the back street, stopping outside number 48. Immediately, the back door opened and a figure dashed out of the house and jumped in the back of the car which drove off, its lights still off until it reached the end of the block where it continued straight ahead and accelerated away before turning its lights on. Scoffer gave pursuit while the second police car remained in position in case the car was a decoy and Mullinder was still in the house. Scoffer, though, soon confirmed the car he was following contained Mullinder as it continued to accelerate and raced down the streets towards the A6069. It soon became clear to the speeding car that it was being followed when the passenger window opened and a weapon, a handgun, was pointed at the pursuit vehicle and three shots were fired, causing Scoffer to throttle back and swerve from side to side. Nevertheless, one bullet smashed through the windscreen. Instinctively, Scoffer ducked and braked hard, slewing his car to the right and momentarily losing sight of the fleeing car. He called Control.

"Christ, he's shooting at me! I'm aborting pursuit. Target heading for A6069."
"OK. Helicopter on way. Backup car will pick you up shortly."

Scoffer cursed and waited impatiently until Andy and Ruth arrived in the other surveillance vehicle. He jumped straight in the back, advising them not to follow too closely, whilst listening as instructions came over the radio.

"Target vehicle on A6069 heading west, approaching junction with A65."

There was a brief period of silence before more instructions came through.

"Target turned left on A65, approaching roundabout, now right on A59 towards Bolton Bridge. Roadblock being organised."

They could now see the lights of the target vehicle ahead in the distance, illuminated by the searchlight from the helicopter. Scoffer reminded his colleagues.

"Keep it in sight, but don't get too close. Don't forget, he's armed, and we're not."

The lights from the brightly illuminated roadblock were now visible in the distance as the two cars raced towards it. The driver of the target vehicle, realising he could go no further, braked hard and threw the vehicle right down Prior's Lane before coming to a rapid halt. Both men got out of the vehicle and ran in different directions into the fields. The pursuit vehicle stopped at the junction, relaying messages to the fleet of police vehicles approaching from different directions before they split into small groups to search for the fleeing criminals.

The driver was quickly found hiding in a hedge and surrendered immediately, though the search continued for the armed Mullinder, with the bright lights from two helicopters illuminating the dark fields as he fired indiscriminately in the direction of his pursuers on the ground until he ran out of ammunition. He was soon located and surrounded, surrendering without a fight, and handcuffed for his trip to the cells in Bradford.

Brian had been alerted at home, following the incident's progress by phone and on his laptop. On hearing of Mullinder's capture, he took a quick shower, dressed and drove to HQ to meet the new arrivals and congratulate his team on their work. He quickly took Scoffer aside.

"I heard he shot at you in the car. Are you OK?"
"A bit shook up, boss. It came as a bit of a shock, but I'll be fine."
"If you need counselling, it's available. Just ask."
"I will, boss. I don't think it's hit me yet."
"The help is there if you need it. Don't feel embarrassed about it, Scoffer. Nobody will think any less of you if you seek help."
"Thanks, boss. I'll keep it in mind. At the moment, I'm OK."

But he wasn't OK. Once he'd got home an hour later and begun to digest what had taken place, he began to shake and poured himself a large whisky to calm himself down.

It came as no surprise to Brian when he called in sick the following day. Brian immediately rang him back.

"Scoffer, I'm not ringing to ask how you're feeling. I *know* how you're feeling. If you wish, I'll come over and keep you company while you try to put into words the trauma you've suffered. If the idea doesn't appeal, I can give you contact details of the counsellor I've been using since my wife and kids were murdered. She's very good and listens patiently while I vent my anger and suggests coping strategies which have helped me. If *that* doesn't appeal, I'm happy to come over and keep you company whenever you wish until you learn how to deal with your situation. Bear in mind; it doesn't go away. You just have to learn how to deal with it. So, do you want me to come over?"

There was a short silence before Scoffer replied.

"I need time, boss. I'll be OK soon, but if you want to call after you finish work, I would appreciate that. I just don't want to feel like a wimp."
"That will never happen, Scoffer. I know you better than that. I'll see you after I finish work."

He sat at his desk, thinking, before picking up the phone and calling Ruth.

"Hi, Ruth. Just a quick question, do you still go running every morning before you come to work?"
"Yes, boss. Well, every day unless I'm called in for an early start. Why are you asking?"
"I'm just wondering if you could take Scoffer with you. I haven't asked him yet, but I think it would do him good, and he might open up to you."
"I'm not sure how to react, boss. I'm not a therapist."
"I know that. I just want to find something to occupy his mind. Running with you would be something he'd enjoy, I'm sure."
"I'll give it a try. What do you want me to do?"
"Will you give him a call and ask if he fancies it? Don't say it's my idea. Just tell him you think it might help take his mind off his recent ordeal."
"OK. I'll do that. I can pick him up and do the Parkrun course at Lister Park. He lives close by, I believe."
"Yes, in Heaton. I'll give you the address."
"OK, thanks."
"You can start work later if he starts opening up to you."
"We'll see how it goes. I'll ring him now."

****

After work, Brian drove to Scoffer's home for a chat, during the course of which Scoffer revealed that he was going to try a regular morning run.

"I'd been thinking about it. You told me once that you ran regularly to clear your mind, so I thought I'd give it a try. And then, lo and behold, I got a call from Ruth asking me if I'd like to join her in the morning. She swears by it, and if it goes OK, we'll do it regularly, workload permitting, of course."

"It's a good idea, Scoffer. I hope it goes well. I'm sure it will. Another thing is that it helps Ruth feel more a part of the team, which is something she really wants to be. So, treat her well,"

"No problem, boss. I'll let you know how it goes. But first, let's just have a small whisky, but just a small one. I really don't want to run with a hangover. I want to enjoy it."

"You will."

After spending time with Scoffer and leaving him in a better mental state than when he arrived, Brian returned to his investigation of Stephen Marks in the certainty that he'd missed something. It was just a feeling that Marks had withheld some information simply for the feeling of power it gave him. He loaded the USB stick and started to read, noting each incident in turn to check the timeline. A thought crossed his mind. The first murder in his book was that of the homeless man in Greengates. He called Teresa, asking if she could send him a contact number for PCSO Marks, and rang her as soon as he had it.

"Hi, Penny. It's Brian Peters. I'm sorry to bother you but something is bothering me. I don't think your father had been totally honest with us. I think he's keeping something back, just for the hell of it. I just want to ask you, when you read his book, what was the first murder he wrote about?"

"It wasn't actually a book. It was an A4 printout of only one event. It was about the murder of a young woman he offered a lift to, then murdered and buried in woods in Calverley."

Brian's heart was pounding, as he continued.

"You're certain. There was only one event?"

"Yes. The next time I saw him, he said he hadn't written about any further events."

"And you read a hard copy?"

"Yes."

"Have you any idea where we could get hold of the file?"

"He just put it in a kitchen drawer."

"Any idea where he kept the original file?"

"I would have thought it would be on his laptop."

"Do you remember, did it have a title?"

"In the header text, he'd called it 'Killing for Pleasure'."

"OK, thanks for your help, Penny. We'll have another look for it."

He called Allen Greaves at the lab.

"Allen, the items you collected from the addresses Marks lived in, did you find a hard copy document titled 'Killing for Pleasure'?"

"Give me a second, Brian, while I have a rummage. Er, no, there's nothing of that name recorded. Is it important?"

"It could be. His daughter read it. It was about a woman killed and buried in woods at Calverley. It may have been his first murder."

"I'll see if we can trace it. We'll have another look at his laptop. I'll get back to you."

"Soon as you can, Allen. Thanks."

Brian was preparing to finish work for the day when he received the call he was waiting for.

"Sorry, Brian. We can't find anything remotely like what you described on his laptop."

"Have we searched all the properties he's previously lived in."

"To the best of our knowledge, yes."

"OK, thanks."

He sat back wondering where the original file might be. He had an idea. It was a long shot, but worth it. He picked up his phone and dialled the number.

"Barry Ramsden."

"Hello, Mr Ramsden. It's DI Peters from Bradford CID. May I ask you about the house in Greengates? The one where Stephen Marks lived?"

"What do you want to know?"

"When you cleared it out after he'd left, did you find a printout, or any data storage devices, such as a USB stick, or disk, or anything similar?"

"No. Sorry."

"Did you clear everything out?"

"Yes. Well, everything which was moveable. I left the wardrobe and kitchen units. That sort of thing."

Brian's pulse rate increased.

"So, there are cupboards, drawers still there?"

"Yes. I cleaned them all out. Emptied all the rubbish out."

"As I remember, there was a wardrobe with drawers at the bottom. Did you look under the drawers?"

"Er, no. I don't think I did."

"Would you please put my mind at rest and pull them out and look carefully underneath."

"OK. I'm there at the moment doing some painting. Hold on."

He could hear Mr Ramsden walking up the stairs and pulling out the drawers.

"No, sorry. There's nothing underneath except dust."
"Please just humour me. Turn the drawers over and look at the base."
"Ah, there's something taped under the left-hand drawer. It's a USB stick."
Don't touch it. I'll be there in twenty minutes."
"OK."

He closed the call and phoned Allen.

"Allen, it's Brian. We've had a break. Can you meet me at Ramsden's house in Greengates. I think we've found the file."
"OK. Don't touch it. I'll be there as soon as I can."

Brian called Teresa to break the news before running to his car and setting off. Traffic was heavy but Mr Ramsden had waited patiently for him and showed him the item of interest. Brian took photos on his phone while he waited for Allen Greaves to arrive. Five minutes later, he had donned his gloves and prised the USB stick from its hiding place, removed the Sellotape and inserted it into the drive of his laptop. He opened it and punched the air in triumph.

"This is it, Brian. As you expected, it's the story Marks's daughter read. Look at the date on it. The first murder. The woman who was killed and buried in the woods at Calverley."
"Send me a copy, please."
"On its way."
"Thanks, Allen."
"No problem. Now is it OK if I go home?"
"Sorry, Allen. I didn't realise the time. I guess I got carried away."

****

Back at his flat, Brian made a snack and a coffee before sitting in front of his PC. He opened his emails, located the one from Allen and opened the attached file, making notes as he read and following the route taken by the car on an online map. His first job in the morning would be to organise a search by Forensics to locate and exhume the body.

****

Brian had made his phone calls and was waiting to hear back from Forensics when they would be ready to set off to the Calverley site when Ruth and Scoffer came into the office, big smiles on their faces. They headed straight towards Brian's desk.

"Morning, boss. I'm happy to say your plan worked and I'm back on active duty."

"I'm glad to hear it, Scoffer. You feel OK?"

"Absolutely, boss. Running this morning in good company has put everything in perspective. Thank you."

"You're welcome, Scoffer. It's good to have you back. If you're ready, would you like to meet Allen and dig up a body? Take Ruth with you."

"Fine by me, boss."

"Ruth, are you OK with it?"

"Yes, boss."

"OK, then, off you go. Take a car; you don't need to run."

"And I was just starting to enjoy it."

"So, is the morning run going to be a regular thing?"

"We both hope so, boss. It really has worked for me, apart from the uphill bits, but I think I'll get used to them. And I think Ruth enjoyed the company."

"I did. I haven't laughed so much for a long time."

No sooner had they left the building than he received a phone call.

"Hello, Brian. It's Senior Officer Arthur Parkinson at Armley. I thought I'd let you know that this Mullinder chap here on remand had a visitor this morning. He signed himself in as Barry Harrison. He looked very, very angry when he left."

"That's a surprise. I didn't know he had any family in the area. What age would he be?"

"Early twenties as a guess, sir."

And his appearance?"

"Smart, clean shaven, tall, black hair."

"Thank you for the info, Sergeant. We'll look into it."

He closed the call and immediately dialled Teresa.

"Can you do a search for me, please, Teresa? A man called Barry Harrison, early twenties, clean shaven, tall, black hair. That's all I've got. Apparently, he called at Armley this morning."

"I'll get straight on it, Brian."

"Thanks."

****

They met the Forensics team where the woods began at the end of Thornhill Drive. It was a massive area where the only chance of success lay with the ability of the cadaver dogs to pick up the scent of decayed human flesh. However, Allen was optimistic.

"These three dogs are highly trained and among the best in the business. I'm confident they'll find something. Besides, it's not often that a body is buried deep in the woods. Normally, it's not far from the track as in general it's one man on his own who drags the body to its resting place."

The dogs were let loose and followed their noses, and it wasn't long before one of the handlers called them over.

"It's a corpse, boss. We'll dislodge the earth around it and take a better look before we remove it from its resting place."

They took photographs and measurements and made copious notes before carefully digging it out and bagging it for examination back at the lab.

Scoffer thanked the Forensics team before handing control to Ruth.

"Call it in, Ruth. You took control of proceedings this morning. You might as well carry on."
"Only if you'll run with me tomorrow."
"Of course. And this time, I'll beat you."
"I very much doubt it. This morning was just a stroll. Tomorrow, we'll see what you're made of."

They called Brian to inform him of the discovery of the body. He thanked them and made an appointment to interview Marks, who by now was back on remand in Armley jail, once again.

The moment he put down the phone, he had an incoming call from Teresa.

"It's an emergency, Brian. Someone's firing a gun on the Ravenscliffe estate. Nobody's been hit yet, but nobody dare leave their home."

"Give me the address and alert the Firearms Unit to meet me there."
"Will do."

****

He called Andy over and they set off at speed. By the time they arrived, the main entrance into the estate from Harrogate Road had been closed to traffic. Brian showed his ID to the constable manning the barrier and was waved through. He parked behind the black Firearms Unit vehicle and was directed to where the officers were positioned. Next to them, in the gutter, was a dead dog. The leader greeted him and told him what had been happening.

"There's a guy we have been made aware of who bought himself a 3-D printer recently and built a gun. He's been using it to shoot pigeons, but now it seems his son has it and he's gone mental. This is one of his test victims. Shot in the head."
"Where is he now?"
"Number 33. He's upstairs, shooting out of the front bedroom window."
"Is there anyone else in the house?"
"His parents and a couple of friends. We understand they've had an all-night party. Their neighbours told us it's a regular event where they all get stoned, though he doesn't know what they use."
"OK. Do what you have to do to safeguard the public. I don't care what happens to the users."
"Thank you, sir. My sentiments exactly."

Brian and Andy sat in the car as the operation was carried out. Armed officers wearing body armour approached the house stealthily from different directions until they reached the back door. They smashed it open and stormed the premises, catching the gunman in the bedroom by surprise and disarming him quickly. He was handcuffed and bustled away. The rest of the family were treated by paramedics who then reported to Brian.

"They're all OK. In all honesty, I don't think they realise what's been happening. They're all stoned. Out of it. Good luck interviewing them."
"We'll take them to HQ, and lock 'em up until they come round. Then, we'll get a psychiatrist to talk to them and after that, we'll have a chat."

Before they left, Brian was called over by the head of the Firearms team.

"This will interest you, Brian. We've found the 3-D printer in his bedroom. He bought in on Amazon! There's a PC next to it. You might want to take it to the lab, because I've a feeling he doesn't use the printer to make toy soldiers with."
"Thanks. We'll do that."

He called Forensics and agreed to wait at the scene for them but in the meantime they decided to have a look around the house, heading immediately for the bedroom where the printer stood on a table in a corner. In a box at the side were two firearms, loosely packaged with addresses attached.

"Looks like they're running a business here. Let's see if we can find any more. Let's start in the loft and work our way down."

Brian pulled down the ladder and climbed into the loft, followed by Andy. Both were wide-eyed at the number of boxes stacked in every usable space.

"Don't touch anything, Andy. We'll let Forensics photograph the scene first."
"I don't think these are Christmas presents, do you?"
"Nope. There's no market for clay pigeon shooting round here, but it wouldn't surprise me to find some bags with 'SWAG' written on them."
"I wonder who the customers are?"
"Let's wait until the Forensics team arrives. I'm sure they'll find an order book somewhere."

Forensics were quickly on the scene, photographing, numbering and bagging every item before loading them in the van to analyse in the Lab. As they left, the leader of the team informed Brian.

"These are not master criminals. They've just seen an opportunity and tried to exploit it. None of this hardware is high specification. I wouldn't bet against it being bought from Aldi."
"It was Amazon, actually. We found the receipt."
"Well, the gun they used to shoot pigeons and dogs was very basic. The two others were a little better, so my thinking is their skills are improving with practice, but I can't see them ever becoming a big business. It's a good job we caught them at the

beginning of their apprenticeship, or the estate would be awash with guns in the hands of teenagers, and they would be lethal."

"I agree, but these will be crushed as soon as the courts have done their job."

"They'll be building bloody tanks next."

"Aye, and none of *them* would have an MOT certificate."

****

They were driving back towards HQ when Teresa phoned.

"Brian, we've just had a call from a PCSO Marks. She and her partner on duty are holding a man accused of 'flashing' at the schoolgirls leaving Immanuel College. They're holding him outside the care home on Ellar Carr Road. You're the nearest officer. Can you help?"

"On our way."

He executed a U-turn and raced to the scene where the man known as Uncle Creepy was being restrained by the two PCSOs. Brian and Andy immediately handcuffed him, took statements, thanked the PCSOs and drove back to HQ, with a weeping dirty old man in the rear seat.

CHAPTER 16

Back at HQ, the members of the family were interviewed in turn by Brian and Andy. It was soon apparent that none of those arrested realised they had committed a criminal act. They had just found a way of making money to buy drugs and alcohol. Brian had no doubt that they'd soon be released back into the community and would start up a similar enterprise the moment their dole money arrived.

"All we can do is keep an eye on them and arrest them for every infringement in the hope they'll get sick of the hassle and move out of the area. We've got more than our share of numpties. So, let's get them interviewed and set up the court appearances so they can get bailed. Then we can start harassing them."
"So, what's next, boss?"
"We've still to interview Stephen Marks again. Would you like to join me on that?"
"Absolutely!"
"OK, let's do it. He's been languishing downstairs for a while. I'll just check if his solicitor's arrived yet, and if the report is through from Forensics."

His phone rang as he walked down the stairs. Allen Greaves from Forensics.

"Brian, we may have a serious problem."
"Go on."
"We've had a look thorough everything we confiscated from the house in Ravenscliffe and we found a receipt book. It appears they've sold three handguns recently."
"Any ID's?"
"No. We're just checking to see if we can lift any prints."
"OK. Keep me informed."
"Will do."

****

Marks's solicitor had been waiting impatiently in Reception for a half-hour and was already in a foul, but combative mood by the time the interview started.

"Can you please explain why you are interviewing my client again?"
"Yes, of course. We've found another body."

"So, you're trying to pin it on my client, just to get it off your 'to-do' list?"

"We have concrete evidence your client is responsible."

"Really? And what might that be?"

"He wrote the story. We have it in writing. We found it on a USB drive in one of the houses he lived in."

"And how do you know he's the author of this 'story'?"

"He told his daughter he'd written it and allowed her to read it."

"A work of fiction, then."

"On the contrary. We've just dug up the body, exactly where his story said it would be. The condition of the body is as you would expect from the beating it took in the story. The victim has been identified and her friends have verified she was with them in the pub the night she was kidnapped and killed. They also stated that Marks was in the pub the same night. So, what do you have to say?"

Marks looked at his solicitor.

"My client has no comment to make at this time."

"I thought not. Let me just remind you where we are with this criminal. We've been showing his photo around. The manager of the retirement complex identified him as the man who looked around the premises on the pretence of applying for a flat only a few days before setting it alight. The owner of his previous rented house in Greengates has also identified him. His laptop is full of stories he's written about his murders. They contain information which has never been made public. His time's up. We've got him. Don't waste your time trying to defend him. He's scum. This interview is over. It's back to Armley for you, Marks. Have a good day."

He turned to Andy.

"The air stinks down here, Andy. Let's go for a cuppa."

On their way down to the canteen, Brian took a call from Teresa.

"Brian, an armed robbery has just taken place at a General Store in Calverley. Can you take it?"

"Have the robbers left the scene?"

"Yes."

"Send Paula and Jo-Jo, if they're free. If not, get back to me."

"OK."

He closed the call and continued his chat with Andy.

"I thought we'd take some time for a quiet discussion, Andy. So, how are you enjoying your time in CID?"

"I'm loving it, boss. I've learnt so much. Everybody's treated me really well. I don't think there's anyone I don't get on with."

"I've been keeping an eye on you, and I have to say, I'm impressed by what you've done. I've spoken to your colleagues, and they all hold you in high regard. Just remember, though, you're still learning, so continue to take advice if it's given."

"I will, boss. And I want to thank you personally for giving me this chance. I won't let you down."

"That's good to hear."

He spent the rest of the afternoon, speaking individually with the rest of the team. He gave them all a glowing evaluation and was about to pack in for the day when his phone rang. It was Teresa.

"Mullinder's visitor, Brian. It's his son."

"I didn't know he had a son."

"He had a girlfriend, Sheila Harrison, for a short time. As soon as she got pregnant, he dumped her and she brought the child up. He first crossed paths with Mullinder when they met for the first time in Strangeways. After they realised they were father and son, they kept loosely in touch. It seems that Joe Mullinder got in touch with him and he visited him at Armley. I wouldn't put it past him to have asked his son to get revenge on you. I'd seriously think about having a minder."

"Have you got a photo of him by any chance?"

"Yes. From his driving licence. I'm sending it."

"Thanks, Teresa. Send me all you've got on him. I wouldn't be surprised if there isn't some criminal enterprise he's involved in."

"Will do."

He was about to leave when Paula and Jo-Jo returned.

"Three masked men burst in brandishing handguns. They emptied the till and forced the manageress to open the safe. They shoved everything into a holdall and ran out. An eye-witness said they jumped into a black BMW and raced away towards Rodley. He didn't get the number plate. No usable description. Just masked men, white. Average height, weight. Usual stuff. Nothing to go on unless we can get some CCTV footage from Traffic."

"OK. Stay on it, please. Keep me informed."

Driving home, he was still thinking about Barry Harrison when he had an idea. He swung off the road into the Ravenscliffe Estate and soon parked outside the house where Eileen Davies lived. He rang the bell, then banged on the door when nobody answered. There was still no response so he went round to the back, peeping in through the kitchen window where he could see the body of a woman slumped at the kitchen table, her head in her hands. He tried the door; it was unlocked, so he entered. He recognised the occupant so shook her shoulder.

"Mrs Davies. Wake up."

She didn't respond so he lifted her head to find her face covered in dried blood. She groaned.

"Mrs Davies. It's the police. Are you OK?"

Once again there was no response so he called for an ambulance and left a message at HQ, informing them of the situation before following the ambulance and its injured occupant to the BRI.

He sat in Reception until he was called. Mrs Davies was conscious and fairly lucid. He went to a recovery bay to speak to her.

"Hello, Mrs Davies. I'm DI Peters from Bradford CID. Can you tell me what happened?"
"I can't remember."
"No? So, let me have a guess. You owe money again. And when the man came for it, you didn't have any, so he beat you up. Does that sound right?"
"More or less."
"OK. Tell me, who's the collector these days? We know it's not Mullinder because we've got him locked up. So, who's taken his job?"
"I don't know his name. A young bloke. He said Mullinder had sent him."

He took out his phone and showed her Barry Harrison's photo.

"Is this him?"
"Yes."
"Is this the first time he's been here?"
"Yes. I thought it was finished when I heard Mullinder had been banged up."

"It's a family business, love. Passed down through the generations. I dare say, if he ever gets out of prison, his dad will resume control."

"Well, this lad threatened if I don't pay next week, he'll cut my ear off."

"Then, I suggest you tell us when he's coming, and we'll arrest him. I'm assuming he gives you some warning so you've a chance to borrow some money from another source."

"Sometimes."

"OK, if you see his car, make sure your door's locked and give me a call. Stay out of sight till we get here. OK."

"Can't I have a guard?"

"No. Not twenty-four hours a day. Sorry. All we can do is ask a patrol car to drive past at regular intervals and report anything unusual."

****

At home that evening, Brian was notified of another armed robbery at a filling station in Rawdon. CCTV captured nothing of any use apart from the fact that it appeared to be the same car, and the same criminals. Paula and Jo-Jo had attended the scene and Paula called Brian later to bring him up to date.

"They parked on the road outside the forecourt, Brian. A blind spot for the cameras. The CCTV in the shop picked them up but once again they were masked. Three armed masked men, plus the driver. Same make of car. Same gang."

"OK, Paula. Thanks. Stay on it. I'm guessing we'll hear more of these guys. I'll see if Teresa can help identify them."

Teresa was on the case as soon as she arrived at work. She had received a copy of all the files on the gun seller's computer on a hard drive sent from Forensics and was examining the data when Brian arrived.

"Any luck, Teresa?"

"I'm making progress. They weren't very secretive about the fact they were selling weapons. They just posted on a Marketplace and got replies on Facebook Messenger. Not exactly professional. I'm just trying to trace the identities of those who replied and actually bought the guns. They had loads of replies, but just took the first offer. I guess they needed the money to make more weapons."

"OK, thanks."

"Oh, wait a second, Brian. A call's just come in. Another robbery at a mini-market on Otley Road. Paula and Jo-Jo are on their way."
"OK. Keep me informed."

The officers reported back an hour later.

"Same team, Brian, but this time we got a partial plate. We're running it through the system now."
"Well done, ladies. Stay on it. Teresa's working to identify the buyer at the moment. I'm expecting we'll be able to organise a raid by the end of the day."

By mid-afternoon, Teresa had an address for the buyer. Not surprisingly, it was on the Ravenscliffe estate. Brian decided to lead the raid, along with Paula and Jo-Jo, and an armed unit. He had already sent an unmarked patrol car to check the address, and confirmation had been received that the car was parked outside the house and the criminals were inside, probably counting the proceeds of their activities. The team set off immediately, with backup on alert, and Forensics ready to move in afterwards.

The operation went without a hitch. Two armed officers knocked on the door, which was opened by a man munching a sandwich. He was overpowered and the team stormed in and arrested the four robbers without any resistance. They were taken away in handcuffs and bussed down to HQ while Forensics loaded their van with all the evidence they required for a successful court case. The criminals were quickly identified as illegal Albanian immigrants. Before they returned to HQ, Brian delegated the task of briefing the TV and press crews about the operation to Paula and Jo-Jo. It would be good experience for them.

****

It had not gone unnoticed by Brian how his team had paired off and worked most effectively with their chosen partner. He actively encouraged it and the atmosphere at work was pleasant as well as professional.

He was relaxing at home in the evening when his door entry system buzzed. He walked over to answer it.

"Hello?"
"Is that DI Peters?"
"Yes."

"It's PC Bland and PC Hartley from Traffic, sir. Could we please come up and speak to you?"

"What's it about?"

"There's been an incident we need to discuss with you, sir."

"OK, I'm opening the door. Come up."

He pressed the button to release the entrance door, then walked over to the door to his flat, opening it to the two officers.

"OK. Come in. Take a seat. How can I help you?"

"Please sit down, sir. We have some bad news."

"What is it?"

"There's been an accident."

Brian's heart skipped a beat. He almost knew what was coming. He worried every time his parents rang to say they were driving to Bridlington for the day, but never dreamt his worries would one day be realised.

"Is it my parents? Are they.... OK?"

"I'm sorry, sir."

"Oh, Christ! What happened?"

"They were driving back towards Bradford along the M62, just past the junction with the M1 when there was an accident. An HGV ploughed into their car. They died instantly, sir. We're very sorry. An ambulance was there within ten minutes, but there was nothing anyone could do."

Brian sat and wept for a minute before recovering his composure.

"Anyone else injured?"

"The driver of the HGV suffered minor injuries, sir."

"What caused the accident?"

"The HGV driver fell asleep at the wheel, sir. He's been arrested and will be charged. Apparently, he'd been driving almost non-stop for the last twenty-four hours."

"Where are my parents now?"

"Leeds, sir. If you feel up to it, we'll take you and bring you back."

"I'll get my coat."

They drove in silence to the mortuary where the bodies of his parents were lying side by side. He identified them and completed the necessary forms, something he'd watched other grieving relatives do so many times before they drove him home, and left him, alone and feeling devastated. He felt he had no option but to pour a glass of whisky, but, bearing in mind his responsibilities at work, he downed it in one and went to bed.

In the morning, he gave the news to Teresa, informing her that he had to go to his parents' home to sort out their affairs, and he would be back at work as soon as possible. She offered her sympathy and said she would call him after work to see if he needed any assistance. She gave him a hug and watched him leave, a broken man.

He spent the day sorting out paperwork and making phone calls. Fortunately, his father had previously informed him where all the important documents were kept, should anything ever happen, and everything was exactly as he had expected. They were prepared for this event and instructions were very clear and logical. Nonetheless, it was a heart-breaking experience for Brian. He knew there were only two beneficiaries, himself and a charity they had supported for decades, but he was surprised at the amount of wealth they had accumulated over the years. Brian didn't need that amount of money and had no family to pass it on to. He would have to give it some thought.

****

He returned to work on Monday, his weekend having been spent clearing out his parents' house before putting it on the market. In doing so, he'd found an album of photographs and sat down to look through it. It started with photos of his parents early in their relationship with more added at key points of their life together, their engagement, holidays together, their marriage, his mother's pregnancy, Brian's birth and his subsequent growth. There were many photographs of Brian's wife and his children as they grew up. And then there were several blank pages evidently reserved for future events which would never now occur. His thoughts at that time were mainly about the accident which killed his parents. The only good thing was they died together. Neither would have ever been able to enjoy their life without their partner.

He was jolted back to reality by a phone call from Eileen Davies.

"He's coming for his money tomorrow afternoon. I haven't got it. What do I do?"
"I'll sort it out. Did he say what time?"
"Two o'clock."

"We'll be there and ready. Keep your doors locked until I call to let you know exactly what's going to happen. And don't worry. We'll get it sorted."

He called the team over and explained the situation.

"We have a situation tomorrow where Barry Harrison, Mullinder's son, intends to collect money from Eileen Davies. She doesn't have it, so at the very least she is in for a severe beating, and very possibly will be killed, if he's anything like his father. I want you to liaise with the Armed Unit to prevent this happening and I'd like the villains to be caught rather than killed. Lynn, you'll be in charge. Work it out between yourselves how you're going to handle it and check in with me before the end of today."

"Aren't you leading this, boss?"

"No. Unfortunately, my parents are being cremated tomorrow. I have to be there."

"Sorry, boss. I didn't realise."

"That's OK. You're capable of carrying out the task without me. Any more questions? No? OK, get to it. And call Mrs Davies to tell her what's going to happen. Good luck with it. You're well equipped to carry this out without a problem."

****

At 1.15 the next day, Brian parked up close to the Crematorium accompanied by Teresa who had insisted she would be with him. He was grateful. He wasn't certain he could get through it alone but with Teresa at his side, he managed to keep the tears to a minimum. There were six other attendees, close friends of his parents, with whom he chatted after the service, and accepted their condolences. Then he returned to work, leaving the funeral urn in the car boot. He went straight to his desk and called Lynn for a progress report.

"The mission was successful, boss. We have four men, including Harrison, in cuffs at the scene. Mrs Davies is unharmed and minimal violence occurred, thanks mainly to the amount of artillery pointed at them by the Armed Unit. Like clockwork, boss."

"Congratulations, Lynn. Please inform everybody I'm delighted with the result. You can all be very proud of yourselves."

"We had a good teacher, boss."

"Thank you, Lynn. We'll see if we can get you into our Hall of Fame for this."

"That'll be the day."

"Well, anyway, when you interview Harrison, don't forget to tell him what a useless pile of crap he is. He's only been on the job a matter of weeks and he's already been arrested and set for a prison sentence. His dad will be *so* disappointed."

"OK, boss."

"*You're* the boss, Lynn. You ran the operation today. And very well too."

"Thank you."

"One more job for you and your team. There's a large network of drug users in the area. We've established that one of Marks's victims, Karl Stokes, along with his mate Keiran Donnelly, acted as a distributor for his dad, Dave Carlton and his mother, Mrs Stokes. Come down hard on Carlton and Stokes. Keep harassing them until they pack it in or move away from our patch. Have a word with young Keiran to see if he's found himself another supplier. Talk to the headmaster at their school. Identify as many users as you can. Make sure all their parents are aware. Make them aware we'll keep hounding them until they stop using. Let's see if we can stop the supply by stopping the demand."

"We'll do what we can, boss."

****

Brian was the last one to leave the office, but before leaving he placed a sealed envelope on the desk of each member of his team. Each one contained a personal hand-written note for the recipient, thanking them for their hard work and praising their talents. He was also honest enough to mention areas in which they could improve. The one he left for the DCI sang the praises of his team members and made recommendations for promotion for those he thought deserved it. In the note he left for Teresa he asked again if she'd managed to find any details about the death of Mike Thomas, and if so, to pass them to Ruth to follow up. He placed his ID card on his desk, took a last look around, smiled and left the building.

He drove straight home, parked up and walked around his flat, performing a final check. He'd spent the previous few days throwing away what he no longer needed and boxing up items he wished to leave for his friends. He had left an itemised list on each box along with the name of the intended recipient. He had also ensured all his bills were paid and his final wishes were clearly conveyed to his solicitor. He was ready to join his family.

He looked at the funeral urn which stood on the table, a note underneath it addressed to Teresa, asking if she'd kindly scatter the ashes from the Cow and Calf. He took out the bottle of Speyside malt he'd bought specially for the occasion, opened it and poured a generous measure. He raised the glass and silently toasted his friends and family before downing it in one, and refilling the glass, taking it to the sofa and placing bottle and glass on the table alongside. He sat in silence, taking the occasional sip while he thought about his life, concentrating on the happy events and glossing over the bad times. He felt proud of his achievements and sad about his failures. But now it was time. He'd served his purpose and lost the will to continue. He stood up and walked, hesitantly, to the kitchen where he took a box of tablets from a cupboard and returned with them to the sofa.

He took a final look around, filled the glass, and swallowed all the tablets, washing them down with whisky. He closed his eyes and lay back. His torment would soon be over.

****

In the next few days, the mood in HQ was sombre. Members of staff would burst into tears spontaneously until, eventually, they individually came to terms with the tragedy. Teresa felt it most, but coped thanks to the support her wife, Nikki, gave her. Deep down, she knew it would happen eventually. She found it difficult to believe that anybody could continue after bearing so much personal tragedy and trying to deal with the trauma of losing all those family members who were closest to him. Scoffer was in pieces but gradually, with help from Ruth, came to realise how Brian had prepared him for this eventuality, by carefully tutoring him, and got the DCI's permission to hang a picture of Brian in their Hall of Fame, as a mark of respect.

Gradually, the team learned to cope without Brian and were once again an effective unit, led by Lynn who had been promoted to DI. And life went on.

There was one more thing, however. Apart from the instruction he left for Teresa regarding the death of Mike Thomas, he'd also left special instructions for both Lynn and Scoffer asking them to tie up all the loose ends of the cases they'd tackled in his last months. The two met in the canteen to discuss the matter.

"I'm with Brian on this, Lynn. We've disrupted the supply chain of drugs around Thorpe Edge, but I know for sure that, unless we make more arrests and get some convictions, it will continue."

"OK. I agree. Take it on. Team up with Ruth, if that's OK."

"That's fine."

"I'll see what we can do regarding the murder of the young boy, Paul Bastow. We need to get on top of our investigation into the paedophile ring. We've let ourselves get side-tracked by recent events.

"I know. But Brian would have wanted everything sorted. He just ran out of time."

"So, let's get to it. Let's talk to Teresa and make sure she's aware."

They explained their plans to Teresa who was in full agreement and promised to manage their resources regarding any new cases, which she would pass to Paula and Jo-Jo. Lynn spoke to both officers, who promised their full support.

****

After lunch, Scoffer and Ruth drove up to Ravenscliffe, accompanied by members of the Forensics team. Watched by a growing crowd of neighbours, they hammered on Dave Carlton's door, demanding access, and, being denied, smashed down the door, finding Carlton in the toilet desperately flushing small packages of powder down the pan. He was arrested and the house searched. A car was summoned to take the prisoner to HQ, while Scoffer and his party moved on to Mrs Stokes's address where the process was repeated with the same result. Their next stop was the school, from where Keiran Donnelly was dragged out of class and bundled into the back of the car for the trip down to HQ.

At the same time. Lynn and Andy were going through the information they had regarding the death of Paul Bastow. They agreed it was pointless talking to Marks about it, as it would have been included in his written work by now if he had been the murderer. Instead, they focused on members of the paedophile ring, poring through online discussions for clues. Eventually, they struck gold, following a link which contained some photos of the victim. There were horrific images of abuse, in some of which the abusers could be clearly seen. Teresa was instructed to determine their identities as her top priority, and by the end of the day had provided the names of three men, along with their addresses.

A dawn raid was planned for each address. One man was not home; his neighbour said he was on holiday, but could not say where, only that he was due back on Saturday. The other two were brought to HQ and held in separate cells so they were unable to communicate with each other. When interviewed, each blamed the other. They were all left to stew until their next interview could be arranged, but the officers were desperate for a breakthrough. Teresa, as usual, provided it. Contacting several airlines and holiday companies, she was able to ascertain that their third suspect had taken a holiday in Spain, and that his return flight was due to land at Leeds Bradford airport at 10.40am on Saturday. Lynn and Andy would be waiting.

The third man, William Burton, was arrested as he exited the Customs Hall, and transported to HQ, where each of the three men were seated alongside a legal representative as the interviews started. Scoffer and Ruth were assigned to interview a nervous Harry Crouch in Room One, Lynn and Andy had a cocky Malcolm Black in Room Two and Paula and Jo-Jo took the suntanned William Burton. After the formalities, interviewing commenced in earnest with each interviewer asking questions from a list shared by each team. The answers were recorded and forwarded to the other two teams, and the responses compared when the officers took a break.

"It's no surprise that each interviewee had given a different answer to the questions, so who do we believe?"
"Crouch is very nervous. He's been almost in tears at times. I think he'll be the first to crack."
"OK, so we tell the other two that Crouch has come clean and admitted all three of them were complicit in the abuse and murder of Paul Bastow. We tell Black that the other two have stated he killed Bastow. Then we tell Burton he's been blamed. And the same with Crouch. If we tell him the other two have blamed him, he'll tell us all we need to know."
"OK, let's do it."

Scoffer went straight on the attack.

"You know the other two call you 'Hairy Crotch', don't you? You know they've both, without conferring, told us you killed the lad after you'd finished abusing him? And we believe them. So, let's get this over with. Tell us exactly what you did."

"They're lying! OK, I admit I sexually assaulted him. And I'm sorry for that. I'll take my punishment for that. It was my first time! But I didn't *kill* him. It was Burton. Burton hit him with the hammer. And that was it. The lad was dead! And Burton was standing over him, a huge grin on his face. I was sick, vomiting all over the place, while the other two buried him."

"OK. What did they do with the hammer?"

"Black took it. He said it was a souvenir."

"Why didn't you report the crime?"

"They said they'd come for me unless I stayed silent. They said they'd tell the police I did it. So, I kept quiet. I was frightened."

"OK, we'll take a break. Take your time and think about what you've told us. Think about whether you want a life sentence in a jail where they hate kiddie-fiddlers, or whether the other two should take the blame."

Scoffer was adamant that Crouch had told the truth. The officers held a quick meeting where it was agreed that Scoffer and Ruth would continue with the sexual abuse investigation, while Lynn and Andy would return to the drugs investigation. Paula and Jo-Jo would pick up any other activity.

Scoffer was already beginning to have regrets about taking on the case. He and Ruth had failed to make any headway during the afternoon. Both Black and Burton were adamant the other committed the murder. Fortunately, Teresa solved the problem by virtue of her perseverance in uncovering a further batch of images from the Dark Web, one of which clearly showed Burton striking the boy's head with a hammer. When the image was presented to Burton, he admitted to the murder.

Ruth and Andy finally extracted a confession from Dave Carlton, after Forensics had taken samples from the WC where he'd tried in vain to flush away the evidence. They'd found sufficient 'trace' to prove a significant amount of cocaine and heroin had been emptied, and a search of his house uncovered an even larger cache of ecstasy and other drugs. He implicated Mrs Stokes and Keiran Donnelly, who both, eventually, admitted their guilt.

The team held a muted celebration that evening during which Teresa revealed she had discovered that a man named Mike Thomas had been hit by a car and killed over a decade ago. The car and its driver were never traced. She presumed Marks was responsible.

CHAPTER 17

The CID team had gathered at Scholemoor Cemetery for the service. The mood, naturally, was sombre, and the weather cool and breezy but at least dry. They filed into the crematorium for the short but emotion-filled service.

Afterwards, they adjourned to The Ainsbury which had opened specially for the occasion. As the drinks flowed, the mood lightened, and the team spoke about their memories of working with Brian. There were tears and laughter and Springsteen's songs playing in the background. As the afternoon progressed, they were joined by customers who had known Brian and come to pay their respects. Early in the evening, Teresa left along with Scoffer to carry out Brian's last wishes.

They drove in silence to Ilkley, parking below the Cow and Calf rocks and climbing to the top. They gazed for a while at the panoramic view before taking the urns from the bag. Scoffer found the Bruce Springsteen song Brian had requested on his phone as Teresa removed the lid containing the ashes of Brian's parents, then did the same with the second urn. They listened to the lyrics, the tears welling up as Teresa scattered the ashes from both urns into the wind.

"We said we'd walk together baby come what may
That come the twilight should we lose our way
If as we're walking a hand should slip free
I'll wait for you
And should I fall behind
Wait for me

We swore we'd travel darlin' side by side
We'd help each other stay in stride
But each lover's steps fall so differently
But I'll wait for you
And if I should fall behind
Wait for me"

Through his tears, Scoffer said,

"You're together now. You're with your family. Rest in peace, boss. You'll be missed, but never forgotten."

Teresa was unable to speak, but nodded and sobbed as Scoffer escorted her back to the car to drive her home. She knew she still had someone to go home to and would forever be grateful for that. At the same time, she recalled the first time she met Brian, when she was a mere clerical assistant for CID, generally unpopular due to the fact she was black and a lesbian, but Brian was kind and considerate and treated her as an equal. He gave her the confidence to push herself to become anybody's equal and quickly became a valuable member of staff performing a critical role in the department. She would never forget him.

THE END

Previous novels by Ian McKnight

CRIME

Premonition (Dec 2017)

A fast-paced crime thriller centred on a terrorist plot to explode a bomb in Bradford City Centre and the CTU's attempt to thwart it.

The Devil Finds Work (Oct 2018)

A routine investigation into a girl's death from a drug overdose escalates into the search for an international drugs smuggler in a fast-moving tale of corruption.

Games People Play (Oct 2019)

DI Peters and his team investigate a series of murders while dealing with cases of missing persons, when they become aware of an international human trafficking ring operating on their patch.

Unfinished Business (Jul 2020)

The discovery of an amputated foot leads DI Peters on a trail of crimes involving Climate Change Activists with a hidden agenda, international drugs smuggling; a serial child abuser; corruption in local government, and a computer hacker terrorising and blackmailing innocent victims.

The Pandora Program (Jun 2021)

The team chase people smugglers enslaving immigrants and uncover a paedophile ring.

Retribution (Dec 2021)

DI Peters finds his family slain after a brutal attack, the first of many, and must hunt down the killer and his paymaster in this fast-moving and emotional tale of revenge.

The Darkness of Night (Oct 2022)

A figure from DI Peters' past contacts him when female members of his family, fleeing the war in Ukraine, inexplicably disappear.

ADULT HUMOUR

The Ray Light trilogy: **(2017)**

Losing Lucy
Light Years On
Light At The End Of The Road

A philandering widower seeks to rebuild his life following the death of his wife. A hilarious trilogy full of twists and turns.

SATIRICAL HUMOUR

The Forkham Predicament (Nov 2020)

A madcap comedy set against the background of a pandemic.

All available from Amazon, in paperback and Kindle.

Printed in Great Britain
by Amazon

23261194R10126